MESYÉ KWIK! KWAK!

A Collection of Short Stories

GIFTUS R. JOHN

This book is a work of fiction. Any resemblance to actual events or persons, living or dead, is entirely coincidental.

Edited by Vaughn E. James

Cover illustration by Ronald "Baba" Deschamps

"Mesye Kwik! Kwak," by Giftus R. John. ISBN 1-58939-764-9.

Published 2005 by Virtualbookworm.com Publishing Inc., P.O. Box 9949, College Station, TX 77842, US. ©2005, Giftus R. John. All rights reserved. No part of this publication may be reproduced, stored in a retrieval system, or transmitted in any form or by any means, electronic, mechanical, recording or otherwise, without the prior written permission of Giftus R. John.

Manufactured in the United States of America.

Mesyé Kwik!

Kwak!

Also by Giftus John:
The Dawn
Words in the Quiet Moments
The Island Man Sings His Song

Dedication

*This book is dedicated to the memory of my baby sister, Glorine;
to a dear friend Anthony Esquith "Tall Boy" Pierre
and to a dear uncle, Frank Julien.*

*The flames are gone
But the fires still glow.
In our hearts and minds
Your flowers forever grow.*

Rest in Peace

Giftus

Table of Contents

Foreword i
Acknowledgement v
The Stone 1
Converted 24
Three Young Friends 43
The Street 59
The Final Hour 73
A Life Wasted 84
Grandpa Was in America 95
Trouble in the Channel 113
Flying to Barbados 132
Hurricane 142
A Thief in the Night 155
The Pilgrim 168
A Father's Hope 184
Glossary 191
About the Author .... Back Cover

Foreword

"Mesyé Kwik!"

"Kwak!"

I have lost count of the number of times I have heard this exchange between a story-teller and his audience as he stood on stage at one of the *conte* competitions in Dominica, West Indies. This exchange established a bond between the story-teller and the audience. "Mesyé Kwik!" could well be translated, "Ladies and Gentlemen, I bring you some fiction!" "Kwak!" could then be translated, "Yes, it is fiction!" or "Fine, let me hear it!" Indeed, the "Kwik-Kwak" relationship has become so ingrained in Dominican culture that when one's friends determine that he is exaggerating about a particular event, rather than using the brash admonition, "You are lying!" the friends gently say, "Man, you making Kwik!"

After all, to "make a Kwik" or "tell a Kwik" is not something too bad. To do so would be to follow in the tradition of the *conte*-tellers, those men and women who, with much bravado and gusto, recount tales of Dominican folklore: tales of the *soucouyan*, *la diabless* and *lougarou*, and of cunning animals out-foxing their timid four-legged relatives—and even some humans, too. What tales those story-tellers tell!

In *Mesyé Kwik! Kwak!*, Giftus John does not tell stories of cunning rabbits and wily spiders. He does not recount tales of *soucouyans* flying at night or of *la diabless* with goat's feet. Still, his stories reflect the richness of Dominica's folklore. Correction: the stories reflect the richness of West Indian folklore. At the same time, the stories also deliver some potent messages, messages that extol the virtues of faith, hope and determination and, in a not-too-subtle manner, call for socio-economic and political change in Dominica and the rest of the Caribbean.

The stories in *Mesyé Kwik! Kwak!* are set in—or at least somehow relate to—the relatively large village of St. Joseph, Dominica, its neighboring much smaller village of Layou, and the adjoining Hillsborough Estate and Hillsborough Agricultural Center (a.k.a. "Cocoa Center"). But these Dominican communities could well be Collins, Evesham and Riley in St. Vincent; Laventille, Barataria and San Juan in Trinidad; or Liberta, Tyrell and Swetes in Antigua. Indeed, one could find any of the characters in *Meysé Kwik!* on any of the Caribbean islands, and their adventures and mishaps could well be replicated any where in the Caribbean—or even, in the cases of Thomas Jones (*Grandpa Was In America*) and James and Jane (*A Life Wasted*)—in New York City, London or Paris. But I am getting ahead of myself....

Giftus John's new collection begins with *The Stone*, a story of Joseph, a young boy who encounters a dreaded *lougarou* on his way home one night—or does he, really? The story is steeped in the folklore of the Caribbean islands and, although the reader may laugh at poor Joseph and his predicament, many Caribbean children who grew up before the age of television could relate to the young student's plight. Undoubtedly, some readers may dismiss Joseph's adventure as mere island superstition. That may well be, but superstitions are part of the island's folklore. Indeed, in Dominica and the rest of the Caribbean, superstition and religion often go hand-in-hand. Accordingly, we are not surprised when we read *The Pilgrim*, a story wherein young Jason accompanies a group of aging women on a pilgrimage across the island in the hope of saving an alleged criminal from conviction and a prison term. Surely, we wonder, is this exercise mere superstition, or is it an exercise of great faith?

Certainly, faith—a Caribbean virtue—takes center stage in *Converted*, as we see John giving up alcohol consumption in his quest to serve Jesus and to live a better life. Faith's sister, Hope, comes into play in *Hurricane* as members of the narrator's family gather in their home to watch and pray as Hurricane David, the killer storm that hit Dominica on August 29, 1979, unleashes its fury on the village of St. Joseph. Any reader who has ever experienced the wrath of a hurricane will understand the narrator's mother's hope—and desperation—as she reads her prayer book and rolls the beads of her rosary.

That same hope—though without the element of audible prayer—comes shining through in several of the other stories Giftus weaves in *Mesyé Kwik!* In *A Father's Hope*, two hopes conflict. On the one hand, Michael's father hopes that his son will emulate him and one day become a farmer. On the other hand, Michael, arguing that the day of the farmer is history, hopes for a better life by either furthering his academic career or taking a job "away from the land." It is that same hope that leads Grandpa Thomas Jones (*Grandpa was in America*) to migrate to the United States in search of a better life; that leads Joel and Wally (*Trouble in the Channel*) to traverse the Guadeloupe Channel conducting trade with the Guadeloupeans; and causes Joel to devise a secret plan to migrate to Guadeloupe permanently. And yes, it is that same hope that led the narrator in *Flying to Barbados* to show up at Melville Hall Airport, Dominica, with an empty wallet in his quest to obtain a visitor's visa from the United States Embassy in *Bridgetown, Barbados*!

The hope theme that Giftus presents in *Mesyé Kwik!* exemplifies more than hope. Certainly, Giftus paints a picture of determination by his characters to succeed in spite of the odds. In a sense, Giftus uses *Mesyé Kwik!* to re-write the Apostle Paul's proclamation of I Corinthians 13 that "now remaineth faith, hope and charity" (*The Holy Bible*, King James Version) to a more meaningful declaration for a Caribbean people seeking to better their lot: "You have three things to help you on your way – faith, hope and determination."

Maybe determination, as the third member of the trio of virtues, could, like charity in Paul's discourse to the Corinthians, be deemed the greatest of the lot. After all, in almost every story Giftus relates here, his characters—both heroes and villains—succeed because of their determination to do so. And even when they do not succeed, their lack of success does not stem from a lack of determination on their part, but from forces beyond their control. Thus, in *A Thief in the Night*, Mr. Philip, after much determined effort, sees the chicken thief under arrest with a criminal trial pending. By the same token, Mal, notwithstanding *his* determined efforts to keep stealing chickens, is finally apprehended. In *The Street*, Sandra and the other members of The Concerned Seven youth organization try to rename a village street in honor of a late politician. While the group members undoubtedly ignore proper protocol in their attempts at renaming the street, the reader will surely admire their determination. Alas, on this occasion, determination proves insufficient and the group's efforts are thwarted by a group of unknown opponents equally determined to prevent the renaming of the street. Giftus hints—but does not say outright—that the unknown opponents have the support of the government of the day. This subtle hint gives the story political overtones, and introduces us to the politics of Dominica and the wider Caribbean.

Few things divide Caribbean people as much as politics does. People often become bitter enemies over political leanings and because of differences of opinion on political matters. It is commendable, therefore, that Giftus broaches the subject in not one, but two, of his stories. While the political overtones are subtle in *The Street*, *The Final Hour* presents a humorous yet serious look at island politics. The story takes us through the final days of an election campaign right up to election night. Using the campaign speeches, Giftus also gives us a view of the incumbent's tenure in office—his failures, his successes, and the contrasting views thereof. The story also gives the reader a glimpse of the celebration—and sorrow—of election night. But above all, in *The Final Hour*, we get a glimpse of Giftus's disgust with Dominican politics. Referring to the electorate's ability to "do their civic responsibility" and the system that governs Dominican politics, Giftus writes:

> It was something that many had fought for after the abolition of slavery when Universal Adult Suffrage was granted to all free slaves. But for some, they were still slaves to a system that did not give any hope nor did it provide, but instead just kept taking away and giving to the rich. It was a system that, for many, stunk and reeked of corruption.
>
> Yet, every five years there were more promises—and more empty promises at that. Promises that politicians never delivered. It was a system that allowed illiterate individuals to become elected and make policies that defined the future of the country. A system that allowed people to vote for politicians not because of what they could do for the country, but what they could offer under the table. It was a system that allowed politicians to hire lackeys to hold positions they were incapable of having. It was a system where the blind led those who could see.

Surely, this statement from *The Final Hour* says much about *Mesyé Kwik!* *Mesyé Kwik!* is not merely about culture; it is not merely about folklore; it is not merely for entertainment. Rather, it is a collection of stories with serious themes and messages, a collection which proclaims that faith, hope and determination will conquer and that yes, oh yes, Dominica and the Caribbean need change, change to socio-economic and political systems that will better suit the island and the region. Whether or not one agrees with Giftus, we must at the very least commend him for sharing his thoughts, and for letting his characters express them for him.

The Final Hour ends in a rather sad and mournful manner. After all the activities of the campaign, Kevin—the losing incumbent—and his wife are alone. He wipes her tears, and kisses her.

Somewhere in the village a bell sounded. It had a haunting sound. It sounded like a death knell was being rung for Kevin.

I somehow imagine that the bell being rung was the huge bell at the Roman Catholic Church in St. Joseph. I also imagine that the bell was not just being rung, but was being tolled—tolled just as Trigg, Gabby Hayes, Keys and others have been known to toll it. Such a sound would indeed signal a changing of the guard, the death of the politics of hate and destruction, the death of the system Giftus dislikes so much, and the ushering in of a newer, better and brighter day for the people of Dominica and the Caribbean.

That said, I acknowledge that the bell now tolls for me. I must leave you to read this masterpiece by one of the Caribbean's finest authors, Giftus John. Mark my words: this is no Kwik!

Professor Vaughn E. James
Texas Tech University
Lubbock, Texas

Acknowledgement

I want to take this opportunity to thank all who assisted in the final product; a book that I hope we all will enjoy and have felt good about working on.

To The Almighty for giving me the talent and the ability to share my words with You; to my wife Theresa, my daughter, Mandy and my son, Jamal, my first editors and critics; to members of my family in St. Joseph, whose inspiration figured in most of the stories in the book; to Professor Vaughn James, (aka King Shakey) for his invaluable assistance and support in the final stages of the book; to Ron Deschamps for his help with the cover illustration; and to all of you who helped by reading the manuscript throughout its many stages. Finally, to all of you who have given me the support and encouragement, not only now, but also throughout my literary journey, I also say Thank You.

I hope that "Mesyé Kwik! Kwak!" will rekindle some aspects of our lives that we can share with those who have not experienced Dominica's lure, its folklore, its charm and its mix of everything. I hope I can bring some of that to you. Mesyé Kwik! Kwak!

Geejay 2005

The Stone

Joseph prayed that Mr. Thompson would call an end to the class for the day. He wanted to raise his hand to ask for permission to leave, but he could not muster the courage to do so. Out of fear, or sheer respect for the burly principal, he could not fathom the courage to face Mr. Thompson. He knew that the longer he stayed in class, the darker it would be when he would begin his journey to Cocoa Center.

His sisters, Clare and Verne, had already left. They had taken a ride, as always, with La Bleu, the truck driver, and by now they would all have been home. He had seen La Bleu return to the village, his box truck loaded with farmers and laborers and their bags of provisions; enough proof that his sisters were safe at home.

His family had been living at the Cocoa Center for the past twelve years. His father was the estate's foreman. The Agricultural Department of the Ministry of Agriculture ran the station, which was commonly referred to as "Center." It was the main agricultural station on the West Coast, serving the farmers and garden enthusiasts in that area, mainly with citrus, cocoa and grafted mango plants. Workers from the villages of Layou and St. Joseph worked at the station five days a week, Monday to Friday.

On the weekends, Joseph and his family, together with the manager of the estate, Mr. Burt; Mr. Burt's brother, Burnet; Mr. Burt's maid, Ma Denise; and his yardman, Mr. Poe, were the only ones left at the Center. Sometimes, during the summer vacations, Mr. Burt's family, who lived in Roseau, the capital, would join him for a few weeks. There were other times too, during the year, when they would come up for just a day or two in order to get away from life in the city. It was a very quiet and relaxing place to be, right along the banks of the Layou River, one of the longest rivers on the island.

Every morning, from Monday to Friday, Joseph and his two sisters, Verne, who was ten years old, and Clare, who was nine, traveled four miles to St. Joseph where they attended the St. Joseph Government

School. Usually, they rode by truck with La Bleu or, when he was late or unable to provide a ride, with Mr. Harryman. When that was not possible or when they were too late to catch either La Bleu or Mr. Harryman, sometimes because they overslept or sometimes because they were just too slow to get going, they walked all the way to St. Joseph, book bags slung across their shoulders. They did not mind walking because along the way they had the opportunity to collect mangoes, papayas or oranges on the Hillsborough Estate, something they couldn't do when they traveled by truck.

The Robler family owned the Hillsborough Estate: a vast expanse of land on either side of the Layou River. It was there that most of the island's cocoa was harvested for shipment overseas and where coconut meat was dried and made into copra. That, too, was shipped overseas for use in making oil products, animal feed or soap. Sometimes, when they got to the Hillsborough Bridge that spanned the Layou River from North to South, Joseph and his sisters would get a ride on one of the trucks returning from Roseau after having transported commuters to the town. Otherwise, they just went along their own merry way until they got to St. Joseph.

Now, here he was in this class, hoping to get out and begin his journey home. But apparently, Mr. Thompson had other ideas that afternoon and he did not seem to be in any hurry to end the class. Mr. Thompson had just been transferred to the St. Joseph Government School from the Marigot Government School. He was a native of St. Joseph but had spent most of his teaching life in other districts around the island. He was a very stern man and the villagers were happy that he was in charge of the school. They hoped that his presence would turn around the fortunes of the students at the Common Entrance and School Leaving Exams, since the school had not been faring too well lately.

Joseph began to believe that maybe Mr. Thompson was unaware that he did not reside in St. Joseph. He also thought that maybe Mr. Thompson was punishing him. But what would he be punishing him for? He could think of nothing that he had done, and if he had done anything, Mr. Thompson would have called him to his desk and, in front of the whole school, he would have used his tamarind whip against his little butt.

He looked out a window and could see the greater part of the village of St. Joseph bathed in the soft glow of the late afternoon sunlight. He could see The Morne, the hills above the village and the rather placid silvery waters of the Caribbean Sea kissing the western coastline. For a while his eyes focused on the house of the girl he had started having a liking for. He wished he could see her from where he was, maybe standing on that tall step at the entrance to her house. They had just started speaking to each other. She was in Standard Six, one class lower than he was, and he had watched her leave for home earlier that afternoon. She had looked at him and he had winked to her. He was excited. For a while he let his imaginations run wild.

The village of St. Joseph was alive that afternoon. The Somerset Cricket Club was conducting its usual practice for its members on the playing field. On the grounds of the lower school as well as on the most easterly part of the field, the younger boys were playing their own games, every now and then skillfully avoiding being hit by the leather and cork balls that zoomed past their heads. The field was not the best, with hardly any grass growing, except for the northern part where water usually collected when it rained and where a ravine bordered the Catholic cemetery. Then there was the area close to a swamp on the easterly part of the field. The swamp was fed with water from the septic tanks and other wastewater from both the police station and the Cable and Wireless telephone exchange. The area in the vicinity of the swamp was the greenest part of the field. Other than that it was all dirt and stones. If any of the young boys fell on the field in one of these bare spots, he was sure to find small pebbles lodged in his knees or elbows or the palm of his hands. It was horrible, but that was all they had and they made the best of it.

The box trucks laden with workers returning home from Roseau and other areas were now arriving. Some stopped next to the tall palmiste tree that stood like a guard at the foot of the paved, cement road leading to the Catholic Church. Others stopped in the middle of the village as weary passengers disembarked. Some trucks, loaded with folks coming home from their garden plots in the interior of the island, also made their way through the village. Fishermen who had been out chasing fish all day were pulling their boats and seines into the boathouse on the bank of the St. Joseph River. A few others were mending some nets that had been broken, working feverishly to get as much as they could before darkness fell. Thick, black smoke bellowed from the chimney of Mr. Brown's bakery on Back Street as the bakers were preparing to make bread. The swirling smoke drifted in an easterly direction indicating that the wind was blowing in from the Caribbean Sea this afternoon.

The long shadows were beginning to stretch into various areas as the sun descended lower over the Caribbean Sea. Suddenly there was a loud bang on the roof of the school building. Everyone instinctively ducked and then laughed as they realized what had happened. The player who was at bat on the practice field had hit a ball that had landed on the galvanized roof. There was no ceiling to muffle the sound of anything falling on the roof. The noise was earsplitting. This was expected, with the school building in such close proximity to the playing field. When matches were played, the building served as a boundary line. A ball that landed on the roof would be worth six runs to the batsman. The noise jolted Joseph back to the business at hand.

"Okay guys, that's enough for today," said Mr. Thompson as the students regained their composure. Mr. Thompson hitched his pants up to his waistline and pushed his shirttails deeper into his pants below his bulging stomach. "Tomorrow we will continue doing some more problems. In the meantime let me give you some practice problems for homework. Make sure it's done and I want no excuses," he said, as his voice bellowed throughout the almost empty schoolroom.

Although this was called the St. Joseph Government School (or "Up School" as most people referred to it, or "Aurora" still by others), the building was in fact owned by the Catholic Church and was rented by the Government for the purpose of conducting classes. At the end of the school day and when school was out, it served as a community center. It was there that community meetings were held, movies shown on weekends and cultural shows staged at Easter and Christmas.

There was no luxury for separate classrooms and students from Standard Two to Standard Seven all shared this one large room, a blackboard, on most occasions, serving as the only divider between classes. But honestly, there was no real division. On a bright day teachers would take their classes outside under the trees among the stones and shrubbery or beneath the long overhanging eaves of the building and hold classes there in an effort to avoid the noise. When it rained, there was no choice. Nonetheless, the kids learnt and here was Mr. Thompson trying to prove that point.

Joseph grew more concerned. He thought that it was the end of the day, but apparently it was not. Mr. Thompson was giving him and the other students more work to do at home. He wondered if he would have time to complete the work when he got home. He was beginning to get a little more concerned. He remembered that his mother was worried at the time that he had arrived home last night. He had gotten a ride from a man whom he did not know, but the man said that he knew his daddy. However, his mother was very concerned. The man had met him at the big corner soon after he had passed the Hillsborough Bridge and just before he got to the big *lapo anmè* mango tree. The man had stopped when he saw Joseph. But Joseph could not remember the man's name.

His mother was still worried that he was coming home all by himself. He was only eleven years old. She was caught in a tough situation and she was not sure which was the best way to work it out.

"Your daddy will have to do something or talk to Mr. Thompson," she said, the concern showing on her face. "I hope you don't have to do that after this week," she continued.

Joseph was one of the twenty-five students selected by Mr. Thompson to be in a special class to prepare for the Common Entrance Exams later that year. The students who did well at these exams, which were held in Roseau, the capital, were awarded Government scholarships and bursaries. They would then attend one of the four high schools: The St. Mary's Academy and the Dominica Grammar School for boys, and the Wesley High School and the Convent High School for girls. The Catholic Church ran the St. Mary's Academy, while the Grammar School was government owned. The Catholic Church also ran the Convent High while the Methodist Church ran the Wesley High.

Joseph's mother was happy that he had been selected to prepare for the exam, but she was concerned about him walking up to the Center all by himself. She had been trying to arrange for him to spend the next few months, until the exams, with his grandmother or his uncle in St. Joseph, but she was waiting for Joseph's daddy to make the final decision. That had not yet been done, but this episode only helped make her have a greater concern for her son's well-being.

Joseph, too, was worried because on his way up to Cocoa Center last night, a young man had told him that there was a man sitting on the big Stone waiting for him. He did not ask the man which big Stone, but he guessed he was referring to the big Stone at Louison—part of the Hillsborough Estate. He remembered hearing the kids at his school talk about a man dressed all in black sitting on a big stone. He had heard them talk of such a man on Morne Pican, the hill overlooking the village from the northeast. He had also heard the kids talking about such a man on the big Stone at Louison, along the road that he traveled and just a few minutes from where he lived. He never really worried about any of that until now. He had no need to, and honestly, he never cared. This had never bothered him before because until he started staying over for classes in the afternoons, he and his sisters always got a ride home with Mr. Jeremiah. They never had to walk to Centre by themselves, at night. Was this the night he was going to meet the *man*?

Mr. Jeremiah was the overseer of the neighboring Clarke Hall Estates. He drove a Unimog and he would travel to St. Joseph to pick up his daughter and also his niece who was a teacher at the Lower School and who had recently been transferred from the southeastern village of La Plaine. Joseph and his sisters, Mr. Jeremiah's daughter and a few other kids who lived on the estate, would crowd into the back of the strange looking vehicle as it wound its way to Clarke Hall. Some days, if Mr. Jeremiah did not show up, they would travel with La Bleu or Mr. Harryman. In the event of inclement weather, that is, if it rained heavily or there was a thunderstorm, he and his sisters would spend the night with their grandmother (their mother's mom), Ma Missie. That was preplanned, so they had no problems making up their minds when such situations arose.

You think they're talking about the same man? he had asked himself as he walked alone last night. He had had no answer. He had been spared thinking of it because of the ride he had received from the man whose name he could not remember. He had climbed into the back of the old Land Rover and sat among groceries the man had bought in Roseau. Joseph had tried guessing where the man was going, but there was nothing to give him a hint. He had stretched his legs over a bag of onions and the smell, together with the smell of codfish, had filled the back of the Land Rover. Joseph did not mind the smell or sitting among the man's groceries. He was getting a ride home and he was not going to come across any man on any big Stone tonight.

He and the driver had engaged in some conversation about school, with the man doing most of the talking. Joseph had given short, quick answers to all the questions the man had asked then. Before he realized it, they were approaching the final curve just below the area where the station's cowshed was located. He realized that he had gone past the Stone and had forgotten to look for any sign of the *man*. It was too late then. The jeep had then come to a dragging halt among the loose macadam that marked the entrance to the Center.

"Okay, tell daddy and mammy I say hello," the driver had said to him, as he crawled out from the back of the jeep. "And good luck in the common entrance, eh," he continued. He then pulled out onto the narrow asphalt road and headed up along the Layou Valley, the headlamps of the jeep brightening the mango and bamboo trees that lined the banks of the Layou River.

Joseph had walked up the small hill to his home, which was nestled between two tall hedges: one on the east and one on the west. The family dog had sensed his arrival, barked and ran to meet him. He had heard his brothers and sisters screaming his name. It seemed like everyone was expectantly looking out for him. He was happy to be home at last. He had told his mother of the man who had given him a ride, but he could not remember his name, no matter how hard he tried.

"Mr. Lander? Mr. Cuffy? Mr. Toussaint? Which one of them?" his mother had asked. But Joseph drew a blank. Finally, his mother had given up trying to figure out who it was who had given him a ride. "Maybe someday the person will tell your daddy that he gave you a vep," she said. "So why didn't you ask him his name?" she had asked Joseph.

"I don't know!" he had replied, shrugging his shoulders.

Then it was time for him to get something to eat, get his homework done and get set for bed. But Joseph never mentioned anything to his mother or to his brothers and sisters about what the young man had told him. Was he scared or did he just not bother?

But now, as he sat in the classroom, waiting for Mr. Thompson to give the final word, the thought started bothering him. *What if there was really a man on the big Stone? Was it a jombie, or a lougaroo? What if what the man had told him last night was really true?* He blamed himself for not having asked his mother about it last night. He shivered and goose bumps covered his body. He bent his head unto the wooden desk that he shared with Elvue. He heard the classmates giggle and he lifted his head. Standing next to him was the imposing figure of Mr. Thompson.

"What's the problem, Joe?" Mr. Thompson asked, as he put his left hand on Joseph's shoulder.

"Um, um ..." he hesitated. "Nothing sir, I was just wondering."

"Wondering what?" Mr. Thompson asked sternly.

"Just wondering sir about ..." But before he could finish, Mr. Thompson continued.

"Let this be the last time I catch you with your head on the desk. If this happens again, I will surely see to it that you get the message. Do you understand that, mister?" Joseph looked at him and nodded his head slowly.

"Don't shake your head. Don't you have a tongue in your mouth?" he asked Joseph.

"Yes, sir," Joseph answered.

"Then use it!" the principal retorted, as he placed the end of the tamarind whip that he always carried against the left side of his face. "Did you copy the homework?" he asked, this time in a much stronger and disgusted tone.

"Some of it sir, not all," Joseph replied, fear gripping him.

Mr. Thompson glared at him and walked away, shaking his head slowly and slapping the tamarind whip against his left pant leg, as he moved up to the front of the class. He looked back at Joseph when he got there, a frown now on his face. Joseph looked away trying to avoid his threatening glare.

When everyone had copied the homework, Mr. Thompson randomly picked some of the students to close the windows and doors throughout the building. Joseph cursed silently within after he was the one selected to shut the doors at the farthest end of the room. "Why me?" he asked himself. "I am trying to get out of here and I cannot. I am sure he knows that I have to go to Center," he muttered under his breath, as he finished packing his exercise workbooks into his school bag.

He got up from his seat and ran down the room, hurdling over some benches as he did so. He removed the two stones that kept the doors open, pulled the doors in and bolted them shut. He rushed back to his seat, picked up his bag and sped out the door as Mr. Thompson watched, wondering what was going on.

———————

The shadows were getting longer and that meant one thing: Joseph's chances of getting home before sunset were getting smaller. He looked down the road towards the village to see if there was any sign of a vehicle coming his way. The idea of the man on the big Stone was beginning to sound as a probability. But there was no sign of anything moving, except a Public Works dump truck that was roaring through the village. He wasn't going to thumb the driver. There was no way that he was going to try to get in the back of this thing. He would take his chances of getting a more comfortable ride along the way.

And so he started his lone journey home. He walked along the St. Joseph cliffs, sometimes in shade of the tall sea grape trees that grew along the shore; and then in sun, getting the full blast of the sun's rays against his face. Vehicles loaded with everything from passengers to goods heading to St. Joseph and the other villages farther west, zipped past. Some of the drivers who knew him honked their horns as they sped past him.

His school bag felt heavier now and the weight on his shoulder seemed to slow him down just a bit. Was it just his legs or his mind beginning to play games with him? He started to run. After about three minutes, he stopped, then walked a few more minutes, then ran again until he finally decided that he would walk until he had passed Layou. He was also getting a bit tired.

Layou is a hamlet at the mouth of the Layou River along the coastline of the Caribbean Sea. It is a fishing community and the local fishermen make use of both the sea and the river. These are the men who usually catch *titiri* that is used to make a fish cake delicacy or *ackra*, as it is commonly known. Layou River is noted for *titiri*, that little strange fish that make their way up river from the sea to lay their eggs. The men would go out very early in the morning and cast their nets—nets that look like those used to fend off mosquitoes—and would catch hundreds of these small, grayish and slimy creatures at the mouth of the river as they began their migration up stream. The fishermen would then travel to St. Joseph and other villages or sometimes to the fish market in Roseau, to sell their catch.

The children from Layou traveled to St. Joseph to school while the grown ups traveled there to conduct most of their other activities: visits to the doctor, attending court cases at the St. Joseph Court room; grocery shopping to some extent, and attending services at the Catholic and Adventist churches. The main road linking the West Coast villages passed right through the middle of Layou, just like it did with most of the villages along the west coast, from Massacre to Colihaut. It was a very narrow road and it was a miracle that there were hardly any accidents in the village.

Joseph knew some of the villagers in Layou. His father had a few friends there and Joseph would always say hello to them as he passed by. But there was one lady that he knew very well. She lived on the hill a few feet from the road just as you were about to exit Layou if you were coming from St. Joseph. Her name was Yvonne and she also worked at Cocoa Center. She was the one who always helped his mother with some of her chores and even when the other workers had left for their homes after their day's work, she and his parents would sit and talk until she was ready to make the trek down to Layou.

Joseph was now sweating profusely both from running and a bit from his anxiety or fear of meeting the man on the big Stone. Along the road, very close to where Yvonne lived, he stopped for a drink of water at one of the only two standpipes in Layou. He waited as an old man filled his bucket with water. When the man was done, Joseph bent over, throwing the school bag over his back. He cupped his hands under the water, put his mouth into the cupped hands and gulped down a few pints of water. He stood up and belched loudly. As he moved away from the standpipe, he looked up towards Yvonne's house. As was customary, she was sitting in the yard with Paula, the youngest of her three daughters. Joseph waved to them.

"How comes you goin' up so late?" Yvonne shouted at Joseph. "Where's your sistah an' dem?" she continued, as she stood up, shaking dust from the back of her dress.

"I had class today," Joseph responded. "The head teacher kept us in after school class."

"So you couldn' tell him you hav' to go up Center all by yourself? A big man like you!" she admonished. "You musn' 'fraid to speak. Anyhow take care," she warned, her tone changing to one of concern. Joseph nodded his head. "Wait awhile," she continued, "Let me give you a bread so you can eat. Wait dere for if a vep comin'. I will bring it for you," she shouted, as she disappeared into her house.

Joseph waited for both the bread and the ride wishing that he would get the ride instead. He didn't mind the bread, but with the predicament that now faced him, he could sacrifice the bread. But just as fate would have it, no ride came.

Yvonne walked down the narrow stone track from her home towards him. "Okay, I put some peanut butter on it. I know you like peanut butter," she said, smiling at Joseph, as she handed him the bread, wrapped in a brown paper bag.

"Thanks," said Joseph, as he took the bread and bid goodnight to Yvonne and continued his trip to Cocoa Center. A few moments later, Joseph removed the loaf of bread from the bag and bit into it.

Joseph had not been walking for more than about ten minutes since saying goodbye to Yvonne when he saw a man approaching along the road. The man looked familiar. Was it fate or was it misfortune? This was the same man who had told him about the Stone the night before. Joseph's skin crawled one more time and he felt his stomach tighten up.

"What's up with this guy?" Joseph asked himself.

Was this man out for him or was it just fate that had brought them together two days in a row? He tried to remain calm, but he felt his legs shaking. He could not control himself even if he tried. The man was almost upon him. Joseph looked straight on, trying not to make any eye contact. He was now less than ten feet away and it looked like the man was walking straight towards him. Joseph instinctively moved towards the edge of the road as the man came nearer.

"Why you walkin' up to Center by yourself boy?" the man asked, a grin on his rather bony and narrow face. He stopped, but Joseph kept on walking, scared to engage in any conversation with him. *Who was he anyway?* Joseph could not remember seeing this man anytime before last night. "I talkin' to you, Joseph. You deaf? Anyhow do what you want; de *man* waitin' for you on de big Stone at Louison."

Joseph was more scared than surprised when the man called him by name. How did he know his name? *Who tell mister my name non, boy?* he pondered as the man continued.

"De *lougarou* waitin' for you boy! You not hearin'?" he shouted. Joseph did not stop. Instead his pace quickened as the man shouted again, "An' he goin' to take you with him tonight."

Joseph started running as the strange man laughed and seemed to be enjoying what he was doing to the youngster. Joseph was worried that the man mentioned Louison. If that was where the man on the Stone was, then he was in trouble. He knew what Stone that the man was talking about. The same one the kids would speak about but which he never really paid attention to. Not until now.

He did not stop running until he got to the Hillsborough Bridge. He was hoping that by getting to the junction at the bridge, his chances of getting a ride home would improve. At that junction the West Coast Road joined with the Transinsular Road that led to the Northern and Eastern villages of the island. Maybe he would meet another of his father's friends or somebody who knew his parents. He was breathless. He slowed down but continued walking. Getting home was foremost on his mind.

As he approached the area called Cocoa where a lot of the cocoa trees grew, right along the fertile banks of the river, he noticed some very dark clouds forming in the distance over the lush green mountains. If he were lucky, this was only a sign of rain in the hinterlands. If not, chances were he stood the risk of being caught in a downpour. He had grown accustomed to seeing the swollen river rushing to the sea while the sun was beating down at Cocoa Center. Maybe that was going to be the case. He also was aware that it rained quite a lot when it was least expected. He fervently wished that this would not happen today. If it started raining it would only help darkness fall more quickly, plus he had no protection from Mother Nature. All he had was a plastic bag to protect his books from getting wet. He would get drenched to the bone if the rain came his way.

Before he could gather his thoughts, he saw a quick bright streak zip across the sky. Was it really what he thought it was? Then he heard the rumble in the distance.

"Oh man!" he whispered to himself. "Oh boy, I'm in trouble. See what's happening to me!"

He was so engrossed in his thoughts that he didn't notice the lady who was walking towards him with a bamboo basket on her head. He was startled as she spoke. "Careful sonny, it goin' to rain. Get home safely," she said to him, a smile appearing on her small wrinkled face.

"Yes, ma'am," Joseph answered. "Goodnight ma'am," he respectfully continued as he recovered from the initial surprise.

"Goodnight to you, too. Tell mammy I say goodnight, eh. I didn' see her when I was passin'," she said.

"Yes, ma'am, I will tell her," Joseph answered, as the lady passed him by.

He knew this lady. Her name was Ma Boboy. She was from St. Joseph and a few times a week went to her small agricultural plot in Café, a few miles farther up along the banks of the river than was Cocoa Center. Café was also the place, besides being the area where people like Ma Boboy did their subsistence farming, where the Water Authority had one of its water catchments. That catchment, which was inexplicably accessible to anyone who wished, served the villages of Layou, St. Joseph, Tarreau and Mero. Some days, her husband, Mr. Boboy, accompanied Ma Boboy to Café. They had a donkey and usually when they both traveled together, the donkey would be loaded with a bag or two filled with provisions, bundles of dry wood, and grass for the donkey itself. But tonight Ma Boboy was alone. Apparently, Mr. Boboy had decided to spend the night in Café all by himself like he had been accustomed to, sometimes for as long as a month.

Ma Boboy knew Joseph's grandmother. They were neighbors. She was one of the very few people that his grandmother confided in. The two ladies would usually meet, especially in the late afternoons, under the breadfruit tree in his grandparents' yard. There they would talk for hours while his grandfather banged and soldered as he repaired the leaking and damaged pots and pans brought to him by villagers who could not afford to throw away these utensils and buy new ones.

Joseph turned his head to look as Ma Boboy rounded the corner and disappeared behind the bushes growing along the roadside. Then he heard it again: a distant rumbling peal of thunder. "God moving his chair," he thought to himself, as he remembered a local saying, told whenever there was thunder.

Back home, his mother was becoming very concerned. It was now almost half past six and Joseph had not shown up. She was aware of the thunderstorm heading their way and she realized that if Joseph did not get home on time, he was surely going to get a nice drenching. "Verne, close the kitchen and come inside," she cried out to her eldest daughter who was standing at the kitchen door cooling down a cup of hot tea. Clare was inside doing her homework and the youngest girl and the two boys were looking through old magazines. The General Electric battery-operated multi-wave band radio was on and the evening news was being broadcast from the Windward Islands Broadcasting Service (WIBS) radio station. His daddy was not at home. He had traveled to St. Joseph like he always did every afternoon. There he met his friends, played dominoes and draughts, and then after they would have a few drinks in Teacher Ellen's shop. Sometimes, he did a little bit of grocery shopping. Maybe he had no idea what predicament now faced Joseph.

The dark clouds were moving in rapidly across the sky. There was still sunlight bathing the cliffs overlooking the river, a sign that the dark clouds had not fully enveloped the western sky. But by the looks of it, that was inevitable. Darkness and the storm were not going to be long coming. Joseph saw the rain approaching as sheets of white, covering the hills, quickly drew nearer. He heard the ominous sound as rain began falling on the mango and cocoa trees as it approached from the valley. He hurriedly opened his school bag and took out the plastic bag he had in there to protect his books. He placed the school bag into the plastic bag and braced himself for the inevitable. Within minutes, there was rain all around him. It was a torrential downpour and there was no sign that this was going to ease up very soon.

"Oh God, help me please," Joseph begged, as he realized the situation that faced him. He did not only have to contend with meeting the man on the big Stone, but he also had to deal with this thunderstorm. He started running again. His tennis shoes were now soaked and his feet made a slopping sound with each step he took. He was beginning to feel cold too, as the water quickly soaked through his shirt, vest, pants and underpants. As he ran, he stepped into puddles and the water splashed against his exposed legs.

The headlights of a vehicle loomed behind him. He turned around and stopped, raising his right hand as he did so. But the driver only seemed to speed up more. Water splashed over him as the vehicle passed in a puddle of water. Joseph became angry but he was powerless to do anything or to retaliate. He wiped the water off his face.

After the van had passed him, Joseph started running again. It was dark, but not dark enough not to see where he was going. Besides, the trees growing along the roadside gave him enough of an idea as to where he was. He had traveled this road enough to know it by heart now. He could hear the sounds of cwabo (white crabs), rushing over the fallen cocoa leaves back into their holes as he approached. The male frogs croaked noisily on the river's banks. Even with all this rain, the fireflies were everywhere, their little dots of lights now glowing and then disappearing and appearing again. The crickets seemed to be happy for the rain as they hissed noisily from wherever they were.

A great streak of lightning lit up the sky, brightening up everywhere. It was followed by a powerful blast of thunder that seemed to rock the night. Joseph became more frightened. Everything seemed to grow quiet except the river that was getting louder as it rushed along. It was now swollen. Joseph began blaming Mr. Thompson for the situation he now found himself in.

"If only he had let us go out early I would not be here," he cried, as a bead of water dripped into his left eye. He was crying out of fear, frustration and anger. For the first time it dawned upon him that his mother must be wondering where he was and why he had not yet shown up. He remembered that she was worried last night although he had gotten a ride. What would she be wondering now? He bit on his lip in anger.

The rain kept falling at a steady rate and the thunder and lightning seemed to be intensifying. There seemed no chance that this was going to let up any time soon. His legs were beginning to get tired, more from the running than anything else. They felt heavy. It was like he had lead in his shoes. He was now very close to the area where the Stone was. The sound of the night animals and the swishing of the leaves only seemed to unnerve him more. His skin crawled and his heart raced a bit faster. Should he just stand here and wait for a ride or should he turn back? But what if a ride did not show up, especially with this weather, or if one showed up and the driver did to him what the one in the van had done previously?

"I have to get home," he whispered to himself, as the leaves of the mango trees rustled in the wind that was now blowing stronger. He stood trembling and he felt something warm running down his leg: "Oh man!" he cried as he realized what was happening and the urine collected in his left tennis shoe. He felt stupid. He started walking again.

He was almost twenty feet from the Stone when he heard the sound of a vehicle approaching from the opposite direction. Should he use that opportunity to run past the Stone? Here was his chance to get away from the man on the Stone. But before he had time to make up his mind, the blinding lights of the vehicle were upon him. He tried shielding his eyes, but that was of no use. As the vehicle drove past, the driver honked his horn. Joseph waved back, although he did not know who it was. "Why isn't he coming from the other way instead," he asked himself, as the van disappeared behind the mango groves.

It now seemed like an eternity that he had been on the road. He had no idea what time it was. He had no watch. All he needed now was to get past this Stone and get home safely. Somewhere on that Stone or behind that Stone or thereabout, *that* man must be waiting. Maybe the man had already seen him and was just there waiting for his moment. There was no shortcut. He had to go through this route. He wished he had a flashlight. Maybe he would ask his daddy to get him one like he used when he came home from St. Joseph late at night.

"Would he be here in all that rain?" Joseph asked himself, wondering if the man would be brave enough to be out in this weather. But he had no answer to his own question. He had no choice but to keep going home. He could neither turn back nor could he stay out here alone. He had to keep walking.

Joseph was about ten feet away from the Stone when he heard something move. Then he heard a rattle. At the same time, thunder rumbled and seemed to be rolling towards him. That was followed by an earsplitting blast. Fear gripped him.

"Oh God, help me," he screamed, but no sound came from his mouth. He started running. He tripped over some loose macadam and landed on the wet roadside. His bag flew from his hands. He got up hurriedly, pain in his knees, and picked up the bag. He looked back and it appeared to him that somebody was following him. He started running again, stepping into puddles and streams of water flowing from the cliffs above. His heart raced quickly, like it was going to jump out of his chest.

He came to the narrow corner where many vehicular accidents had taken place and where landslides usually occurred, blocking the road. He was cognizant of the fact that he should stay clear of the edge of the road and at the same time should look out for any mudslides or loose stones coming from above. He still heard what he thought were pounding footsteps behind him. His chest was hurting, but he did not dare stop. The man on the Stone was coming to get him.

"Why is this happening to me? Oh God, why?" he cried as he splashed into a mound of mud. *Maybe I shouldn't go back to class again,* he thought to himself, although he knew that his parents would have none of it. They had hoped that some day he would be able to attend high school and get a decent education. They wanted something better in life for him and his sisters than they had for themselves and if this was the way it was going to happen, so be it.

———————

Back home, his brothers and sisters were beginning to miss him.

"Mama, where's Joseph?" Verne asked her mother who was sitting in a chair next to the door to the verandah looking out for her son.

"Oh, I don't know. Maybe he's with his daddy," her mother answered, hoping that by some miracle Joseph was with his daddy. There was no way she could be sure because she did not have any means of communicating with her husband. The only telephone on the station was in the office building and she had no access to it. She prayed silently that the Good Lord would guide her son home safely.

Joseph did not stop running until he got to the area below the cowshed. He was very breathless and could not get his legs to keep running. He bent over for a few seconds and then he heard a loud noise. He turned back but there was nothing that he could make out in the darkness. Then he heard it getting louder. It was a vehicle coming towards him. It sounded like one of those Public Works dump trucks, similar to the one that had passed him earlier in afternoon in St. Joseph. He panicked. He had to get out from there. This was a narrow and dangerous spot to be in. On his right, the rushing river, on his left, the cliff.

Whenever he and his sisters had to walk to school they always hurriedly moved away from this spot because it was so dangerous. There was a drop of almost fifty feet from the edge of the road to the

16

water below. The basin, too, was so deep, the water looked blue. The water seemed like it hardly moved. Just looking at it was scary. People bathed and swam all along the length of the river, but few dared try this part.

He had to get out of here, and in a hurry. He did not enjoy the prospect of being here face to face with one of those trucks. A boulder rolled in front of him. It only added to his bad luck night. As the sound of the vehicle drew closer, he decided to make a run for it. He had no choice. Ahead of him a roaring dump truck, behind him the *man*. Soon he saw the light of the approaching vehicle as it lit up the trees along the roadside. If only he could get to a safe spot before the dump truck got to him. He momentarily closed his eyes as he imagined himself being pressed against the cliff by this iron monster. He made a dash for it as the truck barreled down the road; the metal box banging against the frame as it fell into one pothole after the other. Just before the truck got to him, Joseph reached a wider part of the road. He jumped over a flooded ravine and landed among a clump of crouton hedges. He felt his arm hurt as it hit something hard. It was too close to home to worry about the pain. Then he thought he heard a voice behind him.

"Oh no, he's coming to get me," he screamed. He got up and began running again, this time along the grass-covered track that led to the cowshed. He slipped but managed to keep his feet under him. Soon he was in the clear as he felt the solid pavement under his feet. He had reached the office compound. He breathed a deep sigh of relief. He was almost home. Just a few more feet to go! Up the hill and he would be home. He bent over and felt his knee. It was raw. He had bruised it when he had fallen. His hand hurt but there was no bruise. He was wet all over. He laughed. "Wet like a chicken," he whispered to himself. The plastic bag that he had placed his school bag in was torn in some places and he prayed that not too much water had penetrated and wet his books.

He did not hear the vibration of the vehicle that was approaching from behind until the headlamps bathed the yard with their lights. The vehicle stopped next to him.

"Only now getting home, Youssie?" a voice asked, referring to him by his pet name. It was Mr. Burt. Mr. Burt had just returned from Roseau where he usually went to departmental meetings at the Botanical Gardens. "Where have you been in this kind of weather?" he continued.

"I had afternoon class and the teacher let us out late," Joseph answered, breathlessly.

"Were you running? Why do you sound so breathless?" Mr. Burt asked him. "Are you okay?" he continued before Joseph had time to answer.

"Umm … yes sir, I'm okay," he hesitated. "I was running so I could get home from the storm." He lied.

"You're wet all over. You need a good dry up," said Mr. Burt as his brother looked on, half asleep in the passenger side of the Land Rover. "Bye, now, and take care." Mr. Burt slowly pulled away and drove up the hill towards his home that was the most northerly of the three houses on the estate.

Joseph could not believe what had just happened to him. After all he had gone through, for it to come to this was incomprehensible. "Man, that's not fair," he said to himself, as he bent over in frustration. "You think that's right, man? After all that and is now Mr. Burt coming? Maybe I should have asked him if he saw the man on the Stone," he chided himself.

Suddenly, he seemed to remember something. He hurriedly looked back as a flash of light lit up the night sky again. But there was nothing behind him. He heard a bark. The family dog came towards him. As usual, the dog had sensed his arrival. Joseph wondered how he did that even if he could not see him in the dark. He felt better because he had heard that dogs scared away jombies and if the man on the stone were really a jombie, the dog would scare him away for sure. The dog jumped all over him, licking him over the face and wagging its tail in delight as they walked up the hill together.

"Joseph home, mammy," he heard Verne shout as he climbed the steps unto the verandah, water dripping from his clothes and hair.

"I thought you were with your father," his mother cried, as she came to the door. "You were in this kind of weather all by yourself? Bondyé! You didn't see your father?" she asked him as his other sisters and brothers came running to the door.

"No ma, I didn't see him," Joseph replied.

"Look at you. You all wet up and dirty. You fall down?" she asked, as she looked him over.

"Yes, ma. I was running to come home. I was afraid of the thunder and lightning," he answered, knowing quite well that he was not telling the truth. But he was not going to bring up the idea of the man on the Stone. Maybe he should wait for a more appropriate time.

Would his mother believe him, and did he really want to deal with the idea of the man and the Stone *thing* now that he was home?

"Come on. Take your shoes off and leave it on the verandah to dry. Take your clothes off. When you finish, wash yourself up and then pass some Bay Rum on your head before you get a cold," his mother said to him, as she took the school bag from him. "Let me make some tea for you."

Joseph was happy to be home. He was on safe grounds now. No man was coming here to meet him. He washed himself and changed into warm clothes. He then had a hot cup of bush tea—*fèy pomad*—as he spoke to his mother about the storm. He had something to eat and then settled down to do his homework. Most of the books in his bag had survived the water but one or two of them would have to be replaced.

But he could not get the work done. The man on the Stone was stuck in his mind. After a while, he decided to talk to his mother about it and ask her if she knew anything about the Stone. He got up from his seat at the dining room table and headed to the living room where everyone else was. But before he made two steps he decided against the idea. Tonight was not the night for it.

Eventually, it was time for him to go to bed. Joseph retired to the little room next to the dining room that doubled-up as a storage room and his bedroom. He knelt at the side of the canvas cot that was his bed, and said a prayer. He then bid his mom goodnight and lay down to sleep.

His mother shut off the lamp and the house was in total darkness. Joseph lay back on the bedding and rested his head on the pillow, but tried as he could, he was not able to fall asleep. He kept hearing a voice. *'There's a man waiting for you at the big Stone.'* It sounded like the same voice he had heard when he fell among the hedges. The rattling sound and the noise that he heard from the bushes next to the Stone came back to him again. He shivered and buried his face into the pillow. Then he wondered: *Did that guy follow me all the way up to Center?* But he checked himself. *How would he have done it?* He pushed that thought aside. Then he wondered again. *Maybe he is the man on the Stone. Maybe he was the man who was going to scare me.* All the weird thoughts about the episode only helped to keep him awake, but not help ease his worries and fears.

He heard when his father came home. Mr. Ranch had taken him home on his dump truck. He heard the sound of the dump truck as it climbed the hill and then stopped in the yard. It reminded him of his encounters earlier with the two dump trucks. But Mr. Ranch had taken his daddy home on many occasions before. They were good friends and Mr. Ranch had once worked with him at Center. Joseph heard them talking, but he had no clue as to what time it was. Then he heard the skidding noise of the tires as the truck momentarily got stuck in the soft mud in the yard. After a few minutes it was out and Mr. Ranch finally headed back to St. Joseph.

His father rapped a few times at the front door until his mother opened it. He heard when they started talking about what had happened to him. He heard his mother plead with his father that they do something. "Sheridan, I was scared all the time," she told him. "I don't want him to be walking home at that time of the night all by himself. Anything can happen to him. You never know," she told his father. "Out there they have wicked people and you don't know what they can do to him," she continued.

"Okay, let me talk to my uncle and see if he can help me. I will go to there tomorrow. His wife had already told me it would not be a problem," his father said.

Joseph realized that his parents were trying to get him to stay at Uncle Lordon's home at Autrobando. He wondered why they were not going to send him to his grandmother like they had done before, until he was punished for staying out too late with his friends. But being at his uncle's home would not be a bad idea either. Still, he would not mind staying with his grandmother again. He'd just have to be careful that he didn't mess up again. Anyhow, whichever worked, he would go with it as long as it prevented him from having to walk home by himself after classes. He knew that would not happen until next week and he squirmed at the idea of being alone on the road again tomorrow.

He tossed about for hours until he finally fell asleep, although not for long. He was soon awakened by the crowing of the roosters that were all about the yard and under the house, and by the birds that were noisily chirping in the Glory Cedar trees and sucking nectar from the flowers outside his window.

The house was soon alive with activity as he and his sisters got ready for school for yet another day. They lit the three-burner kerosene stove that they brought in from the kitchen every night. They boiled some water, scrambled a few eggs (their father raised a lot of chickens), made some cocoa tea and prepared for each of them a loaf of bread filled with butter or eggs or some homemade jam that they would eat at recess. Finally, they bade farewell to their mother, each giving her a kiss on her cheek as they filed out of the house. Their younger sister and two brothers were still asleep. Their father had already left for work.

Outside was still damp and soggy from last night's rain and the morning was cooler, although the sun was out and there was not a cloud in the sky. The air was fresh. As they walked down towards the side of the road to await a ride to school, their father approached them, first to kiss them goodbye, and then to give them some bad news:

"You all better begin to walk down. La Bleu didn't go up this morning and Mr. Harryman is sick," he said to them.

Joseph did not like what he had just heard. He cringed. His stomach churned and his skin crawled just like it did so many times last night. "Oh man, do I have to go past that place again?" he asked himself. *But it impossible for the man to be still there this morning,* he thought. He remembered that the children at school always said that the boogieman did not like the light of day; he ran away at the first sight of daylight. "Maybe they're right," he thought, trying to reassure himself that everything would turn out to be okay.

After they had bid goodbye to their father and to some of the workers who were still on the compound awaiting their daily work details, Joseph and his sisters began their trek to St. Joseph. The Layou River was still muddy but not as swollen as it was last night. The ravines along the road were still flowing with water from the hills above. A cool easterly breeze kept blowing. They maneuvered themselves along the edge of the road, avoiding the small mudslides, stones and also the vehicles that passed them in either way, none of which was suitable or had any space for them to travel on. Joseph silently cursed his luck.

It was not long before they came to the bend in the road just before the spot where the Stone was. His heart skipped a few beats and just as he did last night, he involuntarily moved to the side of the road closer to the bank of the river.

"Where are you going?" Verne asked as she saw him step amid the gravel and mud on the edge of the road. "Why are you walking there?" she asked, rather puzzled at her brother's actions.

"Nowhere! I just ..." but he could not continue. He didn't have the courage to say what he wanted.

They were now directly across from the Stone. The Stone was about twenty feet tall and about fifteen feet wide and twenty feet long. Sometimes, kids who had come to Louison to bathe in the river or accompany their mothers who were doing their laundry, climbed to the top of the Stone. When they got to the top, they would raise their hands in triumph, as if they had conquered Mount Diablotin—the tallest mountain in Dominica. It was easy to climb the Stone, though, compared to the long, difficult and arduous climb to the top of Mount Diablotin.

It looked like someone had just placed the Stone right there, on the side of the road. Some believed that it had broken off from the cliff and remained just where it had landed. Some people believed though, that it was always there and no one bothered to mess with it when the road was being built. The most popular theory, and one that seemed to carry much weight, was that it came down to this spot after the road was built. It seems that every generation in the villages of St. Joseph and Layou spoke of the big Stone, which in fact was a giant rock, and all had stories about it. But whatever the case, what was certain was that it was a landmark along the road. Parasitic plants grew from little fissures. Rainwater collected in small indentations and the birds drank and preened themselves in those mini pools. There were some spots indicating that some unlucky drivers had driven their vehicles unto the Stone. Undoubtedly, the Stone always won.

Joseph slowly turned to look in the direction of the Stone. And there it was! He felt a lump in his throat. He gulped hard. Should he believe what he was seeing? "No! That's not true," he muttered aloud without realizing it.

"What's not true?" Clare asked, looking at her brother somewhat surprised at the expression on his face. "You see a jombie?" she asked, a frown on her face. Then she looked in the direction that he was looking. "What is it? What are you looking at?" she asked him again, as Verne drew closer to them to find out what's was happening.

"You see a jombie?" she repeated her sister's question to Joseph.

Joseph gathered himself. "Oh nothing!" he answered.

He smiled. It was a strange, guilty and embarrassed smile. For there it was. Was this what had caused him all the agony?

"You mean I'm so stupid! Man I let my mind play games with me?" he muttered to himself again. He was not going to let anyone know about this, no matter what. Never!

Across the road from where they were, there was a black cow chained to a stake in the ground, chewing its cud. It was lying under a clump of cocoa trees. As the children passed by, the cow stood up and the chain rattled as it shook its head trying to ward off pestering crows that pecked at teaks on its body. *Was that the sound that he had heard last night? Was that the sound that had caused him all the grief*, he thought to himself.

Someone had tethered a cow among the cocoa trees and left it there overnight. This was a common practice, but Joseph could not ever recall seeing any cows tethered in that area. He cursed under his breath. *So what about the man on the Stone?* He was at a loss to understand what had created such fear in him. *Had he fallen victim to the taunts of the young man he had met on his way to Cocoa Center or had he fallen victim to his own fears of the Man?*

A few tears slowly streamed down his face and Joseph turned away from his sisters towards the river. He quickly dried the tears away, trying not to arouse any more suspicions. His sisters looked at each other, puzzled, but without a clue as to what had just happened. Clare shook her head.

"That's your business. You don't have to answer me, but you acting like you had a bad dream last night," Verne said to him.

Joseph looked at her and shrugged his shoulders. "I am okay. All you asking too many questions," he answered.

He wasn't going to tell them even if his life depended upon it. His sisters looked at him again and laughed. Joseph smiled sheepishly but said nothing as the cow rattled its chain again. The crows flew off, directly over Joseph's head, and finally perched on the top of the Stone.

"Make the sign of the cross," Clare shouted, "that is a bad sign. You see how those birds fly right over your head," she said to Joseph.

"Is true," added Verne, "they say is a bad sign when black birds fly over your head in the morning. Maybe is a *soucouyan* or a *la diabless*. You never know," she said.

Hesitantly, and with a sigh of relief, Joseph crossed himself with the sign of the cross. Maybe he was not alone in his fears. Hopefully he could put away the night's episode behind him as they made their way to another day in St. Joseph.

Converted

The silver rays of the early morning sun sipped through the slits in the wooden house highlighting the bits of dust circling around the room. John rolled over in his bed, reached for the end of the sheet and pulled it over his semi-nude body. His breath reeked of alcohol. Last night, he was carried home by four companions and dumped into his bed as if he were a dead animal.

As National Day approached, the *bèlè*, *quadrille* and *conte* rehearsals were being held at the village community center. Since he was one of the better *lapeau kabwit* drummers in the village, he had become involved in the rehearsals in preparation for island-wide competitions. But he had drunk so much of the free alcohol that was supplied after last night's rehearsals that he had been unable to make his way home. It was therefore left for two of his friends to haul him home.

It was about ten hours since that time, and as he tucked harder at the end of the sheet, he was startled as his wife rushed into the bedroom.

"John, man, get up! It time. I hav' to go to church dis mornin'. Come an' look afta your breakfas'. Today hav' baptism and I want to be dere."

"Oh, what de time?" he asked her, throwing the sheet off his body, his voice still hoarse from the drinking and shouting the night before.

"Doh aks me question about time. Is church I goin'," she replied, as she hurried out of the bedroom.

"Wait, Maria! Wait! Listen to me! I jus' remember. I hav' to go to church today. I is de pawèn for Clem chile. He aks me yesterday. He say de real pawèn sen' an' say he sick yesterday an' Clem doh want to cancel it."

Maria stood silent, mouth agape, not believing what she had just heard. "You what!" she cried after the initial shock. She stood looking at John, her hands on her waist.

Maria and John had been married for the past fifteen years and lived in a small wooden house overlooking the banks of the now dry St. Joseph River. (It was a river only when it rained.) John was a tall dark man who drank heavily. He worked as a laborer on the Macoucherie Estate, about two miles from St. Joseph. He had not been to work the past three weeks because there was a labor dispute between the estate owner and the union representing the workers. He was from the village of Grand Fond, but had moved to St. Joseph in search of work about twenty years ago. It was there that he met Maria. He liked her from the moment he saw her; there was something unique about her, though he was at pains to tell anyone what that was.

Maria, on the other hand, was short and fat and her small eyes sat deeply in their sockets. She was about forty-five years old and had one daughter, an only child, not by John, who was in St. Thomas, Virgin Islands. Maria was a devout Catholic and she was frequently referred to as a *poto catolic*. She hardly ever missed any church activity whether it rained, was weekend or mid-week, early or late. The only time she ever missed church was when she was sick and was unable to get out of bed. The priest had come to see her then.

"Man, John! Man, you drink so much las' nite how you could go stan' for a chile today? God will put a cuss on you. Why you didn' tell me dat all de time? You wait until I get ready an' is when you tellin' me!" she screamed, pausing to catch her breath. "An' when you goin' to hav' time get ready? It a'ready half pas' eight," she continued.

John hurried out to the living room without saying a word and filled a cup with water from the red plastic bucket standing on the table in the corner of the room. He went to the window and splashed some water over his face; filled his mouth with some and after shaking it vigorously, squirted it out on to the pile of stones directly below, wetting the chickens that were scratching in the slimy drain looking for something to eat. He had no toothbrush and even if he did, he would not waste time brushing his teeth now. He rushed back into the bedroom. "Maria, whey my jacket? De one my brudda bring for me from Englan'? Look for it for me. I goin' to clean my shoes. An' look for my tie too. I hav' de pants already."

"But John, how come you pawèn? All you tell fadda? He know dat is you dat is de chile pawèn?" she asked as she searched through a plastic wardrobe hanging by a cord in another corner of the room.

"Well, is not me. Clem say he tell fadda an' he say is me dat is de pawèn an' he doh tell him nothin'. So!" John answered.

"You sure he know is you?" she asked again trying to reassure herself that this was not just a dream.

"Maria, dat is not my problem! If Clem say he tell fadda an' fadda say is okay, is okay! Okay!"

Maria could not believe what she was hearing. Was it really true? What on earth would allow Father Windenberg to accept John as a godfather? Tried all she could, she could not come up with a possible answer.

There was a knock at the front door, the only door to the house, for that matter. The knock was followed by the unmistakable voice of Clem. "John, where you, man?" he asked, a hint of urgency and worry in his voice.

"I comin' man, I comin'. I tyin' my tie. Man I really forget you know ... Oh Maria, whey my hat?" he spoke to both without stopping, as he stood at the door, tugging at the end of his tie, making sure it looked okay.

"Me you aksin'? *Ma sav la chapo la yé.* You go with your hat las' nite. You maybe lose it when you was drunk. *Sarti soula,*" she said, giving him a stern look as she said so. "Go an' aks God for forgiveness for your sins. Go aks for pardon. An' aks him to make you remember where you leave your hat."

"Okay, okay tanks," he replied, as he climbed down the wooden step, followed by Clem. The boards on the step squeaked as they stepped down.

"Is time you fix dat step, man. It will fall down anytime with you!" exclaimed Clem. John looked back at the step, quickly surveyed it, but said nothing.

"I not goin' nowhere with you today. I doh goin' an' make myself feel embarrass with you in church afta what I see las' night. You go alone. An' already I lose all taste," Maria cried.

"How I lookin' Maria? My clothes good?" John asked stopping for a while and turning to face Maria.

"I doh know. Aks Clem. He is a man, he can tell you," Maria answered.

John said nothing.

The two men left quickly and Maria watched as they worked their way between the houses and the pools of muddy water that lined the path to her home. "Is me dat more stupid to go in church with him de

way he is an' for people to say fing about me? An' what de pries' goin'
to say?" she asked herself.

She went into her bedroom and changed her clothes, all the while
talking to herself. "Lord, forgive me oui, but as you make Moses I not
goin' in dat church today," she said, as she worked her way out from
the bedroom to the living room and down the rickety steps to the
detached kitchen. She started singing to herself. "*Kumbaya my Lord,
kumbaya. Kumbaya my Lord, kumbaya. Kumbaya my Lord, kumbaya. Oh
Lord, kumbaya.*" She continued humming the tune to herself since she
could not remember all the words.

In the meantime, John and Clem had joined Clem's wife and the
baby's godmother who were anxiously waiting under a kennip tree,
about a few minutes from John's home. "John, you know dat lady non?"
Clem asked, pointing to the stranger.

"No, I doh know her. She look jus' like you. Your sistah?" John
asked.

"Yes, my sistah, oui. She livin' in Colihaut. Is she I tell you dat in
de village council," Clem beamed.

"Mornin' ma'am, how is you today?" asked John, trying to be his
best. "I am one John Williams originally from Grand Fond, but I livin'
here for de pas' twenty or so odd years," he continued, a broad smile
appearing on his face, revealing his yellow teeth, stained from
excessive smoking.

"Not bad!" answered the lady, a smile also appearing on her face,
revealing her bright white teeth. My name is Cheryl Roberts from
Colihaut."

"Please to meet you makoumè," John answered. They all laughed
when he said so.

Together they started walking to the church; the two men at the
front and the women with the baby following behind.

"Well boy, so long I doh put my foot in a church. I wonda how
inside dere is. Maria always want me to come to church with her,
especially when is Easter or Christmas, but I never goin'," he said,
somewhat ashamedly.

"It not bad. Fadda fix it up a bit. I does go now because dey not
baptizin' de chile if de fadda doh go to church. An' you know Sarah
already. She jus' like your wife. So I hav' no choice," and he glanced at
his wife who seemed undaunted by what he had just said.

They climbed the steps to the church and they met with other
groups who were going to participate in the baptismal ceremony. John
felt very uneasy. He pulled at the end of his jacket, fixed his tie,

straightened himself and pushed his hands into his pockets. He knew the people in the church today would be shocked to see him. He gave Clem a quick, uneasy smile. Clem smiled back.

As they walked up the aisle, they were met by one of the ushers who led them to their seats. The members of the congregation buzzed as they noticed the two men. "Is not John dat up dere?" one woman asked another who sat next to her. They expected to see Clem, but not John. "Eh ben, umm, umm, an' he was so drunk las' nite you know. I see when dey was passin' with him," she continued to whisper.

John nervously took his seat next to Clem. "Wow!" he whispered to himself, hoping that he would be able to relieve himself of the burden he now carried. "Wow, what a place!" he muttered again, as if to reassure himself that he had said it the first time. He looked at his makoumè and she smiled back at him.

The Mass had not started and the few minutes of waiting seemed like an eternity to John. Ten minutes later, the members of the choir stood and started singing. It was the signal that the priest was entering, followed by his servers. The congregation stood, but John remained seated.

"Man, John, get up! De pries' will get vex," whispered Clem, as he tugged at the shoulder of John's jacket.

"Oh, oh, I forget ... so long ...." He could not continue, feeling ashamed of himself and what he was about to say. The voices of the choir members filled the church. John could not recall when last he had heard such singing. He stared, mouth wide open. Then his eyes came in line with those of the priest who was now standing at the altar. Shamefully, he bent his head.

Father Windenberg had been the parish priest for the past five years. He was a Belgian and had served in a number of parishes before being transferred to St. Joseph. He was about six feet tall and for his size was very soft spoken. He was so well liked by the parishioners that when the Bishop decided to transfer him out of St. Joseph, a parish delegation met with the Bishop asking him to extend Father Windenberg's stay. He was very popular with the children most of all. He organized after-school programs and Sunday school activities for them. He also organized a night of games for the youth on Friday nights. The young people played cards, dominoes, and ping-pong and at the end of the night he showed some movies, especially the silent movies starring Charlie Chaplain. That was great fun and the young people looked forward to Friday nights with great anticipation. But Father Windenberg was a very firm man. He was very strict about his faith and beliefs and that was why it was a surprise to Maria that he had agreed for John to be a godfather. It had to be a mistake or Clem had lied to Father Windenberg as to whom he had asked to be the child's godfather.

They did not know each other personally (Father Windenberg and John), but because of Maria's involvement in the church, the priest had some knowledge as to who John was. Like most priests, he did not move about the village too much, except on occasions when he had to visit the sick or to bring communion to them or to administer the last rites to someone who was near death. He remained more or less secluded in his presbytery and usually spent his afternoons in his porch looking at the young people of the village engaged in various forms of sports on the village playground.

John and Father Windenberg had met once though, but in strange circumstances during the funeral of Caesar Williams. Caesar was John's friend. He was a fisherman who had spent almost his entire life fishing. He had just returned from a fishing trip one day when he collapsed on the sand as he hauled his canoe to the shore. People tried to resuscitate him but to no avail. They rubbed him with Limacol and Bay Rum, put smelling salts to his nose, beat his face with salt water, fanned him, and when it seemed that nothing would work, they placed him in the back of a truck and rushed him to the Princess Margaret Hospital in Roseau. He remained at the hospital for a week without uttering a single word. He died without ever regaining consciousness.

There were a number of theories as to the cause of Caesar's death. Some people said that rum had dried up his liver. (He drank rum straight without any mixer.) Some said that he had rheumatism of the brain because he was at sea in rain, thunder, sun, hot or cold, while others said, "*Sé moun ki fè li mal.*" Some had said that he had also died of malnutrition because he never ate the fish he caught. Rather, he sold every bit of it and used the money to fulfill his alcoholic urges.

No priest officiated at Caesar's burial. Instead, a layman conducted the burial. Although his friends wanted to have a funeral mass for him, Father Windenberg had refused, contending that Caesar had never been to any church from the day he made his first communion and therefore did not qualify for the final rites of the Catholic Church. As John watched the coffin being carried to the cemetery that day, he felt hurt. "How could Caesar go that way? Maybe even de pries' eat fish Caesar ketch an' today he refusing to bury him. An' how he get to know all dat about Caesar?" he thought to himself. He decided to have a talk with the priest. He felt he owed it to his dearly departed friend. He left the funeral and made his way to the presbytery.

He stood at the door to the presbytery and he hesitated for a moment before pressing the buzzer. After the third ring, Father Windenberg opened the door. "Yes, what can I do for you?" he asked John, very calmly. "And you don't have to keep squeezing the bell so much. Once is enough. Okay!" he said, looking rather surprised to see that John was the one at the door.

"Fadda," John paused, wondering what next to say "Fadda, I come to bury Caesar, not to pray for him. I cannot even pray for myself, but anyhow dat is not dat. Come an' say a Our Fadda for him before we put him in de hole. Jus' one. Dat is all fadda," he pleaded.

"No, no, no," said the priest, shaking his head from side to side rather demonstratively. "Do not disturb me now. Go away please."

"What do you mean by go away, fadda? I tells you to come an' pray for de man! For Caesar, Mr. Caesar who we puttin' in de hole at this approximate moment."

"Can't you not hear or understand? I, I, I ..." Father Windenberg stammered.

"I hears you fadda," John interrupted, raising the tone of his voice. "I not dead like de damn man in de coffin over dere," pointing in the direction of the cemetery. "But de man is a pusson, fadda, even if he doh have nobody for him. Anyhow man, *zor sé pere sala*," he muttered to himself as he walked away rather dejectedly. He glanced back as Father Windenberg closed the door.

When John returned to the cemetery, it was deserted. Caesar had already been buried. The few mourners had already left and nothing but stones and a lone wreath decorated the grave. John walked to the foot of the grave and knelt down. He did not mind whether onlookers thought that he was mad. This was his friend. They had had good times together and he was paying his last respects to him. He fought with himself to get the most appropriate words to say. Finally, he said, "See you dear Caesar in de Promis' Land. We will soon meet by and by." He was in no way hinting that he wanted to die soon. Nothing close to that. He wished that he could live forever. He made the sign of the cross, kissed his thumb, then slowly got up and walked away with tear-filled eyes.

That was about three years ago. But as he listened to the songs and readings, he was lost in his own world. He remembered the days in Grand Fond when, as a small boy, he accompanied his mother to church in La Plaine. They had to walk, then, because there were no vehicles traveling in that part of the country. As a matter of fact, there were no motorable roads back then. He was happy to tag along even if it took about an hour to get to church. His mother was a very devout Catholic. He also remembered the day he was confirmed. It was such a big occasion in the parish. That was a long time ago. He could not remember, besides the day that he was married, when was the last time he stepped into a church since the day of his confirmation.

He sighed heavily and tried to contain himself; a difficult thing to do in this situation. Maybe the priest had planned it that way. Maybe that was why he had not objected to his being a godfather today. *Dis is a trap*, he thought. Had the priest set him up? The more he thought about it, the more he believed it. *Why else would de pries' break de damn rule?* he thought again. "Is not for Maria's sake. She so important?" he asked himself.

Once again Clem tugged at John's jacket as the congregation stood and the priest came to the lectern. "Stand up, man," Clem whispered. "Is time for de Gospel."

John was so engrossed in his thoughts that he did not even realize that the priest was up at the lectern preparing to deliver the gospel. He shivered. He was unaware that the first and second readings were already done. He was in a different world. He hesitated a while and then abruptly stood up, pulling at the ends of his jacket and then at the tip of the tie. He playfully nudged Clem in return and listened as the priest read the Gospel according to Luke. At the end of the reading everyone sat down. John wondered what was next. Somehow, he believed that the priest had something to say about him.

Father Windenberg climbed down the steps from the altar and stood next to the members of the congregation who sat in the first rows of pews. He looked around, a smile on his face. He again greeted everyone and then he began his sermon.

"Brothers and sisters in the name of Jesus Christ: In today's Gospel, Christ has a message for us in the Parable of the Prodigal Son. In the first reading we also saw him exhorting us to bring the children unto him. 'Suffer the children to come unto me,' ... he said ... and many times we, as Catholics, take these messages, take life generally, for granted and we never put them into practice. Today we are living in troubled times and now, more than ever, we need God. It is time we give up, make sacrifices, and stop pretending we are what we are not. Rum cannot save you from your troubles, marijuana cannot, and cocaine cannot. Only God!" He paused, pulled a handkerchief from his back pocket and mopped his brow. He continued, "Today, brothers and sisters, we have innocent babies in our midst who know nothing of what is happening to them. They hear me, but they don't understand. These children become victims when we do not do what we need to do as parents and godparents." He paused again allowing the congregation to think of what he was saying. Then he continued. "It is the responsibility of **each one of us**, especially the parents and godparents, to lead these infants, these children of God, the true God, to Him. Not the god of drugs, the god of rum, but the God who cares for all of us."

John swallowed hard. He believed that the priest was referring to him. A bead of sweat dripped down his nose and he wiped it off with his middle finger.

"My mind tellin' me to walk out. Oh boy, see my cross today," he muttered under his breath. "Dat pries' is a crook to do dat to me."

Father Windenberg continued his sermon; a mental torture to John. He felt trapped. There was nowhere to go. If he walked out, that was it. And he knew he dared not try to walk out. He had to take it all sitting down. Every now and then he glanced in Clem's direction. But Clem was listening intently to what the priest was saying. Finally, it was over. John was soaked with perspiration. It was like he was out there doing some physical work.

After asking everyone to join him in renewing their baptismal vows, the priest invited the baptismal parties to join him at the baptismal font, one party at a time. When it was time for his party, John stood nervously, almost falling over. He felt like his legs were going to fall from under him. One mistake and he knew he could blow it all. He moved out of his pew slowly, tentatively, but succeeded in keeping himself together.

"Good morning," the priest said in his usual soft manner. Everyone except John answered. He could not get the words out quickly enough and by the time he was ready to do so, the priest was already saying something else. "Jason Hypolite Roberts, I baptize You in The Name of The Father, and The Son and … " he paused as the child screamed and bent back his head as the cold water ran down his forehead. Then he continued. "Of the Holy Spirit." Some members of the congregation laughed as the child screamed again. John wondered whether they were not laughing at him rather than the baby.

He felt uneasy as he walked back to his seat. He felt the pressure of about five hundred pairs of eyes boring through him, seeing through him, but he saw no one, saw nothing but his seat and the world at that moment seemed a big empty prison with everyone free on the outside laughing at him. He was glad to be back in his seat after what seemed like a never-ending trip.

The mass continued without any further incidents and the congregation settled down, although some had inquiring looks as they passed on their way back to their seats after having received communion.

At the conclusion of the mass, the priest stood up to make a few announcements. He began. "First of all, before I make today's announcements, I want to leave a word with you. Something struck me during the mass today. Remember, Christ, the Good Shepherd, is happier when he finds a lost sheep and brings it back to the fold. We, too, must be like shepherds and go out there and find the lost sheep of our flock, bring them back to the fold."

There were whispers among members of the congregation. Even if the priest was trying to be indirect, everyone knew he was referring to John.

"Is you he referrin' to, man," Clem whispered. John didn't answer, but kept staring at the palm of his hands, searching for something that wasn't there.

The priest continued. "Remember, Christ says, '*I am the Good Shepherd*'. Let us be good shepherds to our flock today and everyday." He then read the usual Sunday announcements and when he was finished, he walked down from the altar and went to the baptismal parties and shook the hands of the parents and godparents, congratulating them and thanking them for having been present. When he got to John, he said, "Hi John, glad you came today. I didn't see Maria today. Is she sick?"

John felt a lump in his throat. "No fad-fadda … " he stuttered, "She stay home for me to come today, fadda." He knew that was not true.

As he walked away, the priest patted John on the shoulder. The church was quiet. You could hear a pin drop. People were spellbound. Were they seeing right? John felt relieved but confused. Was the priest sincere in his actions or was he using him as a scapegoat? At least he had said something nice to him.

Finally the mass came to an end and as John walked out of the church, he tried to stay on top of the situation. Although most of the time he had kept his head bent, he tried now to keep it up and show a brave face. The tap on the shoulder was reassuring and he wanted people to see that he was happy to be a godfather.

The church bells pealed loudly to celebrate the joyful occasion. John remembered when on a happier occasion he had heard those bells. It was the day when he had held Maria's hand after they were married. It was in this very church and Father Vanahan had officiated. It was all smiles that day and there was no reason for him to have been ashamed or scared then. He stepped outside into the dazzling sunlight and somebody shouted, "John, John you dat de chile pawèn? Dat chile mus' come a drunkard too."

John tried to block out everything and everyone from his mind. His main concern now was to get out of this area as soon as possible and get to the little bit of privacy in his house. But Clem didn't seem to care. He was in no hurry. He had to show off his child and his sister. Rather than taking the back road to his home, he decided to walk along the main road instead. That did it for John. As he walked with his small party, the fun and verbal abuse continued. For many, this was the first time they had seen him dressed formally. Others remembered him from last night. Some called him just for the fun of it. Now and then he stopped to shake the hand of a friend or that of a well-wisher. He began to feel confident again, but still the discomfort and the hurt of the morning lingered at the back of his mind.

At last, after about forty-five agonizing minutes on the road, they arrived at Clem's house. John was pleased to be out of the limelight. Clem's sister-in-law had prepared breakfast. It smelt good; hot cocoa tea scented with bay leaves, scrambled eggs, bacon, vegetable salad, and some *chodo*. They sat around the table together and enjoyed the meal talking about things as they saw it, but somehow avoiding the incident at church. "You not havin' a fas' one?" Clem asked John just as he made his way to get up from the table after he had consumed enough.

"You hear what de pries' say! Why you makin' de man drink rum?" screamed Clem's wife. "Leave de man alone. *Konpè pa mélé épi Clem, non*," she said, looking at John. John smiled but did not answer.

"Look! Dat is between me an' my konpè. If he doh want rum I hav' some wine," Clem countered.

"Clem, why you troublesome so, non? Listen to your wife," his sister interjected. "Mr. John, doh let Clem make you do what you doh want to. I feel like is me de pries' was talkin' about although I doh drink rum. Doh let Clem make you do what you doh want to do."

"But how all you can say he doh want. Allyou hav' de man mouth? Anyway, I havin' my own." With that said, he poured himself a drink of Macoucherie Rum. He filled his mouth with the spirit, swallowed, closing his eyes as the heat went down his throat. He chased it with some Coca-Cola, wiping his mouth dry with the back of his hand.

Before anyone could say anything more, John got up from his seat at the table. He put his hand into his left coat pocket and pulled out a bundle of crumpled dollar bills. He picked a five-dollar bill and tried to straighten it. "Anyhow makoumè, hold dat for de boy. Buy someting for him," he said, as he handed the bill to the baby's mother.

"Man, you goin' a'ready? Man, what happen? You let Fadda Windburg scare you, man? I cannot believe dat. Since when you does change so easy, John?" Clem asked, as John made his way to the front door.

"Clem, I will come back later, okay!" answered John as he stepped outside into the midday sun. "Oh shit!" he whispered to himself as he realized that he was outside again, exposed to all those who wanted to have a go at him. But no one seemed to bother him as he wound his way between the small wooden houses and the puddles of water along the path leading to his home. Only those who usually sat on the steps of some of the houses, doing nothing else but gossiping most of the time, said anything to him.

"Mr. John, how you today?"

"Anything special today, Mr. John?"

"Aye John, ou sorti légliz?"

"You pray for me, Mr. John?" and so on, and he answered, based on what he was asked, all the while hiding his true feelings inside.

———————

Maria was in the kitchen. She heard John's voice as he spoke to one of his neighbors. From the gaps between some of the boards, she saw John approaching. She was surprised. "What happen he comin' back already?" she asked herself. "I didn' expec' him to come back already. What happen?" she asked again. She watched him all the way and as he started climbing the wooden, squeaky steps to the house, she called to him. "John, what happen you here already?"

He stopped dead in his tracks. For a while he said nothing, deciding whether to answer or not to answer. Then it all burst out; all the frustration and pain that he had held back this morning.

"Fanm kité mwen en po!" he screamed back at her and stepped into the house.

"But what de matta with him? I doh understand. What happen? You see a vision in de church? You turn Pentecostyle? You save! You convort!" laughed Maria, putting her hands on her waist. "God give me strength to laugh. All dose years I goin' to church I never see a vision, you go today an' is like you see de purly gates. You see Saint Peter, non?" she laughed louder.

"Maria, listen, dat is not a joke! I serious. An' doh damn well laugh at me," he shouted at Maria.

Maria realized that John was serious or at least he sounded like that. Never before had he spoken to her in that manner. They had had their differences, but never had they sworn at each other in that manner. John was fuming now.

"Okay mushé, okay!" she said apologetically. She walked out from the kitchen and up the wooden steps into the house to meet John. She wanted to know what had really gone wrong. "You want somethin' to drink? Some tea?" she asked.

"No, I doh want nothin'. I had breakfas' by Clem," John answered, without looking at Maria.

"You mean you a'ready go by Clem, have breakfas' an' come back a'ready! What happen? Somethin' happen? What happen to you John?" she pleaded as she placed her hands on his shoulders.

"Oh Maria, is Fadda Wimbug!"

"Is not Wimbug. Is Windenberg!" Maria corrected him.

"I is not his pawèn. Is not me dat give him his name. Anyhow, he hit me straight on my head with his hammer."

"With what?" Maria screamed, "With his hammer? How dat happen? How comes, John?" she begged him for answers.

"Is not a real hammer, Maria! I mean he attack me right in de church ..." Maria was about to make another of those explosions, but John held her down. "He say things about me infront of all dose stranger dat stand for chilren an' all de rest of dem people. He condem me. He speak of Christ an' all he does do. He speak about me, Maria," as he started crying. "An' he speak about loss sheep. Everybody know is me he was speakin'. He speak of de Prodigan Son," he continued sobbing, his face in his hands.

"De Prodigal Son," Maria corrected him.

"An' Mr. Auguiste an' de choir as if dey know I was comin'. Oh God, Maria, I was so shame. I was tremblin'. He even shake my hand. He aks me if you was sick."

"But how you know is you he was speakin' about?" Maria asked him.

"Maria, even Clem tell me dat an' people was laughin' at me outside de church when we was comin' out."

"Well, what you want me to say? Every Sunday as God make Moses, I does aks you to come with me, but you prefer to go in de *kabawé* or in de boathouse with dose other men. If you was comin' with me, dat would not happen. Is a good thing I didn' go nowhere. Imagine me in church with all dat goin' on. Lord, I would die. All dat is your fault! Now you sorry!" she snarled at John.

John could not answer. He knew that Maria was speaking the truth. What she was saying seemed to be sinking deeper. What could he say to redeem himself? "Maria, whey de Bible?" he asked, with some degree of uncertainty.

Maria was taken by surprise. She had never seen John read a Bible or any book for that matter. She never really cared if he could read either. "It on de shelf where I always puttin' it," she answered.

"Take it for me. Let me sit down an' clear my soul," John said softly. Maria blushed. She realized that she had him where she wanted and she felt like putting it to him in no easy way, but she thought better of it.

"Let him suffer through his own problems," she said to herself as she walked over to the small shelf and took the Bible and handed it to John.

John held the Bible in his hands, rather hesitantly. He wondered whether he was making the right decision. Was he strong enough to fight off the temptations? He remembered the last time he held a Bible was at his confirmation. In fact, it was really a copy of the New Testament which was given to all those who had been confirmed that day. That was the last of it too. Slowly, he opened the book and saw his name and began reading. He read from John 10:14.

I am the Good Shepherd, and know my sheep and I am known of mine as the Father knoweth me, even so I know the Father and lay down my life for the sheep. And other sheep I have, which are not of my fold, them also I must bring, and they shall hear my voice, and there shall be one fold, and one shepherd. After reading the verse, he stared blankly at the ceiling reflecting on what he had just read. These were poignant words. He felt humbled. He flipped some more pages and stopped at Luke 21:33. He read slowly, digesting each word: *Verily I say unto you, this generation shall not pass away, till all be fulfilled. Heaven and earth shall pass away but my words shall not pass away. And take heed to yourselves, least at any time your hearts be over charged with surfeiting and drunkenness and cares of life and so that day come upon you unawares.*

Was this a coincidence or was this a message? It did not seem real. Why was he reading those pages? He sighed deeply. Slowly, he closed the Bible and laid back on the bed. He fell asleep.

Two hours later, Maria came into the room. She had been out there doing her own thing; cooking, meeting neighbors and friends who passed by to say hello and fill themselves with gossip and hear first hand about John's episode at the church. Clem then came looking for John. But John was fast asleep; the Bible lying next to his head. Maria was hesitant to wake him up. She didn't want to face his wrath again today. Quietly, she bent over him and felt his breath against her face. She touched him softly. "John, John, Clem callin' you. He say he waitin' for you," she whispered into his right ear. When she got no response, she spoke louder. "John, Clem callin' you."

"Umm. Umm, what happen? Who? Clem! Tell him I not dere," John said to her, as he rolled to the other side of the bed.

"But he know you dere. I tell him you dere," Maria answered.

"Tell him I not dere, Maria. Tell him I go by de bay." Maria looked at him puzzled. Was he asking her to lie? She looked at him again but John did not blink. She knew that it was wrong to lie so blatantly but if it meant helping John through his worries today, she had no other choice. She walked back out and stood at the front door. Clem was sitting on a stone in the yard in the shade of a breadfruit tree, patiently waiting for John to show up.

"Clem, it look like he go out, oui. I did leave him in de bed when I go by Ma George shop. I thinkin' he was dere all de time. I will tell him you pass when he come back. Maybe he even go to de boatshed."

Somehow Clem did not want to believe Maria. Why would John go to the boatshed today of all Sundays? But how could he tell her that she was not speaking the truth? He respected her and he was not going to doubt her now. "Anyhow, when he come back tell him I an' de fellas waitin' for him an' you, too, makoumè. I hope you come with him."

"Maybe!" Maria answered, as Clem turned and walked away between the small houses and the puddles of muddy water. Maria felt guilty. She knew she had lied, but in this situation what was she going to do? She made the sign of the cross over her chest as Clem turned and walked away. "Forgive me, Lord. You know I didn' want to do dat," she said, as she looked heavenwards.

"Good, Maria, I love you more for dat. Thank you," John said, a broad smile on his face, as Maria returned to the room. Maria blushed and smiled in return. She bent over and kissed John on his forehead.

And so the day went by without John venturing outside. He read. He fell asleep, woke up, listened to cricket on the radio (West Indies was playing Australia at Sabina Park in Jamaica), and ate until finally they both fell asleep, but not before John did what he had not done in years. He knelt down and prayed. Maria was moved, but again she said nothing.

The following morning, John got up and as usual Maria was not there. It had been her ritual every weekday that she went to early morning church service at five o'clock. She always left him in bed and went on her way alone. John stepped to the corner of the living room as he routinely did, filled a cup with water from the plastic bucket and proceeded to wash his face. He vigorously shook water in his mouth and spat it out unto the stones below. The chickens in the gutter below scattered. When he was finished, he stepped out into the kitchen and the strong aroma of black coffee hung in the morning air. He poured himself a cup. He took the enamel cup to his mouth and as if it was the breath of life, drank his fill. He could not start the day without his coffee, strong and black.

As soon as Maria was back from church, John was on his way to the boathouse. It was there that he had spent most of his time during the past two weeks due to the labor unrest on the Macoucherie Estates, but he did not mind it. He and the fishermen were closely watching the movement of a school of tuna. But the school was too far out to catch with the seines. The school went north one day, south the next, but remained out there teasing the fishermen. The fishermen kept hoping that school would get closer before it finally moved out of range. At nights, after being at the boathouse practically for the whole day, John would go to rehearsals for the Independence Celebrations. Life, therefore, from his standpoint, was not too dull at all.

The sun was rising behind the mountains and its rays were beginning to reflect on the newer galvanized roofs and on the glass panes. The air was fresh and clean and villagers were moving about their business. It was another week and everyone had to get back to what he or she did, all over again: farmers, school children, bus drivers, were all on the move. The village was alive with activity. As John rounded the corner next to Mr. Lamber's shop on Back Street, he heard a familiar voice call out his name. He pretended that he had not heard and continued walking. Clem shouted louder. This time John stopped.

He stood to the side of the street until Clem caught up with him.

"John, John, man whey you goin'? Whey you was yesterday? I look up an' down for you. I come at your home an' Maria tell me you wasn' dere although I didn' believe her."

John shrugged his shoulders.

"All dem fellas was at home man! Fellas like Jerry, Sweet Boy, Micky, all dem man," Clem said. "We had a good time," he smiled. "I jus' finish pass by you now, now, now, an' Maria tell me you goin' by Mr. Debor boathouse so I say let me go an' check you out," he said, a wry smile on his face.

John looked at him and smiled too. He was about to answer when Clem started again. "I doh think you still thinkin' of what de pries say? De man hav' his mouth to talk. He wanted somethin' to preach about an' you was dere so he use you as his topic of conversion. You doh see is dat? Dem fellas does drink dey rum too, you know."

John listened and one of the verses that he had read, rather, had glanced at, came to his mind, but he could not remember it fully. He just had a vague idea of what they were. "*For God so loved the world ... will have everlasting life. ...*" He could not remember more.

"Clem, listen to me. Let me tell you de truth. Dey say de truth will set you free. I was at home yesterday. I jus' couldn' go outside. I was shame. I tell Maria to tell everybody dat aks for me I not dere. I stay home an' read de Bible."

Clem laughed.

"Doh laugh, man! Dis is serious business, man! Only me dat know how I was feel infront of all dose people, man! Afta what happen to me, I goin' to try to change my life. You know what de pries' was sayin' is true? I sit down an' check it out, man. I goin' to give it a shot. Maria always aksin' me to come church with her an' I does always say no. If I use to go with her dat would never happen," he said, as he put his hand on Clem's shoulder.

Clem looked at him with mouth wide open. Then he spoke. "So you mean you convort. You is Christian now? So why you doh go an' join Pentecostal or Baptis'? How you convort an' you is still Catolic? Dat doh make sense!"

"If you want to call it so, is up to you, but dat is de bes' for me," answered John.

Clem wanted to say something to John, but what else could he say? It looked like John had made up his mind, no matter what. "Well man, is you. If you want to do your fing, who is me to change your mind? Good luck, man! So where you goin'?" he asked John.

"To de boathouse to see what de fellas an' dem doin' today. We still on strike so I cannot go to work," John answered, as he started walking away.

"Oh ya, is true. When dat strike goin' to finish non, man?" asked Clem.

"I doh know. Is what de union say," replied John.

The labor dispute was now in its third week and there was no sign of a settlement. John was worried that it was not getting better because he could not depend on the meager earnings that Maria got doing housework for Ma Francis. He wanted to be independent of Maria. But he hoped that things would turn for the better and he and other workers would soon be back at work.

"But anyhow, is so it is eh," Clem said. "So dey still behind dat fish?" he asked John.

"Yea, I think so. I goin' to see what dey doin'," John replied.

"Well man, we will see later, non. I goin' an' see what dey doin' on Paul house today. I suppose to give him a hand today. Dey goin' to dig de foundation. By de way, my wife leave a piece of cake for you an' Maria. When you passin' for it? What about dose practice? Who will beat de drum for us? You finish with dat?" he asked John without allowing him to answer.

John only shrugged his shoulders without uttering a word as he moved on. A number of thoughts raced through his mind and once again he wondered whether he was doing the correct thing. Then he turned back and said, "So what you mean? I can still beat de drum. Is not de drum dat is de problem, man. Is what I does do while I beatin' de drum or after we finish practis'. An' if I doh beat it dey can get somebody else to do it. So if I die, all you will stop practis'?" he asked Clem.

"I doh know; maybe, maybe not," Clem answered. The two friends shook hands and for the time being, parted ways.

As he walked along the road next to the river, John saw Father Windenberg crossing over Jubilee Bridge on his way to bring communion to the sick and shut-ins of the village. John wondered whether the priest had seen him with Clem. Maybe not, and even if he had, what would it matter now? He only hoped that the priest did not get the wrong impressions; maybe thinking that they were out for an early morning *eye-opener*. Again, he shrugged his shoulders. "If he see me, he see me; tough luck," he whispered to himself.

41

Somewhere on Church Lane someone had the volume of a radio at its highest. "*Maybe one of those Christians,*" John thought. It was so loud maybe everyone in the village was hearing it. A religious tune that John had heard many times before, was being played on one of the religious stations. Maria sang that song when she was in a good mood. Involuntarily, he started singing along:

> *This is my story, this is my song*
> *Praising my savior all the day long*
> *This is my story this is my song*
> *Praising my savior all the day long.*

And just like Maria did when she could not remember the lines, he too, hummed the remaining lines. He laughed. He wondered what Maria would think if she would hear him now.

He crossed Main Street, now alive with people getting ready to go to Roseau and those heading to their garden plots, and headed towards the bay front. The fresh smell of the air kissed his face. He heard shouting coming from the sea. He saw men in the water and men in boats banging against the sides of the boats. The sea was alive with activity. He saw the buoys that were attached to the seines in the water. He saw the heads of the fishermen bobbing above the water. The fish had come in. The sunlight glistened on the crest of the waves as they rolled in and splashed against the moss-covered stones and the black sand. As they did they seemed to echo the words

"*This is my story, this is my song.*"

John smiled and walked towards the boathouse to join his friends.

Three Young Friends

The copper shades mingling with the dark shadows that covered the land mass and the silhouettes of frigate birds lazily flying overhead indicated it would soon be night. Three young boys sat on exposed roots of a Campeche tree as a steady breeze rustled through its leaves. They were on the top of the hill opposite the St. Joseph Police Station, taking stock of their day's activities. This would possibly be their last stop before heading home. They had been out practically the whole day and it was time to head home. But with them, anything could happen.

"What we gonna do later, non, man?" asked Peter, the youngest in the group. After some silence he said, "So nobody answering me? Well, forget it man!"

"What you mean forget it? What you have in mind?" asked Simon as he stood up and walked to the front of the group, stumbling over some of the protruding roots in the process.

"Watch where you going, man," cried Peter as Simon leaned against him for support.

"By the way, I hear that they're playing another cricket picture next week," said Tony. "I don't know if is true but that's what I heard a man saying this morning."

"Oh ya, right!" replied Simon, "I don't know pal. Not after what happen, non, boy."

"You coward, man. What did the man say? 'Cowards die many times before their death', something like that," replied Peter.

"I ain't care. Maybe is our bad luck," replied Simon. "Who know what will happen this time," he continued.

"Come on, man. What happen? You some sissy boy?" asked Peter. "It happen and it finish," he continued.

"No, not that. It was real close, man; all that happen. We better stay low for a while. Let things cool down a little," Simon replied.

43

Peter, Simon and Tony were classmates and lived very close to each other in the village of St. Joseph. They did almost everything together and if you didn't know it, you would think they were brothers. They got to know each other and bonded their friendship when they were in Standard One at the St. Joseph Government School. Tony and Simon had just completed their first year at the St. Joseph Secondary School and Peter had succeeded at the Common Entrance Exams held earlier that year. He would begin his first year at the high school in September. There were the inevitable fights, of course, for boys of their age, but no matter what, they were buddies and stuck together, always looking to set up another prank.

Simon was the oldest, tallest and strongest of the three, and when he spoke the others usually listened. He was thirteen, although he looked older. Tony was also thirteen, but four months younger than Simon. He was also the most talkative. Although he was not big in stature, he had a deep voice that did not do much for him within the group. Peter was the baby of the group, so to speak, and he was twelve. He always made sure that he was part of everything and whenever he was left out, he felt betrayed.

They had been out all day and now, as the sun was disappearing below the horizon, they were "chilling out," more or less, calming down from the hectic activities of the day. This was Saturday, the day when they joined all the other young boys of the village in all sorts of activities.

They liked the idea of going to school, but like all kids of the village, they were now enjoying the summer vacation. Besides the usual day-to-day stuff, weekends were special and held great expectations. On some Saturdays, they would travel to Roseau to see a matinee movie depending on how good the movie was. The movie rating: good, bad or "so-so," was based on the reviews they got from the adults or from their older friends who were brave enough to venture to the movies during the week without their parents knowing. If they did not go to the movies, they would play soccer for most of the day or make their way to the Layou River at Louison where they would bathe and swim for the greater part of the day. On Sunday, after they had attended church services, they would travel to the beach at the Castaways Hotel in the neighboring village of Mero. There, they would swim in the sea, mingle with tourists and hotel guests and frolic with other boys and girls from the village. There, too, they would make their bold advances at the young girls that they were attracted to. The weekend was fun time and today was no exception.

Peter was the first who had awakened that day. He knew that it was his kind of day from the time he looked out his bedroom window and saw the sun climbing over the Hillsborough hills. It was a beautiful morning. He smiled. His brother and sister were still asleep but his mother was out sweeping the yard. He went outside, next to the detached kitchen where he washed his face and brushed his teeth. When he was finished he proceeded to help his mother do some of the work, at the same time ensuring that he was earning time to go out later.

The air smelled of fresh black coffee being brewed in pots all over the village, as was the custom in this community. People were moving about their business: selling fruits, leaving to go to the city for their Saturday shopping and collecting water at the village stand pipes. Everyone seemed to have something to do.

It was Peter's job, as the eldest, to take care of the family's small herd of goats—all five of them. His mother had an adult male and a female and three kids. He went to the cellar and opened the pen where the goats were kept. He led the bigger goats out of the yard by their tethers and allowed the kids to follow. He led them down the street and across the dry bed of the river to the Church Lane area and after finding a good feeding spot, tethered each adult goat to a separate tree, and left the kids to roam freely. He would return at dusk to bring them back home.

It was about ten o'clock, after he had had breakfast that Tony and Simon showed up. Tony was carrying a hand of ripe bananas and Simon had four grafted mangoes: two in his pants pockets and one in each hand.

"Eh man, what's up?" asked Simon, as they joined Peter who was sitting on a pile of stones in the yard. "You was cleaning all you yard this morning?" he asked. "We was waiting for you to come so when we see you not coming to check us, we decide to come and check you," he continued, a bit of sarcasm in his voice.

"You know I have things to do in the morning, man," Peter answered. "You know the scene. I don't want my mother to cramp my style. You know what I mean," he continued.

"What things you have to do? Your mother doing all the work, so what's the big deal?" responded Simon.

"Enough of this nonsense, man. You don't understand. You better off than me. You don't have to do that so you can make fun of me. Bring out the ital, man! Where all you get them?" asked Peter.

"What you mean where we get them? We buy them, ok. Good! We buy some as we was coming," volunteered Tony. "A lady from Colihaut selling them on Teacher Enid step," he continued. Peter eyed them suspiciously. He sensed they might not have been speaking the truth. However, he was not going to push the matter any further. They then proceeded to share the bananas and the mangoes among themselves.

"Hey guys, throw the skin in that pan for the goats. I don't want my mother to go mad at me after she spend all her time cleaning this morning," Peter warned his friends as they peeled the fruits.

His mother walked into the yard, a reed basket in her hand filled with items she had purchased at the village roadside market.

"Hi guys. All you early today. What time it is? Where all you come from already?" she inquired, eyeing them one after the other, a puzzled look on her face. "All you do all you work already?" she asked.

"Yes ma'am," they all answered in unison, knowing quite well that this was not true.

"By the way," she continued, "I hear Mr. Radigan complaining at the market this morning that some boys was climbing his mango tree last night. He say he going to get police. I hope is not all you," she said as she eyed them suspiciously as she made her way to the detached kitchen.

The boys became quiet. Simon and Tony looked at each other and then began pointing at each other. "You know that's what we come to tell you about," said Simon in hushed tones, hoping that Peter's mother would not hear what he was saying. "We was ..." He stopped short as Peter's mother came back out.

She looked at the boys again, trying to get a hint as to whether they were the guilty ones. She shouted the names of her two other children who were awake by now but still inside and asked them to come out to do some work. Then she said to Peter, "You sure you were not the ones picking the mango last nite?"

"Ma, you remember I was by my daddy last night!" he tried to reassure her.

"I hope you talking the truth," she warned, as she made her way out the yard, through the narrow alley between her house and her neighbor's, Ma Simbert. None of the boys answered.

"Oh yeah, man," answered Simon, when he was sure that Peter's mother was out of earshot. "Where you was las nite? We come to look for you but you wasn't there? Where you was?" he asked Peter again.

"You hear me tell my mother where I was, why you still asking me?" barked Peter. "What happen?" he asked, wanting to know what had transpired at the old man's place.

"Ssshh, not too loud," replied Tony. "We go and see a cricket movie, England and West Indies, last night in Up School. So on our way we was passing by Mr. Radigan house and Simon say his mango riping and he not picking dem, so we decide to check dem out. Simon say birds eating all dem mangoes." He stopped as Peter's younger brother came out of the house.

"I hear what you guys do. Philip tell me. You guys lucky," he said as he pulled a T-shirt over his head and headed toward the kitchen.

"Man, I hope everybody don't know about that! Boy, Philip talking too much, you know," moaned Tony, concern now showing on his face.

"So why you tell him?" chided Simon.

"Just so non, man. I didn't know he would tell nobody," answered Tony, a bit repentant and sorry for having let out their secret. "I met him after I left you last night," he confessed to Simon.

Philip was Tony's cousin and when he was not with Simon and Peter, Tony would be hanging out with Philip. Tony didn't see anything wrong to boast to Philip what he and Simon had done, but it seemed like it would come back to haunt him. He shrugged his shoulders in resignation. "I will not tell him nothing again. His mouth too big," he promised his friends.

"So what happen, then?" begged Peter. "Tell me, man! All you just have me waiting."

"Oh well," answered Simon, somewhat worried that their act had been uncovered. "We didn't expect Mr. Ragga to come outside at the time he come out. When I see him I take off, pal."

"Yea! An' he leave me like a dead duck on the tree," said Tony.

They all burst into laughter.

"Why all you laughing like that?" Peter's mother asked them, as she came back into the yard.

"Just a joke Ma, just a joke," Peter answered quickly, hoping that his mother had not heard what they had just said.

"I hope is just a joke, because if is not a joke somebody will be sorry," she warned, as she made her way up the steps into the house. Somehow she had her suspicions that the boys were up to something, but she wasn't sure what it was. The boys looked at each other, wondering whether they were really in trouble. What would they say in defense of their actions if they were discovered?

Mr. Ragga, whose real name was Radigan Julien, lived alone in a small two-room house. He had a large yard where a twenty-five foot tall grafted mango tree stood. In the past he always had someone climb the tree to pick the mangoes that he then sold from a basket on a small stool by the roadside. However, this year he did not get anyone to pick the mangoes. He was not too well and he did not really seem to care. If a mango fell, it lay under the tree until some lucky person came by and picked it up. Sometimes, when his grand kids came down from Mahaut they would pick a few to take back with them. Otherwise, he didn't seem to care one bit what happened, or so it seemed.

Tony and Simon had laid out their plans for the night. They were sure it would work. Get to the scene, get what they wanted and move on to the movies. Easy! Well, so they thought. When they arrived at Mr. Ragga's place, they surveyed the situation very closely. They looked around to make sure no one was watching. Satisfied that it was okay, they slipped quietly into the yard. Simon pulled out the flashlight he had in his back pocket and swept the beam of light around the yard and up the tree. The ripe mangoes were hanging there, waiting to be picked. He switched off the flashlight and placed it in his waist.

The door to Mr. Radigan's home was slightly ajar. From the open window came the sound of a radio. Apparently, Mr. Radigan was listening to the radio or had it on just for companionship. The light from the curtained window was not strong enough to brighten the yard. Tony had a large plastic bag stuffed in his back pocket. The boys walked quietly to the tree. No one saw them. No one heard them. Simon climbed the tree, ensuring that the flashlight in his waist did not drop to the ground. There were low hanging branches and that helped make his climb very easy. He was soon hidden within the foliage. Tony then slid to a dark corner of the yard to avoid being seen by anyone and thus jeopardize the mission.

When he had climbed high enough, Simon took the flashlight from his waist. He turned it on and shone the light and looked among the branches to find out where he could get the mangoes and get out quickly. He found a branch laden with the ripe fruit. He grabbed one and bit into the warm meat. The juice leaked down his hands and he licked it. "Um, boy! Mr. Radigan blood tasting nice," he said to himself, as he took another hurried bite.

"Come on, man!" Tony whispered to himself as he realized what was happening. "Now is not the time to eat mango. Hurry up!" he hissed. "We will have plenty time to eat." Then he heard the leaves rustle and down came some mangoes. Above, Simon stopped and peered through the branches to make sure that Mr. Radigan had not heard the noise. For a while nothing happened. Tony then rushed out of his hiding place, and picked up six mangoes and placed them in the plastic bag. He looked around but there was none left on the ground for him to collect. He rushed back to the safety of his hiding spot. He was not going to stand out there and make himself a sitting target. He whistled. Simon climbed to a higher branch and shook again. This time many more mangoes came raining own. Again he stopped and Tony came rushing out to pick up the prize. He was almost through collecting the mangoes when he heard the squeaking sound of rusty hinges. He spun around.

"Oh, man!" he muttered to himself, as he saw the old man standing at the open door. He whistled. Simon wondered what was going on. He peered through the trees and saw Mr. Radigan. He heard the footsteps as Tony rushed through the yard and to safety. A dog barked next door as he made his hasty escape in the darkness between the houses. He made his way to Back Street and then across the narrow bridge that spanned the St. Joseph River and headed towards the school building. Hopefully, if all went well, Simon would meet up with him.

"Wow!" Simon muttered to himself as he realized the situation that he was in. He switched off the flashlight and placed it back into his waist. Mr. Radigan was not aware that he was up in the tree. He remained quiet, hoping that the old man would have thought that Tony was just one of those regulars who sneaked into his yard to pick up the mangoes that had fallen to the ground. The old man stood at the door for about five minutes, muttering something to himself. It seemed like an eternity to Simon. He prayed for the old man to get back into his house. But the old man kept muttering. Simon did not understand a word he was saying. The old man looked up the tree, but saw nothing. Then he went down the step.

"*Oh man, he see me,*" thought Simon, as the old man slowly moved down the step, grunting in pain, apparently from the arthritis in his knees.

The old man bent over and picked up a pair of shoes that were sitting on a pile of stones just at the entrance to the house. "*Kitay yo volé mango la tojour. Yo ké sav. Mwen ké ba yo sa yo lé yon sé jou la,*" he

49

said aloud. Simon snickered at what the old man was saying. He realized that the old man was not aware that he was up in the tree. He just did not want to make any mistakes. He held on to a branch and prayed that Mr. Radigan would get back into the house real soon. He was beginning to get tired in the position that he was. He wondered where Tony was and whether he had taken the mangoes with him.

Mr. Radigan turned and began another grunting climb. Simon slipped. He grabbed unto another branch to save his fall. Mangoes rained to the ground. Mr. Radigan turned around. This time he knew that something was up. "*Ki moun ki la?*" he shouted. Simon remained quiet, as the old man moved down the step much faster this time than he had just done when he picked up the shoes. The old man moved towards the pile of stones. "*Ki moun ki la?*" he shouted again, as he picked up one of the stones, again grunting as he did so.

Simon realized what was about to happen. He was not going to remain in the tree and be stoned. He had one choice. Get down now! He slid down another branch and tumbled to the ground. He felt his stomach burn. He realized he had bruised it. He got up, pulling his shirt over his face as he did so and ran away into the darkness. He stumbled and he heard a stone hit the ground two feet from him and bang against the rusty galvanize fence of the next-door neighbor. He got up again and ran away as Mr. Radigan swore to kill him. He heard the loud bang as another stone crashed against the side of the neighbor's house. He prayed that Mr. Radigan did not make him out or that anyone else had seen him running away.

Soon he was on Back Street and hopefully in the clear. He hoped again that no one had seen him. He gathered himself and made his way across the bridge and along the cemetery towards the school building. When he got to the school grounds, he sat down on the grass. He was scared. He was breathing heavily. He wondered if anyone besides Mr. Radigan had seen him. He sat alone until he regained his composure. He stood up and whistled, like he always did when he wanted to communicate with Tony or Peter. He heard someone whistle in return. "Where you?" he shouted.

"Over here. You seeing me? I waving my hand," shouted Tony. "I by the ravine."

Simon headed across the playing field to meet his partner. "Wow! Boy that was close!" he said, a sign of guilt on his face and still a bit breathless after this little escapade.

"You think he know is us?" asked Tony.

"I doh know non man. Just doh say nothing to nobody," urged Simon.

"Cross my heart. As God make Moses," answered Tony, as he crossed himself with the sign of the cross.

"Where the mangoes?" asked Simon, when he realized that Tony was empty-handed.

"Man, I throw the plastic in the river. I only have two mango in my pocket. I didn't want nobody to see me running and get suspicious," answered Tony.

"Man, after all that, you leave dem mangoes?" Simon cried, a bit angry with Tony.

"Better mango stay where it is than Mr. Ragga knock me down with a stone, oui pal," Tony answered. "You have the flashlight?" he asked Simon.

"I have it in my waist," Simon answered, as he lifted his shirt to show Tony. "I couldn't leave it behind. Is my father own, man! If I did leave it behind, you know what would happen? That would be evidence boy!" he added.

"Okay man, let's go. It almost time," warned Tony.

They walked together across the playing field and headed up the steps of the building. They got in and disappeared among the audience.

––––––––––

Peter was amazed at what he was hearing. Why did he miss the action? He licked his lips. "How you guys can go through all dat and still lose out, man? All you guys hopeless! If is me, you know I not losing what I work hard for," he boasted.

"Ya, right!" snapped Tony. "You always can do, but you never doing."

"You see that, man?" asked Simon, looking around to make sure no one else was snooping in on their conversation. "You see that?" he said again as he lifted his shirt to show the bruise he had sustained when he fell off the tree. "This is the price I pay, man. So what you mean by what you saying?" he asked rather defiantly, as he looked at Peter.

"Well ... I mean," answered Peter, stopping short his thought as his mother walked out from inside the house with a pile of clothes in her arms. She walked down the steps towards the boys and dropped the pile of clothes on the stones next to them. She glanced at them inquisitively without saying anything and then walked over to talk to her neighbor who lived across the street. The boys waited until they were sure she was out of earshot before they started talking again.

"Okay guys, it's getting late. What are we doing today? It's going to be a nice day today. We doing something?" asked Simon, trying to get out of what could be a tough situation.

"I was thinking maybe we could go to Louison. I going to check a scene out there today, so maybe we all can go," said Peter, a wiry grin on his face.

"Oh ho, that is why we couldn' find you las night. You wasn't by no father. You was by Lucy. Oh ho!" Tony cried.

"Ya, ya, that's true!" piped Simon. "What happen? She goin' to wash clothes today? You sure her mother not goin' with her? You askin' for trouble, man," he continued, playfully rubbing his hand on Peter's head.

"I check all that out already, man. You see stupid write on my forehead? She's going with her big sister. Her mother's going to Roseau today," a smile of exhilaration on his face. "I and her sister cool so is no problem, man." He sounded rather confident. "So what we say? We doing it or not?"

He waited for an answer from his friends. Simon and Tony looked at each other, trying to restrain their amusement. They looked at Peter and shrugged their shoulders.

"Okay, man, if you say is Louison, is Louison. No big deal," answered Tony.

"Count me in, then," said Simon. "What time?" he asked, as he stood.

After deciding to meet at the front of the Catholic Church at noon, the three boys parted ways, agreeing among themselves to remain as quiet as they could even if Peter's brother had heard of the escapade. They knew they could count on him not to tell anyone. They would try to get in touch with Philip and deal with him. They could not let Mr. Radigan or the police or Peter's mother know that they were the ones who had climbed Mr. Radigan's mango tree.

Peter was the first to get to the church grounds, just as John was ringing the church bells to signal that it was midday. John was the priest's helper and also served as the village sexton. He took care of the church grounds and the nearby cemetery and made sure that he rang the bell at five in the morning, midday and six o'clock in the evening. He enjoyed his job and was very passionate about it. Peter looked at him intently as he worked the three bells and then just one as he sounded the hour. *I wonder if I couldn' ring that bell,* he thought to himself.

But he would not have any more time to entertain this thought as both Simon and Tony came running towards him. Simon was the first to speak. "Peter, I hear some guys saying that Nippie going to Louison. They were working on Carlton's truck and they going to bathe in the river. If we run fast we can get a ride when he passing."

"So what we waiting for then? Let's go!" screamed Peter.

Together they all rushed down to the foot of the driveway and waited for Nippie.

When they got to Louison, everyone disembarked and filed down through the grassy track to the bank of the river. There were many people on each bank; some were in the water; some were seated on stones doing their laundry. Some boys and girls were playing catch with a beach ball in the middle of the river. Some other boys, and girls too, were diving from a huge rock into the deepest part of the river. It was a brilliant sunny day and everyone was having a great time.

Peter surveyed the crowd. He looked up, looked down, but could not see Lucy.

"What happen? You lose somebody?" Simon asked him, giggling as he did so. "You cannot see her? You blind, man! Look over there." He held Peter's head and slowly turned it to the right. "Who is the person opening clothes on the stone by those gabion?" he asked.

"You know I didn' see her over there. I was looking for her in the water," answered Peter. He blushed. He whistled, and when Lucy looked his way, he waved. She waved back. Peter smiled with delight.

"You're the man! You're the man!" cried Tony as he patted Peter on his back. Then he, too, waved to Lucy. She waved back. Peter motioned to her that he would come by and then he walked away with Tony and Simon.

They walked down the bank; took off their shirts and hung them on the small trees that grew along the bank. They stepped to the edge of the water and tested it with their hands to see how warm it was. They were standing in an area shaded completely by the tall mango trees growing on the bank of the river and that didn't help their cause too much. They blessed themselves with the sign of the cross and then waded into the water. Peter screamed as the cold water touched his body. Simon winced in pain as the water irritated the bruise.

The boys swam and dove with the other kids. They wrestled each other. That was what they liked the weekends for. It was a time for fun and a time to be themselves. After they had spent about half an hour frolicking in the water, Peter left the group and made his way among the stones and the women doing their laundry until he came to where Lucy and her sister were. He was nervous as he approached them. Lucy smiled as she saw him approach, looking at her sister to see if there was any sign of disapproval. But there was none. The sister smiled and winked at her.

"Hi guys," Peter said nervously. "Can I help?" he asked.

The sister was the first to answer. "Hello, Mister Peter. What are you doing here? Of course, you can help," she responded.

"I always come here with Tony and Simon and sometimes by myself," he answered.

"That's not true!" Lucy jumped in. "He came because Laura told him I was coming to wash today."

"Not really. I'm always here. Ask Tony when you see him," Peter replied.

"I know. I was just joking," Lucy said, her lips parting, showing her bright white teeth. She stood up and walked in Peter's direction.

He looked at her and he felt his heart skip a beat. She looked at him again and she smiled. She was wearing a bikini bathing suit and he looked at her mid-section. Her body looked very smooth. "Wow!" he said to himself. She looked good in that bikini. She walked past him, brushing playfully against him as he did. She walked over to where some clothes lay on a pile of stones and placed them in the plastic basket.

"You are a policeman, non?" Lucy's sister asked Peter, a hint that it was okay to sit down with them.

"No, but I have to go and meet those guys before they leave," he replied.

"They're not going yet," Lucy answered, as she picked up the basket of wet clothes and walked to the water's edge to rinse the laundry. "You don't have to leave with them. Do you?" she asked.

"Not really," Peter answered, "But you know what they'll say," he said, shrugging his shoulders.

"So even if," Lucy answered, trying to convince Peter to stick around a while longer.

But before he could answer, he heard his name being called aloud. He looked around. Tony and Simon were standing on the roadside directly across from where he and Lucy stood. They beckoned to him.

"Time to go, man, or we leaving you behind," Tony shouted, a large grin on his face.

"See what I mean!" Peter said to Lucy.

He could not realize how the time could have passed by so quickly. He had just started to feel comfortable in Lucy's presence and was getting an invitation to hang around. Now Tony and Simon were spoiling that opportunity.

"You can stay and help to carry her clothes down," laughed Simon. "What you doing?"

Peter looked at Lucy and they smiled at each other. He knew that he was not going to stay here all afternoon. He felt tempted to extend his hands but he decided against it. He wished he could kiss her goodbye, but he wasn't sure that he wanted to do that. "I'll see you later," he said nervously, as he started to walk away.

"Maybe, maybe," she answered, her white teeth showing again.

He was on a different world. He liked her and it looked like she didn't mind him being around her. He didn't mind being in her presence either. He waved to her sister and she waved back. He made his way up the riverbank over some gabion baskets. He was excited as he reached the road where Tony and Simon were waiting. He had a broad smile on his face.

"Oh yea, you the man. Things looking cool," cried Simon.

Peter jokingly punched him in the stomach. "Who have my shirt?" he asked. "Did somebody take it for me?"

"Which shirt?" answered Tony, acting as if he did not understand what Peter was talking about.

"My shirt, man. The shirt I had on me. I left it with yours on the tree branch," he said, as he made a move to go back and search for his shirt.

Tony and Simon laughed gleefully. "Okay, sweet boy. What you mean cutting style on us. Like is only you can chat up nice girls, eh?" cried Simon as he and Tony laughed again. "Look over there!" he exclaimed, as he pointed to the shirt hanging from the branches of a small tree along the roadside.

"Aright, aright pal. I'll get you back!" Peter warned, as he playfully shoved Simon aside.

The boys waved to Lucy and her sister and started their trek back home. Nippie had left a long while ago, but that didn't bother them. They had come to have fun and were in no real hurry to return home. That was especially true of Peter who could not but help gazing back and waving to Lucy.

It was now approximately four o'clock in the afternoon. They detoured through the Hillsborough Estate, like all other kids loved doing, in search of oranges, grapefruits and coconuts. They were rewarded when they came upon a young coconut tree laden with fruit. They bent low and peered beneath the trees to ensure there was no watchman patrolling the estate.

Simon was the best climber among them and therefore volunteered to fetch the nuts. He took off his sneakers and threw them to the base of the tree. He had climbed coconut trees on his uncle's plantation in Carholm on many occasions. This tree posed no real challenge to him. Certain that all was clear, Simon started his quick ascent up the tree. Soon, he was easing himself unto the fronds. Peter kept his eyes peeled for any movement among the trees while Tony got set to collect the nuts, the events of last night still fresh in their minds. But they were boys and boys did boy things no matter what the cost they would end up paying.

"Watch out, guys!" cried Simon, as he settled himself on a frond just above a bunch of nuts. He pushed his heel onto the bunch and shook vigorously. The nuts tore off one by one and slammed to the ground—about ten of them. That was more than enough for the three of them. Simon, satisfied with his achievement, worked his way down the tree, making sure he did not aggravate the bruise on his stomach.

They searched around for a rock with which to split the nuts. They found one that weighed approximately ten pounds. Peter repeatedly dropped the rock on the green nuts until the skins came apart. They then pulled the skin from the nuts. They then used a smaller stone to crack the shells, making small openings to allow the milk to flow out. They then drank the milk, some of which spilled unto their chests. When they had drunk their fill, they struck the peeled nuts against the bigger stone, breaking them open. They dug their fingers into the warm meat and filled their mouths. They burped one after the other, stroking their stomachs as they did. After they had eaten enough, it was time to hide the evidence. They picked up the shells and skins and hurled them into a clump of bushes, disposing of any evidence of their act. Mission accomplished, they used their shirts to wipe their mouths and hands clean. They headed home once again.

As they emerged from under the cover of the cocoa trees, they heard the sound of an approaching vehicle. They started running, though slowed a bit by the weight of their own stomachs filled with coconut water and meat. Tony was the first to get to the roadside, followed by Simon and Peter holding the rear. Tony raised his right hand and shouted, "Senjo!"

The truck driver slowed down to a crawl and allowed them to climb in, aided by some stronger kids who pulled them in. The truck was loaded with other youths who had been swimming up river and people who had come from doing their laundry. A mock cheer rose from them as the boys settled in, breathless and tired.

Together, they wound their way to St. Joseph. At the first stop, at the entrance of the village, the boys got off and rather than going home, they decided to hang out next to the Upper School building. There they revisited their exploits of the past eighteen or so hours. The shadows of the buildings and the trees were now getting longer. The sun would soon disappear below the horizon and it would be night again.

Peter waited for an answer, as he stared into the distance, looking at a fishing boat coming towards the shore.

"I don't really care! Whatever all you do is okay with me," answered Tony.

"So when we going to decide what we doing?" asked Peter. "I know what I'm doing if nobody have nothing to do."

"Ya, I know what that is and when you finish say is by your father you going," replied Simon. "Is father that have more malè?" Tony laughed mockingly. Peter blushed.

The breeze blew cooler and Peter shivered a bit. "Is time we go home, man! Is time I go home so my mother doesn't get mad with me," he exclaimed.

"Aye! Watch that, watch that!" Tony screamed, pointing in the direction of the sun that was just easing below the horizon. "Watch the green color, like is a disco florescent. Man, that's pretty!" he cried. A green arc hung above the horizon where the sun was just seconds before.

"Boy, that's irie. First time I see something like that, you know. That is cool," added Peter as he got up and stretched himself, yawning loudly as he did so.

From the village nightclub, the *Sea Blast Disco*, came the sound of the calypso *Good Morning Mr. Walker* by the Mighty Sparrow. The boys joined in, to the amusement of the members of the Girl Guides troop who had just ended their meeting on the steps of the Upper School. It was fun to be young.

The shadows disappeared as dusk came. Everything seemed soft and innocent. A stronger gust of wind ruffled their shirts and a sheet of dust blew in the direction of the boys who turned their faces to avoid the onslaught.

"Is time we go home before I get in trouble," said Simon as he tucked at the collar of his shirt, shielding his face from the gusty breeze.

"And I have to go and get my mother's goats before it gets dark or else is me that will pay for it tonight. I almost forget, you know," said Peter, as he remembered that the goats were still out. Failure to get them in on time could lead to unpleasant situations at home.

"Okay, guys. Let's go. We better go home," urged Simon. This time there was no argument.

The boys got up and started down the hill from the school grounds, holding each other around the waist. Simon began singing:

"Good morning, Mr. Joseph,
I come to see your daughter.
Oye Mr. Joseph, I come to see your daughter
Sweet Lucinda (a reference to Lucy) she promise she go marry me
And now I tired waiting,
I come to fix de wedding."

Simon and Tony playfully pulled at Peter's shirt. They had yet to decide what they would do later that night. Maybe that didn't matter. Sometime down the night they would all end up somewhere, like they always did. They were young and time was on their side.

The Street

Crimson patches led from the sandy beach and ended up in a pool of blood on the wooden step. He did not utter a word but clenched his teeth as the pain surged through his body. He saw his blood gushing out and flowing along the edge of the step. He said nothing and stared innocently at his mother, hoping she would not get mad at him.

"How comes your foot bleeding like that, Henry?" she screamed when she saw Henry standing at the door.

"Cut it cut, mama! Something cut me in the sea," the young boy replied.

"Oh shate! Damn it, boy. I tired telling you to bathe by Mr. Brown, but you insist on going to bathe in the sea. You see what happen now? What cut you?" a tone of anger and yet some concern in her voice, as she bent next to him.

"I don't know," he replied, bending over to brush off some of the wet sand still clinging to his scrawny leg. He lifted his foot and there was a puddle of blood where his foot had been. A stream of blood ran down along the edge of the step and then dropped to the ground. He gritted his teeth and held on to his mother.

"How comes you don't know?" she replied, as she rushed into her bedroom. She lifted the mattress off the bed, pulled out an old skirt and ripped it into strips. She rushed back out, "Come, boy, put your damn foot here," she ordered pointing to her thighs with her chin. "Lord God, see what the boy did to himself," she cried as she realized the extent of his injury. "When you going to listen to me when I talk to you boy?" she continued. But the Henry just clenched his teeth and said nothing. "Look at that, non. See what you do to yourself!" his mother moaned, as a bead of sweat slid down the middle of her nose.

It was Monday morning and eleven-year-old Henry, like so many other boys in the village, loved the idea of bathing in the sea before going to school. There was no fun bathing in a shower. What could you do there? The sea was open. Free. One could swim, dive, do anything and stop only when John (the sexton), rang the church bell letting everyone know that it was seven-thirty and time to get set for school which began at 8:00 a.m.. Moreover, the lack of water in the village continued to be a major problem and there seemed to be no end to it. This was the reason why the youth of the village found it more fun to bathe in the sea than to go begging for a bath at someone's outside shower. When they got out of the sea they would stoop beneath standpipes and wash the salt off their bodies.

The sexton had rung the bell that morning, just like he did every day, but Henry did not pay heed, as he usually did. Instead, he had kept swimming back and forth. He would have enough time, he thought to himself. He was the only one in the sea except for two men in a canoe, cleaning their fishing seines, getting ready for another day at sea. There was no need to hurry and as he slowly swam back and forth, he made bell-like sounds with his mouth. Finally, he decided that he had had enough. He swam towards the shore. He stepped out of the water unto a stone covered with seaweed. His feet slipped. He grimaced as he felt pain shoot through the ball of his right foot. It felt like every nerve in his body had been touched. "Ouch!" he screamed, doubling over in pain, falling back into the water as a wave covered him, filling his mouth with sandy water. He got up coughing and spat out. The water around his foot was red. His heart skipped a few beats and Henry stared in disbelief. He was cut and bleeding. He struggled for a while to steady himself and then agonizingly made his way out of the water. He walked up the sandy beach towards the remains of what was once a canoe, lying askew against some rocks. He picked up his shirt and sneakers that he had placed at the bow of a rotting boat. He grimaced as the pain shot through his body. He limped home, leaving a trail of blood behind him, along the street and in the yards where he had passed. Now he stood before his mother, wondering what would be her next move.

"I wonder if the Health Center is open; and you cannot even walk. How am I going to take you there, boy? Your father's not even here to help me. How am I going to do that?" she asked, feeling a bit helpless. Henry did not answer, but with every curl of the cloth around his heel, he winced in pain. Tears dripped down his face. "Okay! Okay! Come on! Climb on my back," his mother said, as she sat down on the step and urged him to climb unto her back. She had to get him to the Health Center really soon. There was no one she could ask to help her to take him to the clinic; maybe she didn't want anyone to help her either. Henry climbed on and with a heave and a slight moan, his mother stood up and began her trek to the Health Center; a fifteen-minute walk from her home.

That was a month ago. Every day since, she had carried Henry to and from school and every Monday and Thursday to the Health Center, to get his dressings changed. Sometimes she got help from her brother if he was around. His father worked in Roseau as a DOMLEC electrician, so he left home early in the morning and came home late at night and therefore could not be of any help, except if he took time off from the job. That was not an option.

"I am not leaving you home. What are you going to do? Sit there all the time doing nothing? You will sit on a bench or wherever and the teacher will take care of you," she had told him. "I waste my damn time already. I don't want the same thing to happen to you. No, Henry, eh, eh."

Henry had looked at her and smiled. He knew what she was talking about. She had said it to him many times before. It was like a litany and he wondered when was she going to stop. Maybe never. He believed that as long as they were both alive, she would keep saying this to him.

"You don't have to tell me that every time, mama," Henry replied.

"I say what I want. You hear me? And when I talk, don't you dare answer me or I will cut your what I don't want to tell you," she said, some anger showing in her voice. Henry said nothing and watched as his mother walked out, muttering to herself.

Today would be the last time, hopefully, that she would have to carry him to the Health Center. He was going to have the stitches removed. He shivered at the thought. "Ouch," he moaned.

"What happen, Henry?" his mother asked. "You hurt your foot?"

"No ma, nothing," he answered.

"And why the moan? Tell me what happen!" she demanded, as she came out of her bedroom.

"I was just thinking of the nurse taking off those stitches, ma. What will happen if it not cure yet?"

"Ha, ha, I thought you were brave!" she laughed. "Coward, come on! Let's get ready to get over there before it's too late. Come on!" she smiled at him, reassuring him that she loved and cared for him, even though he had not listened to her.

Garbage lined the side of the street. No one seemed to have cleaned the street for a while. Flies hovered over the remains of a dead rat that blocked the drain. The dirty water from the drain overflowed unto the street and as the vehicles rolled by, the dirty water splashed unto unsuspecting bystanders and pedestrians. As she walked past the pile of garbage, Sandra instinctively let off her hold of Henry's right leg and pulled the collar of her blouse over her nose in a vain effort to block the stench. "Oh shate! What the hell is that? How people can stand that?" she asked herself. "That smelling so much!"

"Ma, look. Look that that smelling so." Henry pointed to a dead rat. A swarm of flies buzzed noisily as the rush of air caused by a passing car disturbed them.

"Don't look at that, boy! Umm," she spat to the ground, at the same time grabbing back his leg. "Where is Jonas?" she continued. "The government paying him to clean the street and that is how he leaving the place? Where's the health inspector?" she asked. "He not seeing how the place dirty that bright morning? Is a crying shame!" she said, as she looked for a spot to place her foot so as not to step into the filthy water. She could not jump with Henry on her back "What they paying them for?" she continued, with her outburst.

She was a strong woman. "*She was always a strong woman, that Sandra, from the time she was born,*" her mother had once said. "*That is why she hardly cried when she was a child. She would fall, get up and keep doing what she was doing without saying a word. Whenever she was spanked she just took the blows, cried for a minute or two and stopped like nothing had happened. And she never ever got sick when she was a child. There was something special about her.*"

And Sandra lived up to the words of her mother. She was a tough woman and did not allow things to pass her unnoticed as many in the village had come to find out over the years. "They degrading the man name leaving the street so dirty. What happen, they want people to get sick in this place?" she said loudly so all around her could hear.

"What man, ma?" Henry asked. He had never heard anyone talk about any man's involvement in this street and here was his mother talking about some man. He didn't really know what to think.

"Mr. Eugene," she replied. "We use to call here Eugene Street, boy!"

"Oh!" Henry exclaimed, hoping to put the issue to rest. It didn't really matter to him what the deal was all about. He was more concerned about getting these stitches out of his foot. He had been restrained long enough. He could not go swimming. He could not join his buddies on the playing field to play soccer, and that bothered him. Many times he felt tempted to do something, but then common sense prevailed. He hoped that his foot was healing the way it should and whether his mother believed that there was no respect for the man long dead, he did not care about it.

"So they never told you how come they name those streets with the name they have?" she asked Henry.

"No, ma," he answered. "But ma," he continued, "Is not Hell Street and La Rue L'Enfer they calling here? I never hear nobody call here Eugene Street. I never hear you say nothing about that. Is it because Ma Eugenia was in power, ma?" Henry asked, thinking that the street may have been named after Dominica's former Prime Minister, Eugenia Charles.

"Boy, you crazy! And what Ma Eugenia you're talking about? I am talking about a man, boy. The Prime Minister is not a man. Is she?" she asked Henry.

"No ma, but I didn't know what you talking about," he answered, a bit bewildered, as his mother continued.

"What nonsense you talking about, Henry? As God is in Heaven, if they ever decide to name no street after that lady I myself going up to the House of Assembly and say no. It can Village Council, or Boy Scout, or youth group. Whoever it is. If they want to rename this street, they have better names to choose. Hold me better, Henry," she broke off from her attack on the former Prime Minister and heaved Henry higher unto her back. "You're strangling me, boy!" she said jokingly.

"So why they call it so, Mama?" Henry asked her.

"They never told you at school?" his mother snapped back.

"No mama, no," the boy answered.

"What are they paying those teachers for? They leave high school with all their GCE and CXC. They should study history and tell you about your village. Is time they ban all those history books on Christopher Columbus and Walter Drake and England and America. I am sure you know where Number 10 Downing Street is, eh? And where the White House is? And what about who is this and who is that? What does where the Prime Minister of England live have to do with us? What these countries have to do with us right here after they done reap us out already? Nothing! We're just a drop in the ocean; a speck on the globe, Hen. They came here and took all we had and run us dry and what did we get from them? Nothing, Henry! Nothing! And guess what?" she continued, "Sometimes they don't even have us on the map. So go figure, Henry," she laughed.

"Why you saying that ma?" Henry asked, perplexed at his mother's sudden tirade about the system.

"Why I saying that? Because is so it is, Henry. Is so it is. Nobody knows us even if the Prime Minister went on platform with the American President when they invaded Grenada. People were thinking that she was a Spanish woman because she was from Dominica because they only know Dominican Republic. Some people even say that is Granada in Spain. They never expect us to have people like her. When they send letter to us it still goes to Dominican Republic. After all those years people still don't know the difference between us and them or at least know that we are different from those people in Santo Domingo. Up to this day, when somebody sends a letter to us it goes to Santo Domingo. Then when it finally gets here there is a stamp that says, 'Mal encamiando a Santo Domingo'. I think they say it means 'Missent to Santo Domingo' or something like that. You think I'm stupid, Henry? Even if I didn't finish high school, it doesn't mean that I am stupid. It's my fault it happened. I am paying the price for not listening, but I am not a fool."

"No, ma," Henry answered again. "I don't think you stupid or you foolish, but I don't know what you were talking about."

"How you mean you don't know? Am I speaking in a strange language?"

Henry did not answer.

"You heard what I said?" his mother asked again, but Henry still did not answer. He was wondering what all his mother was talking about had to do with a pile of garbage in the street, a dead stinking rat, water flowing unto the street from people's homes, his teachers, history and most of all, to the stitches in his foot. It all seemed out of place. Yet, maybe she knew what she was saying. She was older and she was his mother. Wasn't she supposed to be wiser? But it seemed like he would never get the reasons from her why the street was named Eugene Street since she was more concerned about the fact that it was dirty and about a man who was not being respected.

"Yes ma, I hear," he finally answered, rather belatedly. His mother said nothing.

Henry knew that his mother was not stupid. She was in the fourth form at the Dominica Grammar School when she became pregnant with him. She was doing well until then. Her plans for a college life were shattered then. She had planned to do something meaningful in Adult Education classes after she had given birth, but that never happened. Instead, she stayed at her mother's home until Henry was five years old and then moved in with his father. She worked intermittently at the Castaways Hotel until she was laid off. She had been home since. She read quite a lot during her spare time or made dresses for women from the village and even some from neighboring villages. She could sew very well. She had learnt at a very early age from her mother who was the main seamstress in the village. Her mother still sewed and sometimes they worked together on certain jobs. There was no reason for Henry to feel that his mother was stupid. In fact he was very proud of her, even if he did not openly show it.

"Get down, boy, you're killing me," she said, as she got to the entrance to the Health Center. "Wow, let me catch my breath. Boy, if you know how I'm glad today is the last day. Thank you, Jesus," she moaned, as she bent down and allowed Henry to ease up unto the step leading into the Health Center. "Go and tell Nurse Joseph you here. Take your time. Tell her I am outside if she wants me."

"Yes ma," Henry answered, as he stood upright. Sandra watched as he slowly made his way to the nurse's desk. She walked away towards the shade of a flamboyant tree, about twenty feet away from the building.

"Oh Lord, what a life! This damn village drives me crazy. Everything's upside down. Not even about their very own village those teachers teaching those children these days. I wonder what they tell them?" she said to herself, as she sat on a pile of stones at the foot of the tree.

A few hundred yards from where she sat, a teacher was conducting a physical education class with a group of students on the playing field. Sandra watched as the children ran, jumped and bent their young bodies in the hot tropical sun. They seemed to be enjoying it. The school bell rang, indicating the end of the session, and there was a mad scramble to the lone standpipe on the southwestern edge of the field. The kids piled over each other, each trying to get to the tap before the other. "If they only waited their turn, wouldn't it be so much easier?" she laughed.

But children loved fun and excitement and challenges and this was a challenge. Later, they would boast about their little conquests at the tap. Sandra smiled. As a child she did that too, and it was an achievement to get there first. Usually, they drank until their bellies bulged. Nothing had changed since. She watched until the last child left the tap and walked along the field and up the steps before disappearing into the school building; a building that was in need of repairs. It was not a pleasant sight to look at, and how the children learned in that type of environment, only God knew. The paint was peeling off the walls and some of the windows were broken. She turned her sights beyond the empty playing field and she had a clear view of Main Street and the buildings that lined it on either side, including the gas station and the post office.

Main Street was not just another street. It was part of the main thoroughfare that snaked its way through the village. The other part was called the Morne Road and that was in the section of the village called The Morne. Main Street started at the bridge over the St. Joseph River, at the beginning of the village, and ended at the foot of The Morne. It was the main center of village activity—besides the schoolroom, of course, which was the cultural or social center for everything imaginable. Main Street was the life of the village. But there was something stranger than that. The street went by two other names: La Rue L'Enfer and Hell Street. And depending on what part of the village you lived, or how old you were, or what political party you belonged to, the street had a different name.

The older people called it La Rue L'Enfer. The younger ones, especially the sports minded ones, Hell Street. To the majority of the villagers it was Main Street, and those who opposed the government, Eugene Street. There had been numerous stories as to why the street was named La Rue L'Enfer. Sandra remembered once talking to her grandfather about La Rue L'Enfer and he gave her a mini history of the street. They had sat down outside (she was only ten then), and as he smoked his tobacco from his bamboo pipe, he told her of the many stories he had heard and the many things he had seen happen there.

He had told her that many years ago, there used to be some serious fights on La Rue L'Enfer. Gangs of men would fight others from other villages if they dared visit St. Joseph. That was most common on Feast days. Situations like these created fear in the minds of everyone in the village. He told her that he was once caught in the middle of one of those fights and he had to sleep with his brother, Roland, that night because he did not dare venture out lest he be attacked. There were times, he had told her, when no one dared walk the village after dark. No one wanted to meet one of these gang members on the street at night. Sandra wondered what her Grandpa, who had died a few weeks after telling her this story, would think now if he were still alive.

It was easier to figure out the reason why it was also called Hell Street. Teachers and the intellectuals (*intellectuals?*), of the village found it low and degrading to talk patois in an English setting such as at school or any place where English was supposed to be the formal language. Anyone who did was admonished. This was a British colony and we had to speak English. Creole was for the "uneducated" and the old. And so the name Hell Street was born.

Main Street, on the other hand, was the official name in almost every quarter. The common story is that it was the first public road built in the village. The village expanded, new roads were built, but Main Street remained Main Street. Any meeting, political or otherwise, was held on that street. Religious zealots wooed people from its sidewalks. Carnival parades went back and forth. People going to Roseau or to the gardens gathered on Main Street. School children attending classes at the high schools in Roseau (everything happened in the capital), congregated there before boarding the wooden box trucks or the one bus at the time that traveled back and forth to the capital.

Vendors from the villages of Salisbury, Colihaut and Coulibistrie sold their grafted mangoes, sugar apples (*pomme carnel*), corn and watermelons, from the steps of *Kay Ka Ka Chyen*—the big store on the corner of La Rue L'Enfer and Back Street. Anything that one wanted was on Main Street. In fact, that was where the first Police Station was ever built. Right there in the middle of the village. It is said that anyone that spoke of the village—outsiders that is—knew only one place, Main Street. That was where they passed through everyday on their way to and from Roseau.

Sandra surveyed the village and the rooftops of the houses, some rusted and in need of repair. Then there were others with new galvanized sheets that shone brilliantly in the mid-morning sun. A car with a bad muffler entered the village. She followed it until she lost it momentarily as it wound its way through Main Street, up the Morne Road and continued on until she could neither hear nor see it as it descended down the hill towards the small village of Mero.

The village was somewhat quiet now; most people would have been preparing lunch for their families, and with the sun as hot as it was, where would anyone be going anyway? Sandra sighed deeply as she remembered the scene at the corner of the street. She bent her head into her hands and thought for a while.

Sandra was one of those who had decided to have the street renamed about ten years ago to Eugene Street. She was a member of the youth organization, The *Concerned Seven* that was observing Community Awareness Week. One of their activities was to try to rename the streets in the village. There were no official names for the streets in the village, besides Main Street/ La Rue L'Enfer. There were four or five streets in the village that all used the same name, Back Street, although they were completely different streets. It was not a problem because villagers still went to the post office (someone's private home), and stood outside on the street, in rain or sun, until the postmistress called their names or the name of someone in their family. It would have been a nightmare if a postman had to go from home to home delivering mail.

But the group's attempt at renaming the streets, especially Main Street, had met with stiff opposition from a number of people, the government most of all, who refused to grant the group permission to do so. But the group had the support of the Village Council, the local government of the village, that saw the move as a good one, since it was a chance to honor one of their own. They were affiliated to the same political party, as was the late minister. They encouraged the group to go ahead with its plans to observe the week. The Council saw this as a way to frustrate the Government in power.

Alexander Thomas Eugene was born in the village sixty-five years ago. He grew up a poor boy and survived the difficulties that school life presented while trying to cope with the outside world. After leaving school at sixteen and his parents being unable to send him to high school, he was appointed as a student teacher. From there, he worked his way up and at forty was appointed as a principal. He worked in a number of schools around the island. His success rate wherever he worked was always very high. However, in 1970, he resigned from teaching to pursue a law degree at the University of the West Indies. On his return to the island, he entered the political arena, contesting the 1975 General Elections for the Labor Party. He won by a wide margin over the Freedom Party candidate. But sadly, after only three years in office, he died suddenly at his home.

As a tribute to him and all his efforts in the community and the country, The *Concerned Seven* had taken the initiative to perpetuate his memory by renaming Main Street in his honor. But that did not work. There was talk that the big new school being built in "Yard", on the hills overlooking the village and the neighboring village of Layou, would be named in his honor. Naming a street after him, some thought, would only duplicate efforts. But the group and the Village

Council saw the school as something in the future while in their opinion the street was already here.

But still, the new street signs were placed on telephone and electric poles along Main Street and some of the other streets, the name written in white against a red background. Sandra and the other members of the group had worked hard to make this a reality. The morning after the signs were put up, not one remained on a pole on Main Street. There was not a trace of where they had ended up or who had removed them. In their places were signs saying HELL STREET written in white against a black background. In small letters below HELL STREET was the word FOREVER. However, the signs on the other streets were surprisingly left untouched. Somebody, or a group of people, had made a point clear. She laughed as she remembered the sequence of events that followed. She did not worry then. Not that she worried now, either, although she still had her very strong opinions about the whole issue.

Undaunted, the group tried one more time to get government's approval, but before any action would be taken, the group ceased to exist. No one knew why, although it was hinted that they were threatened with prosecution if they continued in their efforts to have the street renamed. It was also believed that inter-group problems had a great part to play in the break-up. Neither Sandra nor anyone else from the group would say why they had broken up, leaving the community to speculate on what had transpired. This, then, was where the story of Eugene Street began and ended.

"Boy! That was something else, eh!" Sandra muttered to herself. "This place will never go anywhere with that kind of attitude. What the hell? La Rue L'Enfer, Hell Street, Main Street. In those modern times things have to change. Is time we have something meaningful to identify with," she pondered. She smiled as she remembered the questions that Henry had kept asking her. She did not want him to know that she was one of those who had tried renaming the street. She tried thinking of a way to tell him what was happening and why she was so unhappy. But she did not seem to have the courage to do so. "He will find out in time," she thought to herself.

At that point the church bells rang, indicating that it was now midday. The school bell, as if automatically set off by the church bells, rang too, signaling the end of the morning session. Soon the kids would be crowding Main Street, La Rue L'Enfer, as they headed home for lunch. Those who were fortunate would get something to eat, but there would be many who would have nothing to eat. It was a sorry plight.

Sandra got up, yawned and stretched her body. She felt emotionally and physically drained. She had been sitting out there for almost an hour. It was getting warmer and the shaded area was getting smaller. She did not hear Henry call out to her as she concentrated on the children running down the school steps, shouting and laughing. Memories flashed through her mind.

"Ma!" Henry called again, as he gingerly hobbled down the step towards her. "Ma, I finish. Nurse Joseph say she want to see you before we go home."

"What does she want to see me for?" Sandra asked, as she got up and walked towards him.

"I don't know. She just say she wants to see you," Henry answered.

"Wait for me here. Sit down here," she said. "How's the foot? It okay?" she asked. Henry nodded his head in the affirmative.

Sandra wondered what the nurse wanted to speak to her about. She worked her way to the nurse's office and greeted Nurse Joseph like she'd done so many times those past few weeks.

"I just want to tell you to ask him to be careful with his foot. It is coming on okay, but he must take care. It is still a little sore. He should be okay in a few days. If he doesn't take care of it, I cannot take care of it for him," the nurse warned.

"Okay nurse, thank you. I will keep an eye on him. Anyhow, as you say, is his foot and if he's not going to take care of it, I cannot take care of it for him," Sandra replied, and they both smiled.

She walked out and joined Henry and together they made their way home.

Although the stitches were now removed, the foot was still a bit tender and Henry was still not ready to trust putting all his weight on it. He walked with a slight limp but he was happy that he was going to be okay soon. The visits to the Health Center had come to an end for now, at least. If all went well, he would soon be out there doing the things that he loved.

They took the same route back home along Main Street. There were not as many people as there were earlier in the morning. The street was, for all practical purposes, empty. It was hot out here, too. The pile of garbage was no longer there; only the scraps littered the street. Flies still buzzed in the spot where the dead rat had been. The scavenger had not used any disinfectant; he never used any, anyway.

"They clean it, then. I thought they were going to leave it there like a trophy," Sandra said as she passed by. Henry looked at his mother and somehow she knew what he was thinking. "Okay, Okay, Henry. Yes I speaking too much," she said, looking him straight in the eye, a smile on her face.

"I didn't say that, ma!" he replied.

"I know you didn't say that, but I can see it in your eyes, boy! I always know that smile, Hen. You cannot fool me. Remember, I am your mother."

Henry smiled. "But true, ma, how comes I never hear nobody talk about Eugene Street before. I only hear people call it La Rue L'Enfer or Hell Street or Main Street," he asked her, as he hobbled along, trying to keep up with her.

Sandra paused for a while before answering. "Henry!" she exclaimed, "It's a long story. Sometimes we see things in life one way. Other people see it another way. Some never see it, even if it is written in black and white or red and green, whichever. Remember that. As *Paton* used to say: '*Put it in your pipe and smoke it*' (referring to a popular phrase coined by one of the village's most prominent politicians). One of those days I will tell you everything, but now is not the time for that."

"But ma!" Henry blurted out. But before he could continue, Sandra stopped him short.

"Don't but me, boy! Watch where you going before you hurt your foot," she snapped at him. Henry obliged without saying one more word.

They turned off unto Back Street and then entered one of the narrow alleys, between houses, towards her home. In the yard—if one could call it a yard—of one of these houses, there was a pigeon coop. As she passed by, something caught Sandra's eyes. She stopped and retraced her steps.

"What happen, ma?" Henry asked, as he saw his mother staring in the direction of the coop.

"Nothing, Henry, nothing, and mind your business."

"So why you looking over there like something happen? You want a pigeon ma?" he asked his mother. "I don't like pigeons!" he added.

Sandra did not answer. She pretended that she had not heard what he had said. She had seen something that was of interest to her. A sign or remnants of it on a piece of board, used to make the coop, had caught her eyes. It was one of the signs that she had helped put up when her group had tried to rename Main Street. The piece of board had been split in two, horizontally, but she could easily make out what was written on it. She shook her head and smiled. Henry looked on, not knowing what to think. He did not want to ask his mother any more questions, but he realized, from the intense look on her face, that something was wrong; but he could not see what it was.

Sandra shook her head. "I see!" she said to herself.

She had passed that way so many times before, and why didn't she ever see this? Maybe it had not been there in the first place or maybe whoever it was who had it, now felt that it was safe to show it in the open.

"Oh boy, I tell you. What the hell? All of them is the same, I guess. La Rue L'Enfer, Hell Street, Main Street, Eugene Street, Senjo Street. What else?" she asked, mockingly.

Henry heard, but he chose not to say anything more. He smiled and hobbled on ahead of his mother.

"Wait, Henry," Sandra shouted, "Wait, Hen! I have something to tell you."

But Henry kept limping along, paying no heed to his mother's pleas.

The Final Hour

The crowd roared and the noise echoed in the distance. The man at the microphone raised his hand and said, "Look all around you and you will see what we have done over the last five years. Don't let them tell you otherwise. We shall not be moved come Election Day!" The crowd roared louder and the flags and banners waved frantically in the late evening breeze.

All the political parties were now on that final swing, the *home stretch*, as some called it, trying to win the support of those who had not yet made up their minds as well as trying to strengthen the faith of those who were still in doubt.

It had been a mud-slinging campaign and each candidate and party had accused the other of corruption and foul practices among a myriad of other failings, and had turned the election campaign into one of the worst in many years. Everyone was trying to get, not just a slice, but also the biggest slice of the electorate and it didn't matter how they got it. What mattered was that they got it.

Only two more days remained and that last desperate drive would be on Sunday when all the parties went on their usual island wide motorcade. This was the final push. The tempo was building up, but for the guy at the podium, it was a clash with his destiny. He knew it was going to be a rough road to travel and he wanted to get there. But had he done enough to get there again? "We have to show them that we will do it and let them know who we are," he said, and the crowd cheered louder still.

The electorate throughout the island had been presented with manifestos, promises and pleas by all the parties, and in this constituency of St. Joseph, it was no exception. All the candidates were presenting themselves and what they had to offer to the people. One, an independent, was making his first appearance on the political stage. The Labor Party candidate was giving it a shot in a different constituency from the one he previously represented. The man at the microphone, the incumbent and candidate for the People's United Party, was trying to get re-elected for another five-year term. Many in the village were not sure for whom they should cast their vote. None of those who were asking for their votes seemed convincing enough to do what the people wanted.

For years, the community had seen various politicians take up office promising to do the best to uplift the village. But yet, after five years, there would still be nothing to show for it except more division and pleas to give them one more chance. The man at the microphone, the People's United Party candidate, had had a disappointing term and chances of him being reelected were very slim and getting slimmer as the campaign progressed. The presence of the independent candidate was not making it any easier for him either. He, like the rest of the party, knew that it was going to be a rough road. Yet, he sounded extremely confident.

"Tell all those who doubt my ability to check the records. I caused the farmers at Neba to get better roads so they could get their bananas to the market on time. I got the Health Center, the *little hospital*, built in this village. What else do they want? What did they do when they were in there?"

"Nothinnnng!" the crowd roared back.

"Nothing whatsoever. It took this party, with intelligence and faith to do the things that this community needs and I want you to stand behind your man come Election Day. Go to the polls and cast that vote for me, for a winning party and a winning team. You cannot put the future of your children and this community at ransom. Can you?" he asked, gesturing to the crowd.

The crowd seemed to have lost its sting and vigor, and as if in resignation, answered, "No waaaay!"

There was not the usual lively atmosphere that was always prevalent at People's United Party meetings. It was as if the crowd was waiting for something dramatic to happen. But it was not happening. Maybe they doubted their own minds. Were they at this meeting simply to get out of their homes and the drudgery of life in the village? Or were they patiently waiting for that final plea from Kevin to convince them that he wanted that second chance?

―――――――――――

Five years ago, Kevin Joshua Lambert stormed his way into the political picture. He was a very popular and respected young man in the community. He was a teacher and a sportsman. He was a man of the soil; one of the masses. He won easily then, beating two other candidates. At last it was believed that the person who would help bring change and progress had finally arrived. But tonight that was no longer true and his party followers and the party bosses knew it. He was facing a formidable challenge from a man who had taken the country down the gutters and was now trying to make a political comeback in what he called his adopted constituency.

The two other candidates seemed to have strengthened their position and they were beginning to have larger followings than expected. That was especially true of the Labor candidate. He was not from the village, as had been the case with many parliamentarians who had represented this constituency over the years. He was an outsider, so to speak. He had served a term in jail on fraud charges, yet he was getting the support of the community. This was a bitter pill for the People's United Party and its followers to swallow.

But who else could they blame but the man at the microphone? Some in the village had believed that Kevin did not get the support of the party and its bosses and it was hypocritical of them trying to salvage his political career at this late hour. The other candidate was an ex-schoolteacher, but no one expected him to do anything except to take votes away from Kevin. He was also a former member of Kevin's Party, one who felt slighted when Kevin had been chosen by the Party bosses to represent them again. He felt that he could do a better job than Kevin had done. But the party was sticking to their man and Kevin was *that* man.

Tonight, Kevin's role was being scrutinized. Had he done anything for the constituency during his five years in office? Had he lived up to the people's expectations? Many had argued that he was a failure and there was nothing that they could attribute to his poor showing in office. He had been given a job on a silver platter and now that job was slipping away. He was now standing on shaky grounds. Tonight he was seeking support for another five years.

There had been calls for him to step down and allow a more competent candidate to represent the party, but that met with strong opposition from party brass. Some in the community believed that he was never the man for the job in the first place; but Kevin wanted to prove them all wrong. The task ahead was a difficult one and he knew that. But he wanted desperately to win that seat and prove he could do the job.

At an opposition meeting the night before, Kevin had heard members of the other party deride him and what he had done during his term of office. He was blamed for the poor social conditions that existed in the village and the constituency in general. He heard the other candidate blame him for every thing that had gone wrong during the past five years. He was blamed for poor and inadequate sporting and recreational facilities and even for the poor returns to farmers who had become poorer while the price of bananas kept dropping and the price of producing it went higher. He had listened to all this and tonight he had to try to dispute all their accusations and turn the tide back into his favor.

But tonight Kevin's party was united with him and they wanted his supporters to stand behind their man. They realized his shortcomings but they were hoping against all odds that Kevin would pull this thing out. There was no way they wanted the Labor Party candidate to get this seat, especially as they wanted to prosecute him for fraud when he was a member of the former regime. They had fought for years to get this seat and they had to keep it. Party allegiance to them was more important now than Kevin's shortcomings and his lack of productivity. There were party members who had come from Grand Bay, Portsmouth and even as far away as Marigot to lend their voice and support to Kevin. Even the Prime Minister, Ms. Charleson, was here tonight. They all knew the importance of winning this seat and what it meant to have this constituency in their pocket. This was the final hour.

Speaker after speaker urged the people to make a sensible decision on Monday—Election Day—and vote wisely for the future of their children and their children's children. "*Give the party a chance to complete its program*," they all said, as if this was the motto for the night. In between, anti-freedom remarks would be made by a dissenting voice from a safe distance and Kevin's supporters would shout back, sometimes with obscenities, directed at the heckler. And so it went on through the night from the steps of Teacher Edwina's shop.

The promises being made were the same that had been made five, ten, fifteen years ago and yet not one of these parties had fulfilled any of them. There was still no better water service. In fact, it had deteriorated. Contrary to what they all promised and said, feeder roads were not built and the farmers were getting frustrated. Some supporters could not deal with this poor treatment and had switched parties. And although Kevin was a sportsman, maybe the thing that had won him the seat in the first place, he showed very little interest in developing the sports situation in the village and surrounding communities.

"And what I want to do is make one final plea. I beg you all tonight to go out there on Monday and put that X next to the Hand. Think of what we have gone through together to get here. Our camp has been divided by the man who thinks he is better than I am. If he were a better man he would be here tonight fighting with us to get rid of these Laborites. Maybe he should join them instead," he said. The crowd cheered loudly, waving the flags and banners in the night air. Kevin continued: "So please, I ask you. Vote wisely. Vote intelligently. Make your vote count in that polling booth on Monday. Vote People's United Party! Vote Kevin Lambert on Monday because I am your man for the future. We shall not be moved!" He blew kisses and raised his hand and gestured to the crowd, a huge smile on his face as the emcee for the night led the crowd in singing the chorus to the union song that had become the party's anthem throughout the campaign.

We shall not be, we shall not be moved.
We shall not be, we shall not be moved
Just like a tree that's planted by the water
We shall not be moved.
We're voting for Kevin, we shall not be moved
We're voting for Kevin, we shall not be moved
Just like a tree that's planted by the water
He will not be moved.

The meeting ended and amid the talking and clapping, the people dispersed and made their way back to their homes and the frustrations of life that they were now sadly accustomed to. Some stayed around discussing the pros and cons; the possibilities and improbabilities of a win and urging each other to vote. One woman, dragging her two kids behind her, said, "Well I don't know, non, nothing doh goin' to stop us now, nothing at all." Would Kevin have believed her?

It was now left for the people to decide and, for Kevin, it would be two more agonizing days. Was this the beginning of the end or the end of a poor beginning? Only time would tell. And Kevin and his party knew that too. Could they win this election? That they surely would love to see happen. Their destiny lay in the hands of the people. It was not only in the hands of the people of St. Joseph, who were now walking through the dark alleys still waiting for streetlights to be installed. It was in the hands of those who, at this late hour of the night, were heading to the public standpipes to fill their buckets because after all these years they still did not have pipe-borne water in their homes. That destiny was in the hands of voters all over Dominica who they hoped would give them yet another chance to run this country. But had they done enough as individuals or as a Party?

The music from the public address system filled the night, bouncing off the hills and echoing in the distance. A soca tune, by one of the region's calypsonians, boomed through the night resounding loudly throughout the village:

> "*Raise your hand in the air,*
> *Raise your hand if you want to dance*
> *Raise your hand if you want to prance*
> *Raise your hand if you want to dance*
> *Raise your hand if you want to prance.*"

The music stopped abruptly and a female voice cried out, "Ladies and gentlemen, people of St. Joseph, remember your roots. Vote for Kevin. Vote People's United Party."

And all became quiet in the waning hours of the night.

It was the morning of May 25, 1985. The sun shone brightly over the village and the air was alive with excitement. It was seven o'clock and the early morning risers—churchgoers, farmers, students going to the high schools in Roseau, and fishermen—were all heading about their business, mindful however of what was going on in the country. The day was finally here, one that would hold surprises for many. Who was it going to be? No one knew. The final rallies and motorcades were held all over the island yesterday. Supporters for all parties, in the thousands, had shown their loyalty. All the accusations, mudslinging and *mepuis* were over, for now anyway. Today, only one man would win.

Polling stations all over the constituency were opened and voters were streaming in to cast that important vote for the candidate of their choice. Kevin walked in and cast his vote at the Main Street Polling Station. When he walked out, he had a broad smile of confidence showing on his face; thumbs up in the victory sign. He shook hands with his supporters and friends who stood waiting to enter the small voting station. He, and they, too, wished that they had done enough to pull this thing out. But Kevin knew that he had more work to do and he walked away with two of his campaign buddies determined to go out there and urge more supporters to go to the polls.

It seemed a long day for everyone. The hours seemed to drag on by. The village was bathed in brilliant sunlight and that gave everyone a chance to go out there to do his or her civic responsibility; something they did once every five years except in the case of a death or resignation or expulsion when there would then be a bye-election. It was something many had fought for after the abolition of slavery until Universal Adult Suffrage was granted to all free slaves. But for some, they were still slaves to a system that did not give any hope nor provided for their well-being, but instead just kept taking away and giving to the rich. It was a system that, for many, stunk and reeked of corruption.

Yet, every five years there were more promises and more empty promises, at that. Promises that politicians never delivered. It was a system that allowed illiterate individuals to become elected and make policies that defined the future of the country. A system that allowed people to vote for politicians not because of what they could do for the country but what they could offer under the table. It was a system that allowed politicians to hire lackeys to hold positions that they were incapable of holding. It was a system where the blind led those who could see.

Groups of individuals congregated in various parts of the village: on steps, under breadfruit and mango trees, on the steps of *Kay Kaka Chyen* and at Teacher Edwina's rum shop, discussing what they believed the outcome would be. Party "checkers" stood at polling stations, pen and pads in their hands, making a manual tally of their supporters entering and leaving the polling stations with the hope of getting a hint of what the voting pattern was.

Other party supporters were scurrying about, taking the elderly, the handicapped, the homebound, the sick, people whom they had never visited all those years, to the polling stations to cast their votes, even if these poor souls could not comprehend what was going on. They were taken by car or bus or carried to the polling stations and all they had to do was put an **X** next to the Shoe, (Labor Party) or the Hand (People's United Party) or the Fork (the independent candidate). Who it was that represented these parties did not matter. The symbol spoke volumes. It was *the Party* that mattered. At the end they would be rewarded with something in return for that most important **X**. Every single vote; every single **X,** counted today. This was a "do or die" day for either party.

The voting throughout the constituency and the rest of the island ended at six o'clock that night. Everyone was confident that *his* man had won. Each candidate's people claimed victory.

Behind the closed doors of the polling stations, election officers, party representatives and a police officer closely witnessed the counting of votes. The results would be tallied and escorted to the St. Joseph Police Station where the Chief Returning Officer would tally all the returns from the various polling districts all over the constituency. At the end, the results would be announced over the national radio station.

At approximately 7:30 a.m. the first results from the smallest polling district, Belles, was announced. Kevin had won by only 23 votes, 110 to 87. The independent candidate had received 50 votes. This was closer than was expected. The People's United Party had expected to sweep that district quite easily, since the last time around Kevin had won in a landslide. What had gone wrong this time? Was this going to be a trend? In the meantime results from other constituencies were announced over the radio, and with each announcement there were loud cheers all over the village.

At eight o'clock, the results from Mero and Layou were announced. In Layou, as expected, Kevin had been crushed by the Labor candidate 209 votes to 80. Although he had relatives in Layou, no one expected him to make a dent in what had always been, for some unknown reason, a Labor Party stronghold. Layou was devoid of anything that made one believe that any political party of the past had any concern for this tiny fishing village. Yet, the villagers continued to vote for the Labor Party. In Mero, a community that closely mirrored Layou, Kevin lost by 4 votes. He amassed 67 votes to the Labor candidate's 71. The independent candidate was not a factor in any of these two districts, getting just a handful of votes in either district. But that could be significant in the final analysis. Kevin was not happy nor was the hierarchy of the People's Party.

The Labor camp was excited. Were they pulling this one through? They were ahead now, but they, as well as the supporters of the People's United Party, knew that the results from the People's Party stronghold were yet to be announced; the results from the St. Joseph flat and the Church Lane area. But the Laborites knew they had a good chance of winning if the results from Autrobando reflected the results from the previous election. Both sides were hopeful.

Kevin was at home with his faithful party followers seated around a table listening to the results on the radio. They were also getting unofficial results from their men at the various stations and they were convinced that they, too, would pull this thing through. Kevin paced up and down the room, unable to sit, the pressure too much to handle. His wife urged him to relax, to take it easy, one station at a time, but Kevin knew what this was. Every now and then he sipped a drink from a glass on the table. He needed something to help calm his nerves. The brandy felt good and refreshing. He had a mountain that he wanted to surmount and he was not sure he was going to get to the top of that mountain.

Then the results from the St. Joseph flat—Back Street and environs—were announced. Kevin had held his own but had he done well enough? He had amassed 354 votes to the Labor Party's 185. His supporters erupted in wild cheers. Yet, they were extremely optimistic although they realized that the results from the Morne-Autrobando area, a definite Labor stronghold for years, could easily swing this election. Kevin hoped that he had done well there. A good showing in that area could make his dream come true. His political future depended on what happened at the stations in that polling district. His team made additions and subtractions on the chalkboard resting against the wall in the living room as the different results came in.

This was a roller coaster ride for them. One time they were up the next they were down. This is what they had worked for these past months and they hoped they would reap the harvest tonight. It was a tough campaign. But for some reason the results from these stations were taking a while to be reported and they sat around agonizingly waiting, hoping that the next result would be the one they were hoping for.

At half past nine, the results from Church Lane were announced. It was a stunner. Kevin and his team expected better results than what they heard. It was not a good win. It was not as decisive as they had hoped. Just 128 votes to 115! They had hoped to sweep that area. What had gone wrong? How would that impact his re-election based on the results still to come from Autrobando? All they had to do was wait.

The village was humming with excitement. Vehicle horns blared through the night and now and then the sound of a *lapeau kabwit* drum was heard as a supporter celebrated his party's win. It was hard to pinpoint who was celebrating because both parties were claiming that victory was theirs. Kevin had only a slim lead now. *A mere 72 votes!* Could he maintain that lead? It was going to be tough. He and his party were riding a time bomb. Yet, they were optimistic. It was not over yet.

In the meantime, results from other constituencies all over the island were being announced and the People's United Party seemed to be heading for a decisive victory. They had already won ten of the twenty-one constituencies and the results from Roseau Central, Canefield, Goodwill, Newtown and Grand Fond were not yet in. Would Kevin be part of that victory? Time would surely answer this question. He sat staring at the now empty glass in his hand asking himself questions while everyone around him sat waiting for that one result. He realized that he might have blown his chances, but it was too late to think of that now. He had to think positive. It made him sick thinking of not being the man of the people for another five years. Would his own people let him down for a man who had never cared about them? A man who was facing criminal charges? Had the people listened to him? What else could he have done differently?

He was jolted back to reality when someone called his name. The results from the final polling station were finally in and going to be announced. It was now 10:35 p.m. and the People's United Party had a commanding lead and was poised to be the next government of the country. Only three results were still to be called and Kevin's was one of those. The supporters in the village were in a form of suspended celebration. They wanted to celebrate the party's overall victory but they were unsure as to whether they were going to be part of the bigger picture. The party was being given a mandate by the people, to do what they, the people, wanted. One of this was to continue to bring criminal charges against the members of the old regime, one of whom was contesting the very seat that Kevin so badly needed to win.

The supporters and well-wishers at his home sat at the edge of their seats. Some stood inches from the radio as if wanting to urge the announcer to speak on. They listened as the announcer spoke.

"And now we have the results from the last polling station in the St. Joseph constituency. Kevin Joshua Lambert of the People's United Party, 140 votes; Independent candidate Jeffrey L. Hill 25; and Peter Richard Jacob of the Labor Party 245 votes. The final totals for the St. Joseph constituency are as follows: Kevin J. Lambert of the People's United Party 879 votes; Independent candidate Jeffrey Hill, 155 votes;

and Peter Richard Jacob of the Labor Party, 912 votes. So the St. Joseph constituency, ladies and gentlemen goes to the Labor Party."

The room became quiet. No one uttered a word. They looked at each other in stark disbelief and sadly shook their heads. They looked at the chalkboard as one of their members added up the totals hoping that this was not really true. The glass dropped from Kevin's hands and shattered on the concrete floor, just like his dreams to be re-elected. He stared at the board, shaking his head in disbelief—or was it disappointment? He slumped into a chair, bent his head and placed his face into his cupped hands. The radio station continued giving the other results but no one was listening. No one cared to listen.

Tears streamed down the face of Kevin's wife. A supporter finally got up and switched off the radio. They had heard enough. The stark reality of it all now stared them in the face. It was all gone. All that they had dreamed of had slipped away tonight. So close! But not close enough. Where had they gone wrong? 33 votes!! If only the independent candidate had stuck with them! If Kevin had only done a little more work when he had the chance to do so!

Throughout the village, vehicle horns blared and the beat of the drum continued to sound as the Labor Party supporters reveled in the streets, especially on The Morne. They screamed and shouted from their windows and doors, letting all know how they felt. They waved shoes in the air. They hung shoes: old, new, dirty and clean—any type they could find—around their necks. They knew that once again their party had failed to get control of the government, but their man had won and now, at this moment, this was what mattered. This was their time. Tomorrow would take care of itself.

Kevin's wife walked over to her husband and hugged him tightly. He wiped the tears away from her eyes and kissed her. Time and reality had caught up with him. Without saying a word, he walked around and hugged each of his stunned supporters. Deep down they knew that they had not done enough. Now it was too late. They had let their man down. They had let the party and their supporters down, too. Should they ask for a recount? It was too close to be true. But would it change anything? They had not been invited to the "Big Dance" and that hurt.

Somewhere in the village a bell sounded. It had a haunting sound. It sounded like the death knell was being rung for Kevin.

A Life Wasted

He looked like a man possessed. Nothing seemed to disturb him as he sat on the wet pavement. A damp and unlit cigarette hung limply from his lips and his dreadlocks hung loosely over his shoulders. It was just another day and life for him continued its most recent course; panhandling for a living. He seemed very well at ease doing it and he seemed to have a way of getting what he wanted, even in these conditions.

"Hey, man, wha' you doin' today?" he shouted at me, as a northbound Number 2 train rattled along the overhead tracks and came to a screeching stop at the 225th Street train station before moving on towards its final stop at 241st Street in the Bronx.

He knew me. For about four years we were tenants in the same apartment building on East 213th Street. He was also a Dominican like I was and he was from the village of Mahaut. He had left Dominica at a very early age with his parents who had immigrated to the island of St. Croix in the United States Virgin Islands. He later joined the army and after a spell in Viet Nam he returned home. However after having been back home for only six months, he decided to move to the mainland and to the state of Florida to join his eldest brother.

We had developed a very close relationship although some times I wondered whether he was really suffering from the after effects of being in the army. He was someone I was able to sit with and listen to some Dominican music, talk about cricket and just hang out with when we both were not at work. For the first two years, things seemed to be moving okay with him but then he turned to drugs and alcohol. He wasn't the same James anymore.

It was surprising to see what had happened to him over the years. James had worked as a token clerk for the New York City Transit Authority. He was able to make ends meet and to see him today panhandling at the very doors of the stations where he once worked was extremely pathetic. It was a waste of a human life and resources, if one could call it so.

I walked over to where he sat alone on the sidewalk, his back against the post office building, wondering all the while whether he was on one of his usual highs. As I approached he sat upright and pushed his hands into his pants pockets and pulled them out.

"See, man, tings hard for I. Got some quarters to spare man?" he asked me. "I want to buy some cigarettes and something to eat," he continued.

I knew he was not going to get anything to eat and I was not prepared to compromise either. He looked at me as if pleading his cause, but I was not going to give in to him. "Why don't you get something positive to do?" I asked him. "Get yourself together, man, and things will be better," I continued.

He stared at me, a frown on his face. He got up from the pavement, throwing the unlit cigarette to the ground. I knew that this was going to be it between the two of us, albeit for a while, but I was not bothered. I had to stand by my belief and that was all there was to it.

As he walked away, he muttered something but I didn't understand a word. I suspected that he was swearing at me, but preferred not to bother with him and slowly continued into the post office where I was heading to in the first place. I was going to mail a few letters to some friends whom I had lost touch with since I moved to this part of the world. I was also collecting a parcel which I suspected came from CBS Video Club. I had succumbed to an advertisement and had ordered ten videos at a cheap price, promising to buy some more in the next three years. I felt it was a good deal.

The post office was crowded today and just a few windows were open, which did not help. There did not seem to be any sense of urgency in what was going on. You got the message that if you wanted service you had to stick around and be punished too. And wasn't that true of many government agencies in the city? I guess it must be part of the job. Today seemed slower still.

I stood behind a tall young woman who detested the idea of having to stand in line. She turned to me and in her heavy Jamaican accent said, "Me, ah tired a come to dat place you know. Wha' de time?"

I looked at my wrist and pulled up the sleeves of my sweater but there was no watch. My heart skipped a beat. Had I forgotten it at home or had it dropped off? I could not afford to lose this one or else my wife would go crazy. She had given it to me as my birthday gift just a month ago.

"I forgot my watch at home," I told her apologetically, still wondering what had happened to the watch. "Seems like I left it at home," I said to her. She smiled and turned around to find someone who could tell her the time.

I was so engrossed in my thoughts about the watch that I did not realize that it was my turn until I felt a nudge at my side and a voice saying, "Wake up, man!" I walked to the window, somewhat embarrassed, but happy to finally get there.

After completing my transactions, I was out of the building. I looked for James, but he was gone. I continued walking southward on White Plains Road. It was a beautiful day and I felt that I had time to exercise my legs and do some browsing. As I walked the picture of James hung before me and I could not help but wonder what had really happened to him. What was it that had driven a father of three beautiful kids to do something that had ruined his life? I wondered whether he was still married to Jane, the *dream girl* of his life, as he had once called her. She had gone through rough times with him, especially when he had had too much to drink at the bar that he frequented into the wee hours of the morning. Their marriage was falling apart the last I saw her and I guess by now it might have fallen completely to pieces. I remembered the three little girls and I wondered what their plight was at this moment. They were three cute little girls: Stacey, Samantha, and Jacinta.

There was hardly any space on the sidewalk for one to maneuver. The vegetable stalls, the store stands and people with particularly nowhere to go, crowded the sidewalk. There were people going uptown and downtown standing at the various bus stops, waiting for the Number 41 buses; those who were busy shopping; and those who simply hung around the stores to pass the time. The sun was trying to make an appearance from behind the clouds but it was having no success.

As I walked on I passed the fruit and vegetable stands filled with a wide variety of fruits: apples, tomatoes, mangoes, cherries, peaches and grapes. I passed the fish markets where fly-covered empty carton boxes lay on the sidewalk, yet to be picked up by the sanitation crews. There were the meat shops crowded with patrons picking their choice pieces of meat. Then there were the music stores, their pulsating rhythms (a mixture of reggae and calypso), booming from their sound systems. Young men, most of them seemingly unemployed, *boogied down* to the tunes of their Caribbean music idols. I passed a pizza parlor and I could not resist the temptation to buy a slice of the cheese-laden dough. It was steaming hot but I bit into it as the melted cheese ran down my fingers. Every now and then a train rumbled noisily along on the elevated tracks heading downtown to Brooklyn or uptown to 241st Street, while down below cars and trucks and people competed for room to move about.

After flushing down the pizza with a soda, I continued my journey to nowhere at all. I was just walking at this point. I was now at 222rd Street and had hardly realized the distance I had walked. Then I remembered James.

Whenever we talked in the better days, he always told me that he had wasted his time in The Nam. *Dam dat place!* he would say. He had once showed me a scar on the inside of his left calf. *See this, man! My own gun, man! It misfired. Lucky it was not one of those little guys,* as he referred to the Vietnamese. He told me that he feared for his life every day and that he was the happiest man alive when he was discharged.

During his time in Florida he met a woman—one of the many that he met—whom he would eventually marry. She was from South Carolina and after having graduated from college had moved to Florida with one of her college friends. After getting married, they decided to move to New York, more from the urgings of James, to see if they could get a better life for themselves. He settled in the Bronx because he knew family from back home who were willing to put him up until he found his own apartment. That was ten years ago.

But usually the big city does not hold the promise that we all expect and although James was eventually able to land a job with the Transit Authority, Jane was not so lucky. Sometimes she blamed James, whom she believed wanted her to stay home to take care of their children rather than go to work to earn a living. She did not want to be a housewife. She believed that it was tough to support the family on the pay James brought home. But he insisted that she stayed home.

When they started having problems, Jane threatened to return to South Carolina but she could not afford to raise the necessary cash for moving and to also take her three daughters along. She was not prepared to leave her three girls in New York with James or anyone else for that matter. She knew that James was not prepared to let her go anywhere and she did everything possible to prevent him from getting to know what she had in mind. She knew that if he ever got to know she would have to face his wrath and insults. She was not prepared to deal with that.

Because of my friendship with James, I got to know Jane a lot more than I expected. She was a very intelligent woman and sometimes I realized that she did not deserve the pain James had brought upon her. She loved him very much but she was paying dearly for his insensitivity. She was very fascinated with New York when she first landed there ten years ago but over time she had become scared and disenchanted with the city. She was petrified at what was happening: the mugging, raping, murder and robberies. She was also afraid that James would ruin their lives if he continued the way he did. She always felt that people survived rather than lived in New York. She hoped that someday she would go back to her peaceful life in South Carolina.

Jane was a very proud woman who cared about her three girls and fervently hoped that they would some day attend college. She was a college grad herself and it was after graduating from the University of South Carolina that she traveled to Miami together with a college friend. It was there that she met James. After seeing each other for just six months, they were married. She believed that the move to New York was the biggest mistake of her life. James, however, did not see it so and detested the idea of moving back to Florida or even South Carolina, for that matter. He was determined to make it in the *Big Apple*. "*If not here, where else?*" he would always ask.

Jane believed that she had become a prisoner and sometimes when she explained how she felt about the whole situation, she cried. She wished she could find a way out. She didn't want her parents back in South Carolina to know what was going on because they had not been too thrilled when she decided to marry James. They were proud black folks who cared, but she believed that she had to deal with her own situation. The last time we spoke she had vowed to make a move.

As I walked along the sidewalk and all that was happening on White Plains Road, the reality of it all jolted me. *Had she finally made that move, or had she thrown him out?* I asked myself. I wondered whether she was still trapped within the situation. I felt tempted to turn back at that moment, find James and ask him what had happened. But it was now almost an hour since I had left him at the post office and I doubted whether he would still be there. He was not one who hung around one spot too long. But since I was all the way down here, I decided to visit the apartment where he had last lived to see what I could find out. I also decided to use the opportunity to visit one of my close relatives who lived around the corner from where James had lived.

I walked up to the apartment building at the corner of Holland Ave and 213th Street and squeezed the buzzer at the front door. After a while I realized that it was not working. I stood there hoping that someone would come by. I had been standing there for about five minutes when the door opened and a woman, wearing Rastafarian dread locks, came out of the building.

"Excuse me," I said to her. "Do you live here?"

"No!" she answered rather disgustedly and walked away, looking back at me suspiciously.

Soon after another woman, whom I remembered from my days when I lived in the building, walked up the sidewalk towards me. She was pulling a shopping cart laden with groceries behind her, and on her head she had a large straw hat.

"What you doin' aroun' here?" she asked when she saw me. "Long time me no see you. How you doin'?" she asked.

"I come to see Jane," I answered.

"Oh, your friend dem dat livin' in 3A. You doh want to know," she continued.

"Does she still live here?" I asked her.

"Well to tell you de real truth," she continued, "Is a long time me no see she. Almos' three months now. I hear she got up an' go with her three girls dem afta de husban' beat she up. Cops even get involve. Dey even arres' him too."

I was shocked that it had really gotten to this. She had indeed stayed around with James. "So does he still live here?" I asked her, wondering if she really cared to speak to me anymore.

"Well, I doh tink so. I tink he was owin' de lanlord an' he put him out. He was involve in de drug business and … anyhow dat's all I know," she said, as she pulled out her keys from her bag, opened the door and entered the building before I could ask any more questions. I realized that she did not want to speak to me about it in too much detail. I did not mind. I had the answer I wanted.

This was the first time in over two years that I had been back to this area. Nothing seemed different. Besides a newly cemented sidewalk and a few trees planted along the roadside, nothing had changed. The auto mechanic shop across the street was still operational and I guess the guys still bought and sold their illicit drugs when they were around. I went over to where my cousin lived but he was not around. After a final look, I departed the area, feeling sorry for Jane and her three daughters. I wondered where they were now. Hopefully, they were happier wherever they were.

I knew that some of his friends could not fully comprehend what had really happened that caused James to get so deep into drugs and the booze. Some believed that this was his way to ease the pain and memories of Vietnam. Some believed that he had fallen in with the wrong crowd. But whatever the reason, he was now a victim of his own doing.

James always said that he cared about his family. He said that he loved his wife and was very proud of his daughters. Whenever he was sober, it was a fun loving family; but when the weekends came it all changed. Somewhere along the line it had gotten out of control and he was paying the consequences. He had lost his job and his family and now he was putting his life on the line. What a sad state of affairs!

I remember the day we were together in a park off Gunhill Road and we started talking about his stint in the army, especially about the time he spent in Vietnam. He told me of the times when he and some of his buddies would light it up and that would sometimes help create a sense of false security. It would help take away the distress and fatigue and set them up to face the challenge. He mentioned the day that he lost it in the jungles. He still believed that the drugs he had taken had made him think he wasn't what he was and his foolish actions caused the life of one of his men.

"The man got shot right in front of me," he told me in a repentant voice. "It hurt me so much that's why I stop that shit, man." I remember seeing tears flow down his face as he said so. "I killed that man," he said again. "Boy, you know man weak and sometimes I do a spliff or two or do some pulls. You know what I mean … a little now and then," he said, after a momentary pause.

But today it had turned out to be worse than maybe even James could have imagined and it was now taking hold and charting the path of his life.

By now it was almost midday and I decided that I had walked enough. Sweat was beginning to drain down my face and my shirt was wet. It was a bit warmer now although it was still a bit cloudy. I felt that it would be better to go home and get ready for another day on the job. I started work at 7:30 p.m. Tomorrow would be Thanksgiving and I would be spending the first part of the day on the job. Later, I would join my wife's family to celebrate and give thanks together. People like James would not be able to share in this and understand the warmth and companionship that such a day would bring. Maybe he never did, for that matter.

I walked to the bus stop at 219th Street and joined a group of people waiting for the uptown Number 41 bus. The weather had changed and darker clouds were now covering the sky. It began to rain and a slight drop in temperature was noticeable. I felt the chill go through my body, although I had on a sweater. I hated this weather. Too much clothes to carry about.

The rain was getting stronger and I was beginning to wonder if I should wait until a bus arrived or whether I should take a cab home. I peered down White Plains Road and there was no bus as far as those eyes of mine could see. I decided to take a cab. It was going to cost me more but I needed to get out of this weather. I could no longer stand under the elevated subway tracks waiting for a bus. I stretched out my hand as a *Skylark* taxicab drove in my direction. The driver stopped and in a strong Jamaican accent, inquired of my destination. "Ah whey you a go, boss?"

I got into the cab and shut the door. "4466 Hill Avenue," I told him. He seemed a bit confused and after some slight uncertainty, he indicated that he knew where I wanted to go. His cassette player was blaring Jamaican reggae. I could not understand why he had such loud music in a passenger vehicle. But I guess this was part of him or what helped to keep him going. Jamaicans love music, especially reggae. It started pouring very heavily and although only one wiper on the car worked, he maneuvered his way along the side streets.

Along the way we got into a conversation, which I initiated. I wanted him to tone down the volume of the music but I did not want to offend him in any way. I knew that if we began to talk he would listen and he would have to take down the volume. I asked him about the recent hurricane that had struck Jamaica and whether he had anyone who had suffered loss when Gilbert passed through.

"Ya man, everyting me fadda had done destroy. Me mudda loss all she roof 'pon she house, but beside dat dem awright. You know wha' a mean. By de way, whey you from?" he asked me before allowing me the chance to make any further comment.

"D.A!" I answered, and I a saw a perplexed look on his face. "Dominica!" I continued, this time being a little more emphatic. "Dominica, man! In de West Indies!"

"Oh, you mean Dominican Republic. Oh me know, me know," he answered.

"No! Dominica! An island between Martinique and Guadeloupe," I answered, realizing that he was another West Indian who did not know much of his Caribbean history and geography.

"No, me never hear 'bout Dominik," he answered, finally toning down the volume on the set. "Me know 'bout St. Lucia and Barbados, but me never hear 'bout Dominika," he added. "What language you speak dere," he asked.

"English!" I answered somewhat snobbishly.

It is difficult to comprehend that we are so close to each other yet we do not know that each other exists. Sometimes I believe that it is just a case of insularity. As a boy in primary school, I knew the names of all the islands; the names of their leaders, their capital towns and even the names of their main rivers. Yet, many people from Barbados, Jamaica and Trinidad, the so-called bigger islands of the Caribbean, had never heard of Dominica. I feel it's a damn shame!

Before I could tell him some more of the Dominica that he seemingly had never heard of, we were on Hill Avenue and I directed him to my apartment. "How much is that?" I asked him.

"Five dollars boss. Just five ... see," he answered.

I could not really understand how such a short ride could cost that much. I wondered whether I had really been taken for a *ride* by one of those *fixed* meters or whether this was really the price for the trip. Anyway, I knew I was not going to win or make him change his mind, so I pulled out my wallet and handed him a five-dollar bill. I didn't tip him and I hoped he was not expecting one either. I stepped out of the car, slammed the door shut behind me and scampered across the street to the warmth of my apartment.

I peeled the wet clothes off my body and placed them to dry out in the bathroom. I then went to the refrigerator to fix myself a drink: a mix of Macoucherie Rum and some Coke. I needed something different to add a little warmth inside. The rum always felt good during the cold weather, although it is said that drinking is not the best thing to do when it's cold. But I was inside for now and I didn't think it really mattered. I just wanted a drink as I reflected on my friend's life. I felt very tired; the long walk and the fact that I had not been to bed— since I had worked last night—had worn me out. I tasted the drink. It tasted good and I felt the warmth from the rum burn up the inside of my mouth. That was a potent drink. I switched on the TV and sat back to watch another episode of *Bonanza*. I had become a fan of the program and made sure I watched it every day before I left for work.

I was awakened by the sound of the buzzer in the house. Someone was ringing my doorbell and that person would not release the button for almost thirty seconds. I sat up on the edge of the couch and cursed beneath my breath. I was tired. I had fallen asleep. The glass in which I had my drink was on the floor and there was a wet patch on the rug where the contents had fallen. The bell rang again. "Okay, okay, damn it," I muttered to myself as I headed to the door. I opened the door and there was a deliveryman from UPS with a small package in his hand.

"A parcel for you, sir, sign here," he said. "Sorry to wake you up, man," he continued, as he realized that I was dazed and somewhat disoriented. I looked at the parcel and was about to sign for it when I realized that it belonged to the guy who lived in the basement apartment. He apologized and I showed him the way to the basement. I grudgingly shut the door behind me and went back inside.

It was half-past five. I had slept for almost three hours. I picked up the glass and used some paper towels to soak up whatever liquid was still in the rug. Finished, I sprawled on the couch, as always, and watched the news broadcast on Channel 7, ABC. My wife would be home in a few hours; I would then try to get in a few more hours of sleep before I headed out to work.

What I saw next came like a stab through my heart. Was this yet another drug story, another victim and another senseless murder? I listened in horror as the reporter read a news item. The name of the victim was familiar. "No!" I heard myself shout. "Oh man!" Then a body draped in a white sheet was shown on the screen. I could not believe what I had seen. Was I still asleep? Was this just a dream? I listened intently, wanting to make sure that I was seeing and hearing right. Then the reporter repeated the name of the victim and I shivered. I gazed at the television screen in total disbelief.

James had apparently been involved in a drug deal that afternoon on Gun Hill Road and the deal had gone bad. He was shot outside the same train station where he had once worked. His lifeless body lay on the sidewalk, in the rain. I sat back and just watched in silence.

Somewhere, a wife and three children had lost a part of themselves. Maybe at last they would find peace. Maybe he, too, had found his peace, although in a violent way. I felt sorry for them. I picked up the remote control and switched off the television. I could not bear to watch anymore. The doorbell rang again. I didn't feel like getting up. I sat back on the couch. The bell rang again. I got up and walked to the door and opened it. My wife stood there with our baby daughter on her shoulders. She was home earlier than I had expected.

"Sorry. I didn't expect you so early," I said, as I took our daughter off her shoulder.

"You heard the news?" she asked, as she stepped in. "Heard about James? I heard about it at the baby-sitter," she said.

Our baby-sitter was also a Dominican and from Mahaut. Every now and then James would stop by to say hello and sometimes he would just hang out on the porch of her house with her sons.

"Yea ... I heard," I answered, after a momentary pause. "Oh, what a shame!" I said, and sat back unto the couch. I sat my daughter next to me and I playfully bit her on her face. She giggled.

I remembered James' daughters, now left fatherless and who would no longer have a dad to giggle with. I then kissed her on the cheek. I had lost a friend and a countryman, but his kids had lost more. All I could do now was attend his funeral whenever that was and bid him a final goodbye.

"What a waste!" I heard myself shout aloud as the reality finally set it.

Grandpa Was in America

"Is true Gran'pa, what Mama say about you, dat you was in Amewica?" the little boy asked, as he sucked on the candy his grandfather had given him. "So you was really in Amewica? You see de chuchu train and de President, Gran'pa?" His eyes lit up as his grandfather nodded his head. "When you goin' back Gran'pa?"

The old man looked at him, and smiled. He bent over and picked up the little boy and placed him on his knees. "Grandpa isn't going back, son. Grandpa's days in America are over. Grandpa is going to be here with you for the rest of his life until Grandpa dies," the old man replied as he fondly stroked the little boy's head.

"So why you go to Amewica, Gran'pa?" the little boy continued, looking at his grandfather; waiting for an answer.

"Well, son, is a long story," the grandfather replied. The boy smiled and seemed to be pondering what next to ask his grandfather.

Grandpa's real name was Thomas Jones and the story of his time in America seemed to fascinate Trevor. His face lit up with excitement and wonder as he listened to what his grandfather had to tell him about his years in America. No one had ever told him anything about America until his mother bought a television set and told him that some of the programs that they looked at were coming from America.

"Amewica far, Mammy?" he had asked her and she had told him that it was not. She also mentioned to him that his grandpa had once lived in America. It was his hope then that he would one day ask Grandpa about his days in that strange country.

Grandpa was spending the day at Trevor's home today and Trevor took the opportunity to quiz his grandfather. Trevor was four years old and he was Thomas's only grandson. Thomas had four other grandchildren, all girls: three who resided in the Unites States and Trevor's older sister, Cheryl. Trevor, like all the other kids of the village, had become fascinated with watching television, the latest technological development on the island. He had his favorite shows that he loved to watch and sometimes he sat around while his mother watched the soap operas. As he spoke to his grandfather, the questions he asked were based on what he had seen on the programs that were aired. Grandpa was very impressed with his grandson. He tried his best to answer all the questions that Trevor threw at him, even if it would be painful to do so.

———————

Thomas was born in the village of Colihaut and two years later, his father died. All Thomas remembered of his father was the black and white photograph that adorned the wooden partition of their two-bedroom home. His mother seldom spoke of his father and Thomas never really asked any questions about him either. He only knew that people kept saying that he looked liked his father or he walked like his father, but besides that, there was no other connection. When he was ten, Thomas's mother died after suffering a stroke and from then on, Thomas and his brothers and sisters had to face the world alone. It was never the same without their mother in the house.

The loss of his parents at such an early age may have contributed greatly to Thomas's development. Here he was, a young boy only ten years old having to make it on his own, and totally dependent on his brothers and sisters. Like most boys his age, Thomas lived, despite the loss of his parents, a very normal life, full of adventure and fun. He was the typical village boy. He got involved in fistfights with other boys; played games at night under the moonlight; enjoyed swimming in the sea; and was involved in mischievous acts with his friends.

The eldest of his siblings was Theresa, affectionately called Shortie by all who knew her because of her height—a mere five feet. At seventeen, she took charge of the home and one of her desires was that even if they were facing rough times, Thomas should continue his schooling. It was imperative that someone in the family achieved something meaningful, and to Thomas's siblings, his education was key.

Thomas's brothers and sisters liked him very much, not because he was the *baby*, but also because he was very helpful and bright. In him they saw the word "success" and that was one of the reasons why Shortie made it clear to him that he had to go to school. She believed that if their parents were alive they would have wanted the same thing for Thomas. She made sure that he attended school every day and did his homework whenever he was given work to take home. Almost a year after his mom had passed away, he was one of five students of his class chosen to sit the Common Entrance Exams. No one was more elated than Shortie. She saw this as a giant step for Thomas and hoped that he would make full use of it.

On the day of the exam, Shortie was up early. She woke Thomas up and got him ready for the trip to Roseau where the exam was being held. By 6:30 a.m. they were standing at the truck stop waiting for the truck that transported villagers to Roseau. Soon, Biram came along, and they boarded the vehicle that was already loaded with passengers going to the town. The other four students from his school were also aboard.

The truck rolled towards Roseau and Thomas sat quietly and pensive next to Shortie, gazing at the landscape as it quickly passed him by. He had been on this road before, but today he was not just accompanying his sister to Roseau to get a pair of shoes or to get his Christmas toy as he did with his mother; he was going to do the Common Entrance Exams.

There would be other students from all over the island vying to get into the top fifty spots for scholarships and bursaries offered by the government, plus those who would earn just passes and be granted admission to one of the four high schools. Thomas prayed he would be one of those. He listened as the passengers talked among themselves or to the truck driver. Along the way the driver made a number of stops for a passenger who was embarking or disembarking. Now and then Shortie looked at Thomas and smiled, proud to be with her brother today.

It looked like it was a longer trip than usual, but finally they crossed the new bridge over the Roseau River and Thomas knew they had finally arrived in the town. He, Shortie, the other pupils and their parents disembarked at Queen Mary Street and made their way to the Dominica Grammar School where the exams were being held. After a few turns and twists of what seemed a maze of the streets, they arrived at the compounds of the Grammar School.

Thomas felt a bit overwhelmed by the moment and he was sure that many others felt the same way he did. This was an experience they would always remember. The people of his village knew they were at the exams; in a small village of less than two thousand people, every one knew each other. Everyone was also hoping and praying for the best for them.

Two months later, the results were released and although Thomas did not place in the top fifty students, he was still able to pass the exam. His brother and sisters were proud of him, as was the rest of the village. It was going to be rough, but his siblings were all determined to help him along the way and make things work for him.

In September of that year, Thomas began his secondary education at the Dominica Grammar School. An average student, he was able to work his way through five rough years and it was his determination, plus the support of his siblings, which finally saw him through. There were disappointments and setbacks, but he persevered and was finally able to achieve something for himself. At the end of his five years at the Grammar School, Thomas sat the overseas exams set by the University of Cambridge. The results would be out in August. He was not going to wait. He needed a job. He took the opportunity to spend time before the results came, submitting job applications in the hope that someone would offer him a job. But nothing seemed to work in his favor. However, when the results of the exams were released, Thomas was informed that he had not done well enough to advance to the Sixth Form College. He decided against going back to school to repeat fifth form to obtain the necessary requirements. He didn't think it was worth the time and effort.

Thomas now found himself in the world of the job seekers. It was not an easy task to accomplish. He was turned down by most of the places where he applied for jobs. It was not merely a problem of his qualifications, but that a "country boy" was looking for work in Roseau. But Thomas took it in stride until his break came. A teacher at the village school, Ms. Joseph, was going on maternity leave and the principal of the school, Mr. James, offered Thomas a temporary job as a substitute teacher. It would be for a few months until Ms. Joseph returned. With nothing showing up and a chance to enter the world of work, Thomas accepted the offer.

Teachers were highly respected during those days and Thomas' brothers and sisters were happy that someone within their family had achieved such a distinction. They often wondered what their mother would say if she saw what her *baby* had achieved. The baton now changed hands. Thomas took charge, as he became the main breadwinner of the family, even if for a short while. He was no longer the *baby*. He was Teacher Thomas and that carried some weight in the community. However, during that time, another teacher at the school tendered his resignation, and that opened the door for a full-time job for Thomas. Upon the recommendation of Mr. James and after an interview with the Education Officer for the district, Thomas was offered a full-time teaching position at the school. He was delighted. Finally, he had a real job. After all these years, he was finally going to be his own man.

However, after only three years as a teacher, Thomas decided it was time to move on. He didn't like the job as much as he'd thought he would. Even if there seemed to be some prestige in being a teacher, the real prestige to him was a better paying salary and the chance to further himself. He resigned and got a job with H.H.V Whitmore and Company, a private enterprise in Roseau. The company was the main agent for most of the cargo vessels that docked in the island's harbor bringing in all types of goods. Since it was not practical to commute everyday because of the distance, he shared a room with an ex-classmate from his days at the DGS. He would travel home on weekends.

It was while he was commuting home one of those weekends that he met a young lady from the neighboring village of Du Blanc named Vernel. Thomas was crazy about her. He loved everything about Vernel. Soon, they were dating. On weekends, since they lived so close to each other, he spent a lot of time in DuBlanc. She did the same visiting him in Colihaut. However, their relationship faced a challenge. Vernel's parents were in the United States and she was expected to join them any time. Thomas didn't let this bother him. However, he felt he would cross that bridge when the time came. Now, all he wanted was to enjoy the time with the woman he adored.

They had been dating for almost two years when Vernel broke the news that she had been granted a resident alien visa and would be leaving to join her parents in New York. Her petition had been accepted by the U.S Embassy. It was tough to face reality, but Vernel was determined to join her parents. It was a heartbreaking decision. They contemplated getting married before she left, but Vernel's family felt that this was not in her best interest. Still, they had one option. Vernel could return some day to be married provided that their long distance relationship continued; or he could travel to the United States and get married there. They decided to allow time to run its course.

It was a sad July day as the two embraced and kissed each other goodbye at Melville Hall airport before Vernel boarded the Leeward Islands Air Transport (LIAT) for the first leg of her trip to Antigua. There, she would switch airlines and continue her flight to America on Continental Airlines. The future for them was uncertain but as they bid each other goodbye, they vowed once again to continue loving each other and living for each other.

Thomas wept silently as the plane rolled away to begin its take-off. It was carrying away one woman who had started to make a difference in his life—the only woman, besides his mother and Shortie, who meant the world to him. He gave one final wave as the plane raced along and lifted off the runway to disappear behind the clouds. He walked away, a dejected man.

Life for Thomas continued its usual course, slow and quiet, except for the occasional party or social gathering. Not that he was a reserved individual, but generally, that was just him. His relationship with his brothers and sisters still prevailed. He had remodeled the house and made it more comfortable for him, his brothers and sisters.

It was only a few months after Vernel left that Thomas met and fell in love with another girl. He was torn between the love he had for Vernel and beginning a relationship with this new girl who was from his own village. The young woman knew of Vernel, but that did not matter to her. She was in love with Thomas and Vernel was just a distant concern. Four months later she was pregnant with Thomas' child. Nonetheless, Thomas's long distance relationship with Vernel continued. Vernel eventually got to know of Thomas' new relationship, but although this caused friction, she still had enough faith to continue the relationship, although at times it proved difficult.

The relationship between Thomas and his new girlfriend and child's mother soured, mainly because of his continuing relationship with Vernel that he was not prepared to end. So, sadly, after only a year, they parted ways.

Being away from each other was causing problems. It was not too long later that Thomas and Vernel decided that it was time that they married. That would in turn hasten any process of having Thomas join Vernel in the United States. So after two years in the United States, Vernel returned to Colihaut to marry her man. Hopefully, it wouldn't be too long before Thomas would join her in the Bronx and they would finally share their special moments with each other.

And that moment did come. Eighteen months later, Thomas was heading to New York. The drive to the Melville Hall airport was a

long one that seemed like it would never come to an end. The truck
bent and swayed and the trip reminded Thomas of the day he had gone
to Roseau with Shortie to write his exams—never-ending. The truck
was loaded with his brothers and sisters, their children and a few
friends who were coming along to see him off. They joked and laughed
and spoke of every conceivable thing as the truck made its way along
the winding, mountainous and narrow roads until they arrived at the
Atlantic shoreline and Melville Hall. For Thomas it was a repeat of the
trip he had taken when Vernel had returned to the US after their
wedding, but for many on the truck, it was their first trip to an airport
and they were excited. The truck pulled into the terminal parking lot
an hour and a half after leaving Colihaut.

Thomas worked his way toward the small check-in counter. There were
very few people at the terminal building. The flights at Melville Hall were
few and far between. Not many people traveled during the week. Most
people loved traveling on Sundays. His ticket was checked and his luggage
tagged to Antigua, the first leg of his trip. He walked to the waiting area
where he joined his family. He seemed nervous, but laughed at the
comments made by everyone. Within a few minutes, they heard the roar of
the plane as it landed. A voice on the building intercom announced the
arrival of flight L333 for Antigua. Everyone surrounded Thomas, kissing and
hugging him and wishing him the best in America. Many hoped that he
would return soon to see them. Shortie was the last to kiss him. The tears
dripped down her face and she squeezed him tightly. "Doh forget us, you
know. Take care of yourself an' kiss Vernel for me, she cried." Thomas
hugged her and a tear dripped down his face. He left and made his way to
the departure lounge.

They all stood in a circle, their eyes telling a teary story. The time
had come. Thomas walked to the plane without looking back. He held
on to the railing and moved gingerly up the steps. Only ten passengers
were boarding this flight and he was the last one. As he got to the door
of the aircraft, he stopped, looked back and waved to his family who
were now all gathered on the airport balcony. They waved back.

Thomas took his seat. He looked through the windows and saw
some members of his family still waving. He buckled his seatbelt and
smiled at the stewardess as she checked to make sure he and the other
passengers were okay. A few minutes later the doors to the plane were
closed. Soon, the engines sprung into life. The plane shuddered as the
propellers gathered speed. The plane slowly eased away from the
tarmac towards the runway. At the top of the runway the plane turned
around and faced east. The body of the plane vibrated as the pilot

revved the engines. The plane then started moving, faster and faster as its drone became louder and louder. Thomas felt an empty sinking feeling. He held his breath and grasped his seat.

He looked through his window and saw the land moving away quickly. The houses below were getting smaller. He saw the shoreline and the waves crashing against the land as the plane moved over the Atlantic Ocean. A flash of sunlight whipped across his face. They were airborne. He looked out again and all he saw was water below and clouds and the blue sky above. Melville Hall Airport was behind him. Tears rolled down his cheeks.

After a stopover in Guadeloupe, they arrived in Antigua where he would transfer to a bigger plane. He went through customs and then to the airline counter to check on his flight. Vernel had warned him to do so early and avoid any late minute rush. Everything worked out just fine and after a layover of two hours, he at last boarded a Continental Airlines jet for his trip to America.

He awakened with a start. He looked at his watch. "Wow," he said to himself, as he smiled at the lady seated next to him. It was a little more than four hours since the plane had taken off from Antigua. He had been asleep for most of the flight and when he got up he realized that the plane was not flying as high as it was during the time he was having lunch on the flight. It seemed like the plane was descending through the thick clouds. He peeped through the window and noticed land below. "Are we landing?" he asked the lady. She simply nodded her head. Just then the pilot asked his cabin crew to get ready for landing at Kennedy Airport. Thomas boiled with excitement. Was this America? He was finally going to meet his wife for the first time in almost two years. He felt a tingling sensation through his body as he thought of holding her close to him and feeling the warmth of her body.

He looked out through the window as he felt the plane dip and level out. Then there was a thud directly below him and he saw parts of the wings moving out followed by a funny whining sound. He watched in puzzlement, wondering what was going on. He saw the flaps extend out and realized what was happening. He was amazed by what he saw. He sat back as the plane drew nearer to land and everything seemed to be coming up faster than he expected. He tightened up. His hands sweated and he felt it difficult to control his excitement. He was really going to be in America. He saw the pavement rushing past his window and felt the plane shudder as it touched down. The passengers cheered. Thomas didn't know whether he should join in or not. "Why were they cheering anyway?" he thought. The plane kept rolling until it slowed down, turned around and slowly taxied towards an area where many other planes were parked. Thomas peered through the window and was in total awe at what he saw. The plane rolled for almost five minutes until it came to a stop and then the engines were shut down.

Most of the passengers immediately got up from their seats and headed up the aisles, even if the doors were still closed. Within a few minutes the doors were opened and the passengers streamed their way out as the plane crew thanked them for flying Continental and wished them a nice day. Thomas wondered why such beautiful ladies (the stewardesses), risked their lives to work on planes only to perish when the planes crashed. "Thank you," he answered as one of them wished him the best.

He stepped unto the ramp and made his way with everyone else following the signs that said, "ARRIVING PASSENGERS" until they finally came to a wide opened area where there were passengers standing in long lines. He realized that this was the Immigration Section. He fell in line in one of the queues designated for NON-CITIZENS. A tall blonde woman manned that line. He felt nervous and wondered what she would ask him when he got to her. He hoped that everything was okay.

"Next!" the woman said when it was his turn. Thomas moved up, hauling his hand luggage behind him. "Your documents please, sir," the woman demanded. Thomas nervously handed his passport and other documents to the officer. She looked at him, then at the documents and then at him again. She flipped through the passport and stamped it. She then directed him to a room, which had a sign over the door that read "ARRIVING RESIDENT ALIENS"

"What's wrong?" Thomas asked himself as he nervously moved towards the office. He was too uneasy to ask the woman any questions. He just did what she told him to. He opened the door and walked in. A male officer asked him for his documents and after going through them, he asked Thomas to step forward to get fingerprinted. He was then asked to sign some more documents and given a temporary permit to work in the country. Thomas breathed a sigh of relief when the officer told him it was okay to go.

He made his way to the baggage area to find his suitcase. There was a mass of people and Thomas realized then that there were other flights that landed at about the same time as his. He was stunned. He had never seen so many people at an airport. He worked his way to the front and waited at the carousel until his suitcase showed up. He pulled it out and after making sure that it was really his, made his way to the Customs area.

"Anything to declare, sir?" a Customs Inspector asked him as he made his way out dragging the suitcase behind him. "Any fruits or food?" the inspector added.

"No fruits, just some rum and some cake from back home," Thomas answered. "And some sticks of cocoa, ginger and spice and some smoke fish," he added.

"You've got a lot. Anything else?" the officer asked. Thomas shook his head.

"Okay then, young man," the officer said, as he used a stick of white chalk to write an X on Thomas's bag, indicating that it had been checked. Thomas heaved the strap of his handbag unto his shoulder, lifted up the suitcase by the handle and made his way out. The automatic door swung open, surprising Thomas. He saw another crowd of people who were apparently awaiting their friends and relatives.

"Tom! Tom!" he heard a voice cry out. He knew at once that it was Vernel's. He looked in the direction where that voice had come from. He saw that smile. A chill ran down his spine. He made his way to her and the two embraced each other and *Lost Love* was rediscovered. They kissed, laughed and looked into each other's eyes and kissed again and Vernel cried a bit. Thomas lifted her off the ground and felt happy to be with her again.

After all the kissing and hugging, Vernel introduced Thomas to her brother, Stan, who had stood there quietly while all this was going on. Thomas had heard of him, but this was the first time that they were meeting. Stan had left Dominica when Thomas was still very young. The two men shook hands and exchanged pleasantries. The three of them made their way towards the airport parking lot and to Stan's car. Stan stuffed the luggage into the trunk of the car and they boarded the car and made their way towards the Bronx.

"Welcome to America," said Stan as he entered the VanWyck Expressway.

"Thanks, bro'," replied Thomas. He smiled. He was in America! He watched wide-eyed as cars zipped past on the highway at speeds he had never seen before.

Half an hour later, they were off the highway and driving through local streets of the Bronx. When they got to Monticello Avenue, they pulled to the side of the road, in front of an apartment building.

"Ok bro, that's it!" said Stan. "We're home, man!"

"Yes, that's my mom's home," answered Vernel. "She's on the second floor. We're going to stop there for a while."

They opened the doors and got off. Thomas stretched. "Oh yea, this is it, eh," he cried. He hugged Vernel around the waist and kissed her again.

It was about nine thirty in the morning when Thomas opened his eyes. For a moment he wondered where he was, but Vernel's kiss brought him around. This was really it. He was in America.

The night before, he had recounted all that had happened on his trip to eager in-laws, who seemed glad to have him in their midst. He told them about the drive to Melville Hall Airport and how scared he was when the plane took off. He told them about the long wait in Antigua and how the plane had bounced around after an hour in the flight; how he was afraid, and how excited he was when the plane finally landed and how the immigration folks kept him in their office. But he was in America and with Vernel and he was happy. After all the talk and having had something to eat, Stan had dropped him and Vernel at her apartment.

And here he was after his first night in the country that he had heard so much about; one that he never, in his wildest dreams, thought he would be in today. He got out of bed, knelt down and prayed.

The days seemed longer than twenty-four hours. It was now one month since he had arrived in America and he had not been able to get a job. He had spoken to friends, made numerous telephone calls, sent in applications, but nothing happened and no one called. It was get up, sit all day and listen to the radio, watch television, walk around the block, go home, eat, sleep and wait until Vernel got home from her job with a hardware company. He began to feel bored and wondered whether he had done the right thing—leaving his job in Dominica and coming here. Vernel tried to encourage him, telling him that this is what usually happened to anyone coming up to the US from the islands. It was a slow process to get a job.

"All they keep asking for is if I am experienced," he said to her. "What experience can I have when I just got here? Maybe they'll ask me for experience to clean the streets too," he said to her one day when he was feeling very down.

"That's the way it is, honey," she replied. "It's not easy anymore. But who knows when your turn will come? We'll see," she offered some hope.

Thomas would dress up and ride the train and bus to interviews; fill out the application forms; do tests; but never heard from anyone. He was getting very dejected. On some weekends he went to house parties where he met other Dominicans. It helped him to relax and forget the frustrations for a while. On days when Vernel was fortunate to be off from work, they visited the city, the Statue of Liberty and the Bronx Zoo in order to pass the time, but otherwise, it was not the most pleasant time of his life.

It was nine months since he had arrived in New York and he was slowly getting into the feel of being in a big city with its hassles and its problems. He saw the poverty, felt the racism that existed, openly and in subtle ways, and he tried to stay clear of any problems. He began to realize that contrary to what he had heard, it was a tough place to be in. It was a "man better man system and a black and white system on the other hand". Tried as he would, he could not but help question his decision to come to this country. However, he waited for his turn.

The break that Thomas was hoping for finally came. It was a warm spring morning and the telephone rang just as he was preparing to go out for a walk down White Plains Road like he had done so many times before. He picked up the telephone after it had rung five times. The woman on the other end of the line introduced herself as a secretary for the manager at the Canopy Insurance Company. They had reviewed the application he had sent in for one of their job postings. He was to report to their offices at four o'clock that afternoon.

"When you get there, please ask for Mr. Moore," she told him.

All that had happened at some of the previous interviews quickly flashed before him, but something within him told him that this one would be different. He thanked the lady for calling and then he hung up. He immediately called Vernel to tell her what had happened and to ask her for directions to Canopy Insurance. Soon, with directions in hand, he was on his way to the train station en route to Manhattan.

He was expectant and many thoughts flashed through his mind while he sat on the Number 2 train as it made its way along the elevated tracks in The Bronx. He got off at 42nd Street and worked his way to the office of Canopy Insurance on 45th Street, following the directions he had been given by Vernel. He climbed into the elevator and stepped off on the ninth floor. How many times had he gone through this routine since he had been on the job search? He looked around and saw the sign indicating which way the office was located. He pushed open the glass door and as he entered a young white woman looked up and said, "Yes, may I help you?"

"Yes, I am here to see Mr. Moore," he replied.

"Do you have an appointment with Mr. Moore?" she asked him as she wrote something on a piece of paper.

"Yes ma'am. Someone called to ask me to be here to see him this afternoon at four," Thomas answered.

"Your name please, sir?" the woman asked.

"Thomas Jones," he replied.

"Oh yes, yes, you're here for the interview. I am the one who spoke to you. I am Jeanette. Okay, please have a seat. Mr. Moore will be with you shortly," she said. She fumbled through some files and pulled out a folder and then walked into an office. She came back to her seat and smiled at Thomas.

Thomas felt his heartbeat against his shirt. It was a large office area. Besides Jeanette there were other people seated at desks writing. A number of workers walked back and forth talking and laughing amongst themselves, some with cups of coffee and others with cans of soda. Thomas imagined that they must have been on their break time.

A middle-aged white man walked out of the office that the woman had earlier entered and approached Thomas. "Mr. Jones, I am Sherwin Moore. How are you doing today?" he asked in a deep, slow and deliberate manner, as he extended his hand to Thomas.

"Okay thank you, sir. I am fine," Thomas replied, standing as he said so.

"Okay. Come with me," said Mr. Moore. "Glad you came. Jeanette, please take all calls, thank you," he said, as he stopped at the woman's desk. He ushered Thomas in and pulled the door behind them.

With every word, Thomas's confidence grew. He really felt that this was his chance. Mr. Moore was very pleasant and he was conducting a very interesting interview. It was rather informal, too. He knew of the islands and had been to Barbados on his honeymoon, he told Thomas, but he had never heard of Dominica until Thomas told him where the island was located. He indicated that he had an opening for a clerical officer and a few other jobs and he would decide where best to fit Thomas if he did offer him a job with the company. Thomas was deliberate in each answer he gave. He did not want to mess this one up. He tried to be calm and clear.

"Well, Mr. Jones, you'll hear from us very soon. Possibly within the next week," said Mr. Moore, when he was finished interviewing Thomas. "I can't tell you whether you will be hired, but in all likelihood, it's probable. So long, then, and thanks for coming," he concluded, as he extended his hand to Thomas once again.

"I'll hope for the best, sir," replied Thomas. "I hope that it works out okay. I will keep my fingers crossed." Mr. Moore smiled as he opened the door and allowed Thomas out.

"What does he mean by what he said?" Thomas asked himself as he walked out of the building and headed back to 42nd Street, maneuvering his way among the mass of people crowding the streets of New York City. "Anyhow, I hope this is it. We'll see." He made his way down the subway entrance to catch a northbound train back to the Bronx.

Three days later, the call came. Mr. Moore's secretary, Jeanette, informed Thomas that he had been hired and he should report to work on the Monday of the following week. Thomas was elated. He thanked Jeanette and hung up the phone. He was extremely happy. Was this going to be the end of all those frustrating days waiting for something good to happen? He picked up the phone and called Vernel to tell her of his success and she was happy too. He had no idea what the job entailed or which of the jobs Mr. Moore was offering him, but the mere fact that he was now going to have a job was great news to him.

Thomas spent ten years with the company working in its claims department until he left for a better paying job and promotion at Metro Life Insurance Company. Within that time he changed apartments twice, bought two cars (one for him and one for Vernel), saw the birth of three children and got further exposed to American life. He did not have a rich life, but a comfortable one. He gained promotions and pay raises but was always aware of his role and the rift that existed and the things that were against him: his color and the fact that he was "a resident alien".

Because of the stability that existed within their family, Vernel was able to attend school and although she had to do it and take care of the children (though sometimes she got help from her mother), she was able to obtain a Bachelor of Arts degree from Hunter College. She then got a new job with an insurance company in midtown. They were soon able to buy their own house and moved away from the tiny apartment that they had been renting all those years.

The following years were trying ones for Thomas. Conditions on the new job were not what he expected and after two years, he left and joined another company. That year, Vernel became very ill and it took a very long time before her condition improved. The situation had a telling effect on Thomas and the children and also on the rest of her family. His wife was in and out of doctors' offices and the hospital for three consecutive years. She finally had to quit her job and Thomas found himself having to work two jobs to make ends meet. After his regular day job, he worked for five hours at the local supermarket as the Night Manager.

It was tough. Every possible thing came to his mind, especially the thought of returning home. But it was the concern for his wife's health and the general development of the kids that kept him going. When Vernel was well again, she tried to return to her job but it was tough to face the rigors of the job and take care of her kids. Together, she and Thomas decided that it was in their best interest, however tough it would be, for her to stay home. Thomas had worked alone for three years supporting the family, and he believed that hopefully he could continue doing it. He prayed that God would give him the strength and the health to keep on doing it.

It was a hot summer afternoon when an urgent call came to him on his job. It was about his wife and he had to report to Our Lady of Mercy Hospital immediately. Thomas dropped everything, rushed out and headed for the train station. It seemed like it took forever to get to 233rd Street and he wished that the train could move faster than it was moving. He was trembling and scared. He had no idea what had happened. He wished that it were nothing too serious. But when he entered the lobby of the hospital, he found Vernel's family all huddled together and he realized that it was indeed serious. They were crying and holding on to her mother. As he walked in, they rushed to him. Vernel had been involved in a car accident and she was now in the operating room. Her car had been struck from behind and it slammed into a column that supported the elevated train tracks on White Plains Road. Thomas slumped over and screamed.

Despite the doctors' valiant efforts, Vernel passed away later that day from chest and head injuries. This was a serious setback to Thomas. He had hoped for so much for himself and his family and it was all taken away from him. They did not have the chance to say goodbye to each other. His life had been stolen from him.

Vernel's death, coming as early as it did, shattered Thomas and the rest of the family. There was now a huge void in their lives. They dearly missed Vernel. Thomas continued his job at the insurance company but gave up the second job. He struggled on, doing the best he could for the kids, seeing them through high school and then to college. He knew his wife would be proud of the kids and it hurt him more that she was not around to share in their successes.

When he reached the age of retirement, Thomas decided that he had had enough. He could not deal with the situation any more. The kids had achieved some of their goals. He had paid off his mortgage from money he had received from an insurance company following Vernel's death and he saw no need to remain in America. He felt that the more he remained in America, the more the pain of losing his wife would linger. He had to get away. He decided to return to Dominica.

So, on a wet and rainy fall afternoon, Thomas bade farewell to his children and his in-laws. Filled with emotion, he kissed and hugged each one before disappearing behind the swing doors at the airport's departure lounge to begin his return trip to Dominica.

———————

"It was ten years ago, Trevie, when Grandpa came back," the old man said as he passed his hands over the boy's head.

"So why you doh goin' back Gran'pa?" Trevor asked him.

"Maybe one day, son, Grandpa will go back. But Grandpa likes it here. One day we will go to America to see your cousins. Next time Mammy bring you by Grandpa I will show you your little cousins' pictures."

"So why my mammy wasn' in Amewica Gran'pa?" the little boy asked as he pulled at the old man's beard.

"Well, son it's a long story. Your mama was born before Grandpa went to America." Thomas paused as he remembered the circumstances surrounding his grandson's mom. He felt a bit of guilt, but didn't want to revisit it, yet he was forced to do so by the innocent questions of this little boy. "She was a little girl like Chewo when Grandpa went to America. (Chewo was the pet name for Trevor's sister, Cheryl.) That's why, son ...." He paused again. "So, you see," he continued, "Grandpa spent a lot of time in America and now is time for Grandpa to stay with you. One day, who knows, maybe you will go to America. When Grandpa was a young boy he never thought he would go to America. So you see, maybe you will go there, too. What do you think?" he asked the little boy.

"Mmmm, maybe Gran'pa," the boy hesitated. "I an' Chewo an' my mammy too?" he asked. He continued, "I will see de chuchu train Gran'pa?"

"Yes," his grandfather answered. "You will see many chuchu trains."

"An' I will travel on de ewoplane Gran'pa?" he asked.

"A-e-r-o-p-l-a-n-e!" the old man said slowly, urging the little boy to repeat after him.

"Elloplane. Elloplane. Plane. Plane. When I go I will sen' for you an' Mammy an' Chewo an' evvveryyybody," he screamed.

"What are you doing to Grandpa?" Trevor's mother asked as she walked into the room, a cup of lemonade in her right hand and a piece of bread covered with peanut butter in the other. She had been doing her household chores and it was now time for her to watch the *Guiding Light*, a soap opera from America. This was her time of relaxation. She, like many of the women who were home at this time of day, had become entrapped with this program and the many like it that were being beamed to the island through the local TV station.

"Nothing, Mammy. I was aksing Gran'pa about Amewica," he replied.

"So what did Grandpa tell you?" she asked, as she took her seat on the sofa chair across from the TV set, placing the cup of lemonade and the bread on the small end table next to the sofa.

"Plenty, plenty. Not true Gran'pa? Not true you tell me plenty about Amewica," the boy said. The old man nodded his head in the affirmative.

"Just in time for my program," his mother said. "Boy, I almos' miss de beginnin'!" She raised the volume on the set using the remote control.

"When you goin' to Amewica, Mammy?" Trevor interrupted, not too concerned about his mother's interest in the program on the TV.

"I don't know and now is not time for that," she answered. She wasn't going to explain the reasons to him just yet. She was not too happy with her father for what had happened and for his not giving her the chance to be in America. However, they had worked it out and all had been forgiven. Her mother had never married although she had had other children. But since Thomas had returned he and her mother had rekindled their relationship. She glimpsed over to see if he was watching, but he had dozed off. "And is not Amewica. It is America! Say it again," she said to Trevor. "A-M-E-R-I-C-A!" she said slowly, beckoning him to repeat after her.

"A-m-e-r-i-c-a," he said gleefully. "A-m-e-r-i-c-a!" he said again, a broad smile on his face. "America hav' thing so on dey TV Gran'pa? Eh Gran'pa. It hav' fing so?" he asked again turning towards his grandfather. There was no answer. Grandpa's head had dropped across his shoulders. His eyes were closed. He had fallen asleep. "Wake up, Gran'pa, wake up!" Trevor said, tugging at his grandpa's hand. "Mammy, why Gran'pa sleeping?" he asked his mother.

His mother said nothing. She was consumed with her own American world. Everything else now took second place.

Trouble in the Channel

The island of Guadeloupe lies northwest of Dominica. Over the years, the two islands have shared a similar history. Dominica was on and off controlled by the French until it was finally claimed by the British following one of the many wars the European countries fought to gain control of the islands of the Caribbean. Yet, throughout the colonial years, the French took better care of their subjects than the British did. Years after having exploited the countries of everything: their wealth, produce and their women too, the British turned their backs on the islands, Dominica included, and left them to fend for themselves.

And so, while Dominicans struggled to survive, the people of Guadeloupe (a French *departement*), enjoyed a better life. Life in that country was more appealing to many Dominicans than life in their own country. For years, Dominicans have been able to journey to Guadeloupe on vacation; to seek employment, and to ply in trade, selling whatever they could lay their hands on. It was common business and a thriving one, too, and Dominicans generally saw this practice as a way of securing a better life for themselves.

Joel was one of those people who saw the need to enter into the huckstering business with Guadeloupe. It was a lucrative business and every two weeks he plied the waters of the Guadeloupe Channel to Basse-Terre where he sold his provisions under the watchful eyes of the *gendarme*. He was a member of the Hucksters Association and traveled on a steel-hulled vessel, the *Ocean Queen*, to Guadeloupe. However, it dawned on him that he could do his own thing and develop his own business. He wanted a boat of his own and enough provisions to travel to Guadeloupe. He also needed someone who would be bold enough to traverse the Atlantic Ocean—the Guadeloupe Channel—between Dominica and Guadeloupe.

Joel discussed the idea with his wife, Cassandra. He discussed it with his brother, Lavander. He discussed it with a young man nicknamed Wally whom he wanted to be his assistant. Everyone except Lavander thought it was a great idea.

Joel, Wally and Lavander were all fishermen. Cassandra's father was one, too, until he presumably drowned at sea about five years ago. No one knew what had happened. The day he disappeared, he had left for sea like he had done for so many years, in the early hours of the morning. He never returned. No sightings were ever made nor was his boat ever found.

Cassandra's father had loved fishing. He would set out in the early hours of the morning and return late in the afternoons, all by himself. He had said he loved being out there; just him, the fish, the sky, and his God. He always returned in the afternoon with a good catch of fish that he had caught in the chicken wire pots he had placed along the coastline. He had no problems selling his catch since he had an established clientele unlike some other fishermen who had to walk around the village to get their fish sold.

No one knew what had happened the day he disappeared, although every one speculated as to what may have happened. Some believed maybe he had fallen overboard and drowned; others maybe he was killed by rival fishermen. Some people believed maybe *obeah* had a part to play in his disappearance. It was all conjecture; no one was sure what had happened to him. But still, Cassandra did not mind the plan Joel had made. As she said, "Whatever is destined to happen, will happen. It's all God's work."

Lavander believed that Joel was risking his life for a few dollars by trying to go ahead with his plans. He agreed that his brother was a good fisherman, but he was not sure that he felt good about his brother going to challenge the waves of the Guadeloupe Channel. However, he believed that if this was his brother's great scheme, and if his wife was willing to allow him to go ahead with his plan, he would not get in the way. Still, he cautioned Joel and asked him to reconsider. "I doh want to hav' to hear you drown in de canal," Lavander said to Joel.

"Doh worry about dat, man. It hav' so much people doin' dat. All Portsmouth an' place like Capuchin dey goin' to Guadeloupe all de time an' nothin' happenin'," Joel reassured his brother.

"But you know how long dose people doin' dat? An' is no little boat dey usin'. Dey hav' to hav' boat dat strong an' fas' an' deep an' can clime over dose big lam," Lavander said to him as the two sat on the pile of stones under the breadfruit tree in Joel's yard. They had a bottle of Belfast rum with them and as Joel poured the last bit into his glass, he said to Lavander, "Well I goin' to de fisheries tomorrow an' see if I get de bigga engine dey hav'. An' den I will know what I doin'. Infac', I an' Wally goin' to start to build de boat on Monday."

"But when you finish with de boat, where you goin' to get food to bring to Guadeloupe? You doh hav' enough food to full de boat, how you goin' to do dat?" Lavander asked.

Joel looked at him and smiled. "I do my wok a'ready. I contact some people a'ready. Infac', some people even aks me if is true I buyin' food to take to Guadeloupe because dey hear I goin' to do dat," he said.

"But one fing too ... with all de trouble dey havin' with people dealin' drug, take care dey doh say is dat you goin' to do," Lavander cautioned. "Dey say de *gendarme* doh jokin' with Dominicans because dey spoilin' dey country."

"But when I was dere de las time on de *Ocean Queen*, we didn' hav' no trouble. Every time we go is strickly business an' dey does leave us alone," Joel answered, a little swagger in his voice. "An' when we buyin' fing to bring back, is no problem. I doh hav' no problem with *gendarme!*" he exclaimed.

And so, with his mind made up, Joel embarked on his mission to build a boat that would be fitted with an outboard motor. He had visited the Fisheries Department in Roseau and priced the most powerful machine that he could get for the size of the boat he was planning to build. Then, he recruited help from an unemployed carpenter, a fellow named Toutwell, to help him build the boat that he had already named even before a nail was pinned. He called it the *Ocean Princess*. So, for weeks on end, he and Wally and Toutwell sawed and cut and nailed and unnailed and resawed. They had built a small shed that they covered with a large blue tarp to serve as a roof. The shed was alongside the boathouse where Joel had his fishing boat. The boat was being built on sections of a sawed coconut tree trunk just a few feet from the edge of the shore. The sawed sections would serve as rollers and would make it easy to push the *Ocean Princess* to the water when it was completed.

The news of Joel's plans did not remain a secret anymore. People of the village had gotten wind of it and they were inquisitive as to how things were moving on. People stopped and looked as they passed by and some even offered suggestions, advice and warnings. Everyone had time to speculate and conjecture. But Joel kept his mind on his mission.

Philip "Joel" Williams grew up literally in the sea. His father and his five brothers were raised on the sea, so to speak. They were like human fish. Even when he went to school, Joel spent more days on the sea than in the classroom, especially when the fishermen were chasing schools of jacks and bonitos. There was always action around that time and Joel would not miss that. School to him was secondary. It did not bother him one bit that he had left school in Grade Five. There was a life out there for him as a fisherman. He enjoyed the challenges the sea presented to him. The sea was rich and he wanted to cultivate it. It was a hard life, but he enjoyed it.

Joel and Cassandra had been married ten years and they had two children between them. Joel had five more with three other women. Two of these children were in Salisbury, a village where he also spent time fishing. Joel did not want any of his children to end up working the sea like he did. He wanted them to get an education and get a good job as a teacher, a nurse or a police officer. It was too difficult to be a fisherman. Cassandra was Joel's right hand. She was the one who sold most of the fish that he caught. She was the one who took fish to the Roseau market and sold it there. She knew the *runnings*, so Joel left it all to her.

Joel's assistant was Wally. Wally, too, grew up on the sea, but although he was younger than Joel, he was much bigger in build and size. He had thick muscles all over his body, developed largely from the constant rigors of the sea: pulling in boats, seines, and rowing boats when there was no outboard attached. He was very strong and swam very well. He, too, was a good diver and could stay minutes under the water before coming to the surface. His compatriots called him *Papa Glo*. The sea was all he knew, just like Joel, and on the days when he was not out on the water, he could be found dozing in one of the dugouts in the boathouse. He lived alone in a small one-room shack on the back road of the village, but he hardly spent anytime there, except at night.

Wally was excited about being part of the mission that Joel had decided to embark upon. He knew what it was. Together with a cousin who lived in Lagoon, Portsmouth, he had made two previous trips to Guadeloupe. They had used double outboard motors then and four of them had traveled across the channel. Nothing had happened to them on those trips. They discontinued their trips because Hurricane David had damaged his cousin's boat. His cousin felt very distraught and decided not to build another boat. He had spent too much time and money on the boat to see it destroyed to smithereens by the strong waves that pummeled the shores of Portsmouth that day.

Wally believed that he and Joel should be able to make it to Guadeloupe and back every time without any problems. But their boat-building mission did not go according to plan and along the way there were a few obstacles that delayed their progress. Toutwell was hired as part of a construction team to build a dwelling house in Mero and it took a while for Joel to get a replacement, since the wages were a bit on the low side. Then, there was the month when the bonitos showed up. There was money to be made and Joel wanted a share of it.

―――――

The village of St. Joseph was quite hectic as the fishermen—those at the boathouse in Coubarie and a group from Mero—were chasing a school of fish along the St. Joseph coastline. They played cat and mouse (*or rather fisherman and fish*), with each other since the teams of fishermen had to wait until the fish came close enough where they could be netted. Some days, they spent hours with their boats and seines all ready to pounce, but the fish stayed away. You could see the schools feeding and jumping out in the water, frustrating the fishermen who sat in the boathouses, their eyes peeled on the water. Finally though, the fish did come in and even if the catch was not as great as expected, it was a good one.

And then there was the election. Joel was a strong supporter of the ruling Labor Party and as the days neared when elections were to be held to choose a new government, Joel forgot everything about boat building. He wanted to be out there for his man, Symbert, and he was exerting all energies that he had campaigning for his man. Symbert lost, and although Joel was very disappointed, he settled down and renewed his efforts at boatbuilding and his trips to Guadeloupe.

Cassandra was a bit worried at the way things had turned out because since Joel had started his project, he had stopped doing business in Guadeloupe. He felt that if he was not going on the trip himself, he could not trust anyone with his money in that kind of business. He always wondered what would happen if that person did not return. Cassandra had volunteered to go to Guadeloupe but Joel was not going to give in to her wishes. He wanted her to be there for their two children. Cassandra had suggested letting them stay with her mother, but Joel was against that idea. So, Cassandra stepped aside grudgingly and allowed Joel to do what he felt was right. He believed that he had decided to make a sacrifice for the better and this was all he was concerned with at the moment. If things turned out well, he would easily make back that money. If it did not, then only he would take the blame. Not Cassandra, nor Lavender, nor Wally, either.

Six months after the project started, the *Ocean Princess* was completed. It was a twenty-foot long boat with enough space for two outboard engines to be mounted at the back. There was a small cabin built with just enough room for two. It was painted red and white with yellow stripes along the edges. At the bow, stenciled rather crudely in black, were the words, *Ocean Princess*. The *Ocean Princess* was built deep enough to hold enough cargo so that when loaded it would not submerge too deep into the water. That could be a problem in the choppy waters of the channel.

Joel was proud of what he had done and as he and some friends rolled the *Ocean Princess* toward the water, he felt happy that he had achieved the first part of his goal. He would give it a few test runs in the coming days with the outboard motor he had purchased and he and Wally would get a feel for their new *baby*. He beamed with pride as the boat bobbed in the water, tied to its anchor. It would remain there for all to see and admire.

A month after the launching, Joel was ready to embark on his mission. He and Wally left the village in the dark of the early morning after having loaded the *Ocean Princess* the night before. They had covered the cargo: bags of oranges, dasheen, plantains, pumpkin and grapefruits, with a large tarpaulin safeguarding the cargo from the elements. They waded out naked to the boat under the protection of the darkness. They climbed in and put on dry clothes they had wrapped in the plastic bags they had held above the water as they'd swam to the boat.

They checked to make sure that everything was okay. Joel double-checked that the entry papers given to him at the French Consulate were with him. Without them he would be unable to enter Guadeloupe. There were two large fishermen raincoats in the bow and a few necessary items for the trip: bread, bottled sodas and a large plastic container of water. It would be a few hours before they would set foot in Guadeloupe, and they wanted to ensure they had everything with them, including cigarettes. They pulled on the throttle and after three attempts, the engine sputtered to life. Slowly, Joel opened the throttle and the loaded boat sliced through the still water on its maiden trip to Guadeloupe.

For a month, Joel and Wally plied the water between the two countries. The two had now become well known at the market place in Basse-Terre and Joel renewed the acquaintances he had made when he had first started in the business. He was winning over his old clients and things were looking up. He felt independent. He was able to decide when to leave and how long to stay and when to return without anyone dictating to him and he was a man who did not like being dictated to. Just ask Cassandra. She was well aware of that and usually she and Joel had little feuds between them when she tried to tell him what she felt he should do. In the end, she had to give in even if she felt she was right.

———————

Joel and Wally were preparing for another trip. The business was booming and Joel was even contemplating making more frequent trips to Guadeloupe. He even turned away some farmers who were offering to sell him food, because his boat could only take so much. He was also beginning to contemplate getting a bigger boat, possibly buying one in Guadeloupe or getting one of the boat-builders in Glanvillia, a village on the outskirts of Portsmouth, to build him one. He saw the dollars and francs floating before his eyes and wanted to catch hold of them before they all got blown away. He and Wally did their pre-trip ritual, checking the motor, making sure they had enough fuel and oil, and checking their food rations. They loaded the boat and when they were satisfied that everything was okay, they pushed it out, anchored it a few yards off shore and swam back to land. Each man went his separate way to return in the wee hours of the morning to set out for Guadeloupe.

When Joel got home, his wife did not seem too happy. She would not say anything to Joel. She knew that whatever she said would not be listened to. However, she finally decided to tell him what was on her mind and what had been troubling her all day. "You know, I had a dream las' nite an' all day long I wonderin' what it mean. I did even want to go by Ma Zan to ask her, but I change my mind. An' all day long a big fly jus' keep comin' in de house," she said as she placed his dinner on the table in the room that served as both the dining room and living room.

"So what you sayin', den?" he asked her, as he put a piece of yam into his mouth.

"Well, I know you make up your mind an' no matter what, you goin' Guadeloupe tomorrow. You cannot wait another day. Maybe is a sign why I see de fly," Cassandra answered.

"Oh, dat is all supersision. Ole people fing," Joel mumbled, his mouth full with food. "You know I doh believe in dat," he continued.

"My mother did say de same fing when my father die. She did aks him to go to garden with her an' he tell her he hav' to go on sea. See what happen to him!" Cassandra responded.

"But dat was not supersision. De man didn' wan' to go garden so he doh go. Is jus' a coincident dat he die de same day. An' who know what happen to him? Only God know. An' furthermore, I cannot doh go Guadeloupe. Me an' Wally a'ready pack de boat with all de food for us to leave in de mornin'. If I doh go I will lose all de money I pay a'ready. An' what about dose people dat waitin' for me? I hav' to go. Bondyé bon!" he exclaimed, as he put another piece of food into his mouth.

Once again, Cassandra gave in. She had her fears about his trip but she could not change his mind.

She went to bed but had a very tough time falling asleep. Joel was long gone and he was snoring away. He had nothing to worry about and nothing that she had told him seemed to have fazed him. At four o'clock in the morning, he was up. Soon he was walking out the door, after saying goodbye to his wife and his kids who were now awakened by his moving about the house.

He was alone as he walked through the dark alleyway to the sparsely lit Back Street. He walked briskly and soon was at the bay front. There was light in the boathouse and that meant that Wally had beaten him to it. The two men exchanged greetings and after ensuring that everything was okay, swam naked to the anchored boat and then changed into their dry clothes without drying themselves. The engine kicked into life as Joel pulled on the starter cord. Once again, they were on their way.

St. Joseph and the neighboring villages slowly appeared smaller as the boat sliced towards the ocean. The men said nothing for a while as they both settled in and got ready for the task at hand. Every now and then a startled fish leapt for safety as the outboard closed in on it. The silhouetted outline of the coastline became more prominent as dawn drew closer. Joel guided the boat, keeping his eyes peeled ahead for any floating obstacles. He felt the urge to tell Wally what Cassandra had said to him, but he decided against it. He did not want to have a second guesser working with him. That could spell trouble. It was better that Wally did not know. Instead, they engaged in a discussion about the recently held national elections. Both men supported the same party and were rather unhappy that their man had lost.

Joel spoke. "De fing I doh understand is how people not seein' what goin' on. Fings gettin' harder an' harder day afta day an' is because de goverment is a big man goverment. Dey not wokkin' for people like me an' you. Is for all dose big shots. Wait an' see where de country goin' nex."

"You right, eh. Dat is why people like me not goin' to get job because dey give de job to dere people. So de money stayin' in one place," answered Wally.

"You fink I should be goin' to Guadeloupe an' sell food? De goverment should be buyin' food an' sell for us. Dey should come an' see how Guadeloupe more develop dan Dominica. You think we should hav' to go to Guadeloupe for wok?"

Wally shook his head in agreement. "You know, you talkin' truth man. Is a shame, but is so it is. Who hav' more getting' more an' who doh hav' will never hav'. Is a disgrace!" he said.

The sun was climbing over the distant mountains and the bright rays shone on the water as dawn slowly crept over the island mass. They could see the villages, all nestled in their little coves along the coast. They saw vehicles making their way along the coast and through the winding hills. Life was returning to its usual morning ways. The outboard engine purred nicely and Joel was happy. If all went well they would be in Guadeloupe within the next few hours. He changed his sitting position to help his circulation. Wally yawned, a bit sleepy. They cleared the Cabrits and the villages of Clifton and Capuchin.

They soon found themselves in choppy waters. They were on the fringes of the Channel and the water was quite different from what they had been traveling in earlier. The Caribbean Sea was calm and placid. This was not. The water splashed about as the loaded boat cut a path through. The men each donned a yellow fisherman's coat to avoid getting wet. Joel noticed that the water was much choppier than he had been accustomed to. The weather looked okay. There were clear blue skies overhead and there was no reason, in his mind, why the waves were so choppy so soon into the Channel.

The boat bobbed up and down. Joel held on to the rudder and kept guiding the craft along. He asked Wally to check that everything was okay while he himself kept his eyes wide open. Overhead they heard the drone of a plane apparently heading to one of the airports in Dominica. Wally waved as the plane flew by, knowing quite well that no one would notice him. He smiled.

As they traveled farther, the weather seemed to change. Dark clouds quickly gathered overhead and every now and then the sun would be hidden from view. They could make out the fuzzy mass in the distance that was Guadeloupe, but they were still a few hours away. "Lookin' like we will hav' rain," said Joel as he looked up at the clouds. "Maybe we wouldn' be lucky like the last two time," he added.

"Doh worry man, de rain mus' fall. We will get to Guadeloupe before nothin' happen," answered a confident Wally.

Just then, it began raining; a slow drizzle at first, but then a steady shower. Joel hoped that this was not the start of what he did not want to happen. He began to wonder whether what Cassandra had said might have had some truth to it. He smiled and shook his head.

"What's up?" Wally asked. "What's de joke? Why you laughin' an' shakin' your head?" He waited for an answer from Joel.

"Nothin', really, just somethin' I remember. Somethin' Cassandra tell me las' night," Joel answered, still wondering if he should share Cassandra's warning. But again he decided against it.

But the waves were definitely getting choppier and bigger now than Joel had been accustomed to seeing in this part of the Channel. The bow of the boat dipped and rose as it encountered the waves. It sat well and its crew felt confident that they were safe. They were both experienced men of the sea, good swimmers who lived for the sea. They did not feel one bit worried. "De wave an' dem gettin' bigger dan de las' time, not true?" Joel asked, at the same time looking for confirmation of his suspicions.

"Yes, is dat I notice, but maybe is jus de time of de month. Maybe is de moon," Wally suggested, wondering whether the new moon phase may have been responsible for the rise in the tides.

"I doh think so," replied Joel. "Anyhow, just watch an' see if water collectin' an' bail it out. I doh want us to collect too much water," he directed.

They knew they had to push on. They could not make any detours. The route to Basse-Terre had to be a straight and direct one. Thus, they had to deal with the elements. Joel knew that these were some of the risks he had to face when he decided to embark on this mission.

When he traveled on the *Ocean Queen* he did not have to worry about that. The steel craft wielded its way through the water.

Moreover, they had always traveled at night, so Joel never really had the opportunity to see what was out there. But on the *Princess*, it was a different ball game. This was a wooden craft. It was smaller and therefore an easy prey for the powers of the Channel. He fervently prayed for good luck.

"Watch dat!" cried Wally, as he saw a giant wave rolling toward them. They braced themselves as the little boat rode up and then down with the wave as it passed them. "Wew, man," he moaned. "I doh like dat, non."

Another wave followed immediately behind and the outboard made a sputtering sound as the wave shifted the craft a little to the left. '*Joel! I doh think you should go to Guadeloupe.*' Cassandra's words came back again. *Maybe what she say is true*, thought Joel. The rain showers had stopped as quickly as they had come, but the dark clouds were still lingering above and seemed to be moving a little more towards the direction of Guadeloupe. Joel and Wally wondered whether there was not bad weather brewing from Guadeloupe. Was this the reason why the landmass in the distance looked as fuzzy as it did this morning?

No one listens to the weather reports in Dominica unless a hurricane is approaching. Life went on with no real worry about the weather. If rain came, that was no problem. If a storm came that was no problem either. If it was sunny for days on end, that was okay too, until farmers would begin to complain and implore the Higher Power to send some rain to save their crops. So, whether or not there was an impending storm or bad weather in the area, Joel did not know.

The little boat began to be tossed up and down and their progress was being slowed. This was not what Joel had hoped for at all. He hoped that he had enough gas to keep the outboard going until they got to port in Guadeloupe. He had a reserve tank and hoped that they would not be forced to use all their fuel. It would be disaster to get stalled in the middle of the watery wilderness. He had to make a decision. He was going to wait a while still and then see what happened. If things got worse, he would turn back.

But he hardly had any time to make a decision. A giant wave rolled towards the boat. They both saw it heading towards them. Joel turned the rudder in an effort to ride it, but before he could the wave was upon and over them. It broke right over the boat. The force of the wave slammed both men. Water filled the boat. Wally frantically began bailing water the best he could.

"No frere ... I doh think is a good fing. It gettin' worse. What you say? We turn back an' try later this week, or we continue?" asked Joel.

"I fink we can make it but I doh want to take no chance," he added before Wally could answer. "Las' nite Cassandra tell me not to go because she had a sign. Maybe dat is what she was seein'," said Joel, finally unable to hold on to his little secret any longer.

"You believe in dat, man? Dat doesn' work. Dat is de work of de devil man. What hav' to happen will happen," replied Wally, salt water dripping from his head.

"I doh know, but I doh want to take chance in dat weather. It lookin' like de more we go close to Guadeloupe de more bad de weather gettin'," Joel countered.

"Okay, man, we doh hav' to go all de way back to Senjo. We can pull up in de harbor in Portsmouth an' try again if it calm down tomorrow. What you think?" Wally asked.

"Nah!" screamed Joel, as the wind whipped about and the spray of the salt water blasted his face. "I better go all de way back. I doh have nobody in Grande Anse an' you doh know how long we will stay. I hope de food doh get wet. Les go back, man!" Wally shook his head in resigned acceptance. He felt disappointed. In his opinion they could have survived the waves.

"What you say, man ... it doh matter. If you want to go back, les' go back," he said rather dejectedly.

But there was a reason why Wally wanted to push on. He had a plan up his sleeves and he had hoped that this was the trip to make it work. He didn't want to keep risking his life at sea all the while with Joel while Joel reaped all the benefits. He had joined with Joel because he saw an easy way to enter Guadeloupe. The first two trips went as normal trips. He did all that was expected of him. In the meantime, he had made contact with one of his old friends who was living in Guadeloupe and they had discussed the idea of Wally staying the next time he returned. Everything was set.

Joel had no idea what Wally was up to. He had not the faintest idea that he would be the only one returning to Dominica when this trip was completed because his companion was going to make a run for it. So Wally really prayed that Joel would give it a shot, but that was not going to be. Joel held on to the steering arm of the outboard and Wally watched as he saw his plan go by the wayside. He didn't say another word. As the motor droned, the rough weather behind them, the men set their eyes on Dominica and, hopefully, calmer waters.

Wally continued bailing water from the bottom of the boat. He cursed his luck and wished he had remained the last time they had gone to Guadeloupe. But he had to play the game right. It was just about half an hour after they had decided to turn back, that disaster struck. Joel silently urged the outboard engine on, driven now by fear of his wife's seemingly prophetic words. What if something horrible happened? She would blame him because she had warned him. Somewhere at the back of his mind, he was tempted to believe in her superstition, but the other half of his mind doubted that such things really happened. Still, he did not think he should test the truth or validity of this superstition by hanging around in unfriendly waters.

They did not know what hit them. The wave slammed into the boat, covering them, and within minutes they were in the water. The outboard sputtered and died. Bags filled with produce floated around them. They bobbed as the choppy water thrashed them about. The men watched in disbelief as the boat was hit by another wave and quickly sank to the depths of the ocean, just a few feet away. Joel cursed his luck as he saw months of sacrifice and hard work disappearing before him. He cursed again as he saw the produce that was meant to bring him some French francs float slowly away.

The water was very cold. It began raining again. "Hold on to a bag," Joel cried out to Wally, "Hold on an' float on it," he cried again, as he himself struggled towards a bag of grapefruits that floated near him. He knew that they were up against some tough times. "How long would we last out here?" he asked himself silently. Capuchin was a about a mile away. "*Could we get there before our bodies gave up?*" he thought for a moment. Would they become bait for sharks or other big fish in the Channel? That was a scary thought. "Help! Help! Bondyé, Heeeelppp!" he screamed as loud as he could, hoping that somehow his cries would be heard by anyone. "Help! Save us!" he screamed again, but no one on land was going to hear them from this distance.

They struggled to remove the rain gear that was still over them. It was of a bright yellow, good for being spotted, but it was cumbersome in the predicament they were in. They stripped off their clothes and kept only their underpants on. Each hung on to a bag of produce for dear life. There was nothing else that they could attach themselves to. If any of the bags floated away now, that could be disastrous.

"Maybe what Cassandra say was true," cried Wally. "Maybe she was right man! Maybe de big fly was a messenger of bad luck," he said, as a wave splashed into his face.

Joel said nothing.

The men could see the village of Capuchin, but how long would it take to get there? They were cold and they shivered. The falling rain did not help make things any better. Joel made his SOS pleas one more time, in a vain effort to get someone's attention.

Joel swore as the reality of losing the outboard engine hit him again. He was going to have to pay for something that he no longer had and furthermore, he had no insurance. As they floated, they encouraged each other to hang on. Now more than ever, they needed each other. How would one feel if the other drowned? As they drifted, they were pushed closer to the calmer waters. There was hope, at least some hope, that they would make it. But were they strong enough to endure the rigors of the Channel in this condition? They hung on for dear life, praying God would spare their lives.

When they got to less rough waters, Joel suggested that it was time they made an effort to swim to land. The land ahead was tempting. With land so near, it would be a shame if they failed to make it to shore. Once again, Joel cried out, "Help, help, help us! Somebody help us!"

Wally joined in. "Help! Bondyé, Help!"

Would someone hear them? Would anyone hear them? With nothing to lose, they abandoned their floating bags and began swimming to the shore. Joel watched as the final pieces of his doomed cargo floated away. They would land somewhere, on some shore, or maybe picked up by a vessel. For four hours the men had clung to the bags. They were hungry and tired. Their mouths tasted of nothing but salt. Joel prayed. Now, more than ever, they had this resolve to survive. Joel wanted to get back to land, not to tell Cassandra that she was right, but for a second chance to redeem himself. Maybe Cassandra's dream was just coincidental; just one of those things. He was still caught between wanting to believe in her dream and disbelieving that such things ever happened. They swam, rested, floated, and as the land drew closer, their hopes improved. The will to live kept them going until Wally finally spoke. "I gettin' tired man."

"Jus' take it easy, not much to go again," coaxed Joel.

Did he really believe himself?

They could see the rooftops of houses between the trees in the distance. They also saw vehicles winding along the narrow roads between Clifton and Capuchin. "What if somebody did have a spy glass?" Joel voiced loudly. Wally did not answer. Both men were exhausted, but they did not want to give themselves up as sacrifices to the sea. They had heard many stories of people drowning at sea, even fishermen, because of fear and exhaustion, but never because they could not swim. They did not want to be one of these.

As they drew closer, they summoned all the energy they could. They cried for help once more, hoping that someone would hear them. They were close. Stroke by stroke, kick after kick, they inched closer to shore and the chance of safety. They cheered on each other, coaxed each other. Life was too beautiful to let it be taken away. They wished that they could have rested, but that was not practical. They had to get to the shore or be rescued before that could happen. After that they could rest as much as they wanted.

"Wally, we goin' to make it man, we goin' to make it," said Joel as he slapped the water with his right hand. "We goin' to make it!" he screamed.

"Doh speak too early, man. Doh speak too early. Let me put my two foot on de ground before we can speak like dat. You doh know what can happen."

"What can happen again? Enough doh happen to us a'ready? Is us dat more bad? Is us God hate more dat somethin' will happen again? Look at dat, man. We almos' dere!"

And the shoreline drew closer still. They willed themselves on.

They were about a hundred feet from the shore when Wally, exhausted, and seemingly unable to hold on any longer, stopped swimming and sank below the water. He shot back up and screamed with joy and renewed energy. His feet had hit sand and gravel. He turned and hugged Joel. They screamed aloud. The two men waded to the shore and as they got there they both collapsed on the stony beach. They lay there without saying one word. Joel cried.

As they lay motionless on the beach, they heard the drone of an outboard engine. Joel wondered for a while whether he was having a nightmare. It sounded just like his outboard. Was this real or just his mind? They looked in the direction of the drone. Wally was the first to react. "Help! Help!' he screamed at the top of his lungs, the little bit that he still had left after this ordeal. Joel waved frantically, but they watched in disbelief as the two men in the boat paid no attention to them and calmly kept going.

"Maybe dey didn' hear," volunteered Joel. "Maybe de noise of de engine."

"Yeah, but dey watch us an' dey do like dey doh see us," replied Wally.

"Well, it happen a'ready. We on land. Maybe we can go in de village to de police station an' see if dey will help us. I know where it is. I did go in de village with Lavander de other day," replied Joel.

The two men made their way along the beach, searching for a way to the main road. They could hear voices and the sounds of vehicles coming from somewhere, but they could not see anyone. They did not want to call out anymore. They were safe. All they needed now was some clothes and something to eat, then to find their way home to St. Joseph. Joel wondered what Cassandra must be thinking now. Maybe she was certain that he was in Guadeloupe now, although he knew that she had her dreams. Would she be surprised when he got home?

"I can hear Cassandra now," he said to Wally. "'*I did warn you*' an' all dat crap. I not never goin' to hear de end of de story. Maybe she will begin to *gardé* for people now. But is my fault Wally, is my fault," he sobbed.

Wally did not answer. He stopped, bent over and vomited nothing but water. "I okay, I okay!" he said as Joel tried to support him. "Is jus' de water dat in my belly."

After walking along the beach for a while, they finally found a narrow track that seemed to be leading up toward the road. They followed it. Joel was in front and Wally, like the obedient companion, followed behind. They were naked save for their underpants. It didn't bother them. They were going to walk right into the Police Station just like that. Who would care about being naked after having survived the dreaded Channel?

It was not a long trek up to the road, and they were soon heading towards the village of Capuchin. They could hardly move. Every bone and muscle in their bodies ached. As they neared the village, a group of about twenty people approached them. The men stopped, wondering what was going on. "Is all you dat was shoutin' for help dere?" a man who seemed to be the leader of the group asked.

"Yes, is us," Joel answered. "We was swimmin' to land. We almos' drown in de canal."

"A chile say she hear people shoutin' for help but we didn' believe her, but we say we goin' to see who dat was screamin' for help anyway, after she say is true."

"You men are lucky. What happened?" a woman asked, her hands on her waist.

"We was goin' to Guadeloupe and our boat *shalviway*. We lose everythin' we did hav' in de boat," answered Joel. "We was jus' goin' to de Police Station for help," he added.

"Where all you from?" the man who was the leader asked.

"Senjo," answered Wally.

As they spoke, they heard the vibration of an approaching vehicle on its way to Capuchin. They went to the side of the road as a blue truck approached. The leader of the group and a few others raised their hands and hailed the driver. He stopped. He looked surprised, wondering no doubt what was going on.

"Dose two man dere almos' *néyé* in de canal. Give dem a ride to de police station, please," the leader begged. Joel and Wally and five of the men from the crowd climbed into the back of the truck. The driver sped off as the rest of the people shouted and waved. The men looked very concerned as the two tired swimmers slumped to the floor of the truck, finally getting a chance to rest their weary bodies.

"You tired?" one of them asked Wally.

"You aksin' me again! I more dan tired. I dead!" Wally answered.

The men all laughed. Joel forced a smile, for he, too, was hurting.

About five minutes later, the truck pulled off the main road unto a dirt track that led to the stationhouse. The driver honked his horn and kept his hand on it until two police officers came to the door, looking surprised by the noise on the station grounds.

"What's going on here?" the older-looking one asked.

"Officer Jeremiah, we have two man here dat almos' drown in de canal. Dey was goin' to Guadeloupe and de boat *shalviway*. Dey from Senjo," the leader of the group shouted, as he stood in the back of the open vehicle.

"Well, bring them in," Corporal Jeremiah, the shorter of the two officers said. "Let's see what we can do for them."

The men jumped off, one after the other, and helped Joel and Wally do the same. They hobbled over in pain as they felt the aches and pain of their bodies. Slowly, they walked into the station, followed by the men and the driver of the truck. They filled the office of the small building.

"Okay now, okay now, not everybody," the other officer, Constable Henry, said, rather politely. "All you know de place small already," he continued, shrugging his shoulders.

Corporal Jeremiah questioned Joel and Wally and made a report of the incident in his logbook. Constable Henry left and came back with some clothes and handed it to both men.

"I doh know if it will fit you guys, but when you finish put that on you. It better than nothing, eh," he said, as he patted Joel on the back.

"Thank you, officer," Joel said, "I need it." He smiled broadly and took the bundle of clothes from the police officer.

After questioning the two men, Corporal Jeremiah told them that he was going to send them to the Portsmouth Hospital where a doctor would evaluate them. "Okay! I am going to call Portsmouth Police and ask them to send a jeep to take you guys there. We don't have any ambulance in this area. Go and change your clothes and Officer Henry will give allyou something to eat," he said to the men. "Not many men survive the Channel," he said to Wally. "You men are lucky!" he finished. Joel shook his head and Wally crossed himself with the sign of the cross.

"Come with me, let me show you where you can change off," Constable Henry said to the men as he led them to a spare room in the station house. The men donned their new garbs and didn't mind how it fitted. Their bodies were covered, and that was what was important. Constable Henry took them to the canteen and gave them something to eat: sardines, corned beef and bread, together with some Coca-Cola and a little bit of brandy.

"Dat feel good, officer," Wally said, as he gulped down a shot of brandy. "Dat taste better than de salt water. Everyday, officer! What you say Joe?" he asked Joel, who simply nodded his head, seemingly overwhelmed by the experience. They ate their fill and then returned to the charge room. The men felt much relieved and better, especially among people who seemed to have been so friendly and helpful. For a while, the near tragedy was forgotten. They sat on a bench, tired and sore, waiting for the jeep that would take them to the Portsmouth Hospital. Just then, a woman entered the building, sweat running down her face. The crowd made way for her.

"Officer, I heard the news. Somebody came to call me, so I rushed down to see if the gentlemen are okay. Where are they?" she asked breathlessly.

"Over there, nurse. The two men on the bench," Corporal Jeremiah answered as he pointed to Wally and Joel.

The nurse walked over to the two men and introduced herself. She was the District Nurse based in the village. She asked them how they felt and whether they had swallowed a lot of water. "I don't want you guys to drown when you think you are safe. I want to make sure you don't have water in your lungs. What are you going to do officer? Is the jeep coming to take them to Portsmouth?" she asked, turning to Corporal Jeremiah.

"Yes, Nurse Charles. I call the Portsmouth Police. They should be here anytime soon," Corporal Jeremiah assured her.

"They looking okay but I don't want to take any chances," the nurse said, with some concern in her voice. "Do you feel funny or anything? Does anything hurt you? Your chest or your stomach? You feel you want to throw up?" she asked Wally and Joel, trying to make sure she didn't miss anything that would jeopardize their safety on the way to Portsmouth.

"No, nurse. I feel okay. I jus' tired," Wally answered.

"Me too," said Joel. "But we okay nurse, God is good," he chimed in.

"You can say that again," the nurse replied.

There was a loud roar outside. The crowd had more than doubled. The news had spread around the village and in such a small community every one got to know what was happening quite quickly. The people shouted as the police vehicle sped into the yard, leaving a trail of dust in its wake.

"Dey here, nurse," a voice called out from among the men gathered inside the building. "De Police jeep come," he cried excitedly, as two officers from the Portsmouth station exited the jeep.

"Okay, officer! They seem to be okay, but I won't take any chances. Please get them to the hospital as quickly as you can," the nurse said to Corporal Jeremiah who was standing at the entrance to the building, ensuring that the crowd did not swarm in. "Good luck, gentlemen. You are so lucky! Thank God for that again," she said to Joel and Wally. Joel nodded his head. Wally smiled, the distinct gap in his mouth showing where two of his lower front teeth were missing.

Corporal Jeremiah led Wally and Joel to the waiting jeep as the driver opened the door so they could get in. Joel and Wally looked at each other. They had never wished to be in a police jeep before, but in this circumstance it was a good omen. Corporal Jeremiah shook their hands. "Take care guys, and good luck," he said to them.

The driver kicked the jeep into motion, turned around and sped up the dirt track towards the main road. The crowd followed, cheering loudly. Not too often did a mishap in the Channel end on a happy note; today was different and they were happy for Joel and Wally.

Joel and Wally hugged each other tightly around the neck. "*Merci Bondyé!*" Joel muttered as the jeep entered the main roadway and headed for the Portsmouth Hospital. Once again, Wally crossed himself with the sign of the cross. They both turned to look back and in the distance, from between the trees that lined the roadway, they saw the giant expanse of water that they had just outwitted.

Silently, Joel vowed to try it again.

Flying to Barbados

I settled in my seat and my hands trembled. Honestly, my whole body was shaking.

"Are you okay?" the guy next to me asked as I tried to adjust and buckle my seat belt.

"Yes," I answered. I had lied. I was not okay and I was sure he knew that I was not okay.

Hilaire and I knew each other. We were once classmates at the Saint Mary's Academy, but in the emotional state that I was in, I was unaware of his presence until he spoke to me.

It was less than a week before my mom and I were scheduled to travel to Canada on vacation. I had planned to use the opportunity to visit the United States to see some friends in New York. The temporary visa that I had applied for over two months ago was sitting in a consular's office at the United States Embassy in Bridgetown, Barbados. After discussions with people at the Embassy, it was determined that the visa could not be mailed to me because chances were that I would not get it in time to travel. To make matters more distressing, my passport had also been mailed to the Embassy so that the visa could be stamped into it. At this point, I had no other choice but to find myself in Barbados, one way or the other, to pick up the documents.

A thin, tall stewardess walked along the aisle making sure everyone was properly buckled. She smiled at me as I struggled with the seatbelt. Satisfied that I had gotten it right, she walked along to the back of the plane. I breathed a sigh of relief.

Just about four and a half hours earlier I had walked into the office of the Leeward Islands Air Transport (LIAT) in Roseau and to put it lightly, begged for a flight to Barbados. After some nervous details and the surprising realization that the lady I was talking to was my own relative (one whom I had never met before), my only option was a standby flight. But before I could be allowed to purchase a ticket, I needed a passport. I would not be allowed unto any flight without some document that gave me permission to leave the country or to enter Barbados. I had to get some documents from the Immigration Department.

I rushed through the streets of Roseau towards the Police Headquarters on Bath Road. Once there, and after having waited twenty agonizing minutes in line while other customers were attended to, I explained my predicament to the officer at the counter.

"You have to speak to the sergeant," he said to me. "I cannot do nothing for you."

"Who is he and is he here?" I asked, hardly able to utter the words.

"Over there," he said.

The officer showed me an office at the far end of the room.

"Knock at the door," he said.

I did as I was directed. A huge man sat at a desk. He had a big moustache on his upper lip. His eyes were sunken in their sockets and he gave me an inquiring look.

"Yeah, what can I do for you?" he asked.

I went over my predicament for yet another time. He looked at me in astonishment.

"So why did you send the passport to Barbados?" he asked. I found this a dumb question, since I expected him, as the Chief Immigration Officer, to know how these things happen. But in the situation that I was in, I had to make sure I explained everything.

"Because the US Embassy will only issue a visa with a passport," I answered.

"So why didn't you go to Barbados and get the visa rather than send the passport over there? What if it had never found its way to the Embassy?" he asked me rather nonchalantly.

I shook my shoulder. I just wanted a passport or anything to get me on a plane and I was not ready to delve into anything else. I agree maybe I should have gone to Barbados, but that's in the past and that did not matter now. So I felt.

"When you need it for?" he asked.

"This afternoon, sir, for the one-forty flight on LIAT," I answered.

He looked at his watch and then at me and shook his head. "Umm … I don't know," he said. "Do you know what time it is?" he asked me.

I nodded my head. This was not good news for me. He did not seem too eager to help me and I began to panic. Just as I was about to plead my case a bit further, I heard a familiar voice outside in the waiting area. It sounded like my father. *What was he doing here?* I thought to myself. *Was it coincidence or did he know that I was here?* I pondered.

"I think I heard my father out there, could I ask him to come in," I said to the sergeant.

"Who is your father?" he asked, giving me a look of disdain.

When I told him who my father was, his face lit up. I saw a smile appear at the corner of his mouth. "That's your father?" he cried. "Yeah, you look like him in truth," he smiled again. "Wait here!" he ordered me as he got up from his chair and lumbered to the room where my father was.

"Yes sir," I answered with some confidence, now that I realized he knew my father. I wasn't sure whether this was good or bad. I hoped for the best, nonetheless.

He returned shortly with my father in tow. "You know this boy?" he asked my father as they entered the room.

"Yes, that's my son," my father answered. "What you're doing here?" my father asked in a tone of concern, maybe wondering whether I had found myself in some trouble with the law.

I once again had to go over my story and what had led me to this point. Both men chuckled and shook their heads. I soon realized that the sergeant and my father knew each other very well. At this point, I was no more the issue as they began conversing with each other on other topics that had no relevance to my getting a passport. I was getting very annoyed, yet glad that daddy was here. There seemed to be no sense of urgency on the sergeant's part. I was itching to say something but decided to allow things to take their course. After a while, the sergeant called the officer at the desk to his office and handed him a temporary passport that he pulled out from a drawer in his desk.

"I need this right away," he said to the officer.

"Yes, sir," the young officer replied. "Right back, Sarge!" he continued.

"Was I being helped here because of the connections?" I asked myself, as I watched my father and his police friend laugh with each other. Apparently, my father was there to meet him in the first place, since they began discussing agriculture and plans the Sergeant had in mind for his plot of land in the interior of the island. My father was an agriculturist and worked with the Ministry of Agriculture. What coincidence!

Within a few minutes, I had a temporary passport in my hand. I thanked both officers for their help and bid my father farewell. Daddy wished me good luck and warned me to be careful. He said he would tell my mother that he had met me and everything would be okay.

I stepped into the hot sun, hotter I guess because of my anxiety. I was on my way back to the airline office. Once again, I rushed through the streets of Roseau but first I had to go to the bank to get money to pay for the ticket. I had no money with me. I headed to the Royal Bank of Canada on Bay Front. I was lucky because only a few customers were in line. But still, if I could have pushed them along faster, I would have. It was now five minutes to ten. I had to make up time and I was beginning to feel that I would lose out.

As soon as I had completed my transaction, after about fifteen agonizing minutes, I was on the move one more time. I felt like I was in a daze. When I got to the airline's offices, I asked for my newfound relative. After a few anxious minutes, as she set up the ticket and flight connections, I was set to fly to Barbados. But I was on standby, and had an open ticket. Honestly, worried as I was, I could not complain. That was better than nothing at all. I thanked her and dashed out of the office.

But my troubles were far from over. The airport was roughly an hour away by car, and just maybe I was going to make it on time. I was being optimistic. Hopefully, nothing would happen to make it any longer. It would be better if it were shorter. I had just about sixty dollars left after having paid for the ticket, no clothes, and no address to go to in Barbados, but I was going and hopefully, I would get there.

I headed to the telephone company offices where my sister worked and asked her to call my mom to let her know what had happened. There were no pay phones anywhere about and she was my best bet. I needed a change of undergarments and anything else that my mom could send me. My brother was home and he could take the stuff to the junction where the roads split at the Hillsborough Bridge into the West Coast Road and The Transinsular Road that led towards Melville Hall Airport.

Visits to every taxi service in the town proved futile. All taxis were either at the airport or on their way back to Roseau. I started to panic. I had to get out of town. Time was running out on me. I tried to reach a cousin who worked at A. C. Shillingford & Company to see if he could help me. But that was of no use. He was not on the job today.

My last resort was a taxi driver on Great George Street at Valley Taxi Service who had no plans for the day and who didn't seem too interested in taking me to Melville Hall.

"I not goin' nowhere garcon," he answered when I asked him to take me to the airport.

"I'll pay you, man," I said, but he did not make a move. "I have a one-forty flight," I said to him, but he did not budge. I felt helpless.

However, after some prompting from his friends who were sitting on the steps, he decided to take up the offer. "Okay, come les go," he said, a large grin on his face.

He entered the car and I followed. I got into the back seat as he turned on the engine. The car sputtered and stalled.

"No, God! Please, let it start," I muttered under my breath. He turned the engine again and this time it sprung into life as a cloud of black smoke spewed from the muffler. A roar erupted from his friends. Slowly the car started inching along.

I was off on my *unknown* journey. I checked my watch. It was 11:35 a.m.; just about two hours before my flight was due to depart from Melville Hall. I prayed that he would step on it as the car made its way along the coastline, along Morne Daniel cliffs; the villages of Massacre and Mahaut; sometimes stuck behind wooden box trucks, while at other times chugging along slowly.

"Can we go a little faster, man?" I asked him when I could not take it any longer. "I have to catch that flight," I pleaded.

"Okay! Okay!" he answered, as he put his foot to the pedal. "But I doin' my bess, you know," he added. I was prepared to risk it. I had no other choice or else I would never make that flight. But it hardly made a difference. The old car just limped along, groaning as it climbed one hill after the other. I began to wonder whether this was the reason the driver didn't want to take me to the airport in the first place. The old car did not seem to be in proper working condition. The condition of the inside indicated that he hardly took care of it. The upholstery on the seats was torn in many places and patched in others. Yet he was running a taxi. There was nothing I could do now. I was at his mercy. I sat back as crazy thoughts flew across my mind.

What if we didn't make it?

What if the car stalled along the way?

What if? And it went on and on.

Finally, we got to the Hillsborough Bridge. My brother was waiting as I had hoped. I waved to him. I asked the driver to stop the car and my brother handed me the package that mom had sent for me. On top of it she had written "Good Luck!" I opened the package and peered at the contents: a pair of underpants, a vest, a shirt and twenty dollars. I bid my brother goodbye and we were on our way again as a tear dripped down my face.

I sat at the back of the car without saying a word. I just allowed my thoughts to roam about, staring blankly at the scenery. I could not enjoy the pictures that floated before me. This was no sightseeing tour. I had a plane to catch—and soon—and that was what mattered now. My trip to Canada and the United States depended on what happened today. There was no way else.

I had never been on a plane before, although I had been to the airport to see relatives and friends off. I began to have strange thoughts about the flight. I was so wrapped up in those thoughts that I had no time to even take notice of where we had traveled. I just knew that we were heading to Melville Hall.

The car rounded a corner and before me I saw the churning waters of the Atlantic Ocean. I remembered that area from previous visits. We were close. I felt better. I looked at my watch for maybe the hundredth time on this trip. It would be about another fifty minutes before the plane would take-off. I envisioned getting at the airport at about 1:00 p.m. I had a chance. We still had a bit of traveling time along the Marigot coastline and through the village itself. I silently urged on the car as we inched our way through Marigot and then along the coastline towards Melville Hall.

At long last, we turned left off the major road unto the road that led to the airport compound and pulled into the drop-off area. I hardly waited for the car to come to a full stop before I unlocked the door and was stepping out. But I had forgotten one thing. I had not paid the driver.

"Yowe, yowe," he yelled as he got out of the car.

I realized my folly and walked back to him. "Sorry about that man. I just want to get out," I said to him "How much is that?" I asked him as he stood with his hands in his pockets.

"Seventy-dollars!" he answered. I looked at him in total disbelief.

"Are you serious, man?" I asked him. "That's not the price you guys charge to the airport. So why you charging me so much?" I questioned.

"Yeah, is true, but is a special hire to bring you here," he explained.

"But all I have is this," I said to him, showing him the sixty dollars that I had left in my wallet. I still had the twenty dollars that my mom had sent me stowed away in the plastic bag. That was my security and I would not part with it.

"Is not my problem, man!" he snapped back.

I tried to get him to accept part payment until my return even asking him to contact my sister at the telephone company and explain to her what had happened. But that was to no avail. Finally I gave him all that I had in the wallet. I stood at the entrance to the terminal building, tears ready to stream down my eyes. I could not envisage such a situation happening to me. What had I done to deserve being in this predicament? What was I going to do with only twenty dollars in my pocket?

I felt a touch on my shoulder. I turned around and standing behind me was my girlfriend's sister and her husband, Rony. They were both friends of my father. They had seen the exchange between the taxi driver and me and inquired of the situation. I explained to them my dilemma especially what had just happened.

"Okay, relax ... you will be okay ... you will make it," Rony said, trying to reassure me. He pulled out his wallet from his back pocket. "Here! Take this," he said, as he handed me seventy Trinidad and Tobago dollars. Evidently, he was heading to Trinidad on business and his wife had taken him to the airport.

"Why didn't I know that?" I thought to myself. "It would have saved me this embarrassment that now faced me. I could have had a free ride to the airport," I thought quietly. But it did me no good thinking about it now.

"Don't worry, you can use it in Barbados," Rony's wife assured me, as she sensed my hesitation. I felt the weight taken off my shoulders. "Don't worry, you'll be okay. God is good," she continued.

I thanked them both for helping me out of a very bad situation and together we walked into the terminal towards the airline's counter. But nothing was coming easy for me today. Since I was on a standby flight, I was informed by the airline agent that I had to wait until all confirmed passengers had checked in before I could get an available seat on the plane. Subconsciously, I hoped that someone had cancelled or was running later than I was. I knew I was being selfish, but at this point, anything that worked in my favor would be a big plus. I became very nervous. I looked at my watch again. It was 1:05 p.m. That plane would be landing very soon. The what-ifs came back to me again. Rony checked in without any problems and he wished me Good Luck as he made his way towards the departure lounge.

"Take care and I will see you if you get on," he said.

"God is good," his wife repeated. "You will get on. Have faith," she said rather convincingly.

I walked over to an empty chair and sat there by myself pondering on the events of the morning. My legs trembled and my back was wet with dripping sweat. After what seemed like an eternity—although in reality it was only fifteen minutes—the ticket agent called me to the counter.

"Your passport and ticket please," she said to me.

"Am I getting on?" I asked her excitedly.

"Yes ... we have a few empty seats, so you're okay," she said, as I handed her the documents.

I was elated. I was going to be on the flight. There was room for me. I made the sign of cross. *What luck! Or was it Divine intervention?* I asked myself quietly. I wondered if my cousin, back at the airline office in Roseau, had played a part in my getting on this flight. I wasn't going to ask either, preferring to let things remain the way they were. I prayed that whatever it was, it would stay with me until I returned home.

I was processed with no problems. No questions asked.

"This is your boarding pass," the young lady smiled at me as she handed me my boarding pass. "Remember to check in at the counter in Barbados when you're coming back because you will still be on standby. Have a safe trip," she smiled at me.

"Thank you for helping me get on," I replied nervously, as sweat dripped slowly down my cheeks.

"You're quite welcome," she replied. I smiled again, sheepishly. I walked away unsure of what my next move was. I just wanted to be on the flight. I would worry about returning when that time came. My goal now was to get to *Bimshire*, as we sometimes referred to Barbados. Then I heard the drone of an airplane as it landed on the runway. *Was that the plane?* I asked myself.

Within minutes, I heard the announcement for all those booked on LIAT Flight 0367 to Grenada and points in between to head to the departure lounge. That was my flight! I made my way to the Immigration area following the other people who were taking the same flight out of Dominica.

"You can't travel today," the Immigration Officer who was manning the desk said to me. My heart skipped a few beats.

What had gone wrong this time? I asked myself. I looked at him, unsure of what to say or what to ask him.

"Were you born today?" the officer laughed, as he showed me the date I had written down in the space for my *Date of Birth* on the immigration card that I had filled out. "Relax! Why you look so nervous? You will get on the flight. Don't worry," he said, a smile on his long, bony face. "They won't leave without you," he said, as he handed me the form and asked me to write in the correct date.

I fixed my error and handed the card back to him. He looked at it closely and then he looked at me. "Okay, young man, you can go now," he smiled again, as he patted me on the shoulder. "Have a safe trip," he said, as I moved towards the departure area. I nodded my head but said nothing.

When I got to the departure lounge, I looked for Rony but he was engaged in a conversation with another man and I did not feel like disturbing him. I stood by myself again, peering across to the airstrip and saw the plane that I was about to board. The ground crew was loading suitcases and boxes. I had none of that to worry about. All I had was a plastic bag! I was really traveling light. A shiver ran down my spine. I was really going to be on the plane. A tear dripped down my face and I wiped it away.

After what seemed forever, an employee of the airline asked us to present our boarding passes. I showed him mine, hoping he would find nothing wrong.

"Okay, go 'head," he said, as he waved me on. I felt relieved.

I followed the line of passengers heading to the aircraft. I didn't want to seem like a *country-bookie* so I acted like I knew what I was doing. Rony and his friend were up front. I was not going to catch up with them, deliberately, since I didn't want to revisit the events of the morning. I gingerly climbed the steps of the plane, holding on to the railing. I was sweating uncontrollably now. Sweat dripped down my face unto my lips and eyes. Even my arms were wet with sweat. I entered the plane and sat down at the first available seat next to a window until I realized that I had to match my seat with the number on the boarding pass. I got up and found the correct seat, five rows down and next to a window. I flopped into the seat. I was exhausted.

"Okay!" someone shouted from outside. I then heard a thud, as the door of the plane was shut. I felt sweat drip down my neck. I welled up inside. The plane's engines sprung into life as the whirring propellers cut through the air.

I made the sign of the cross and said a silent prayer. I then buried my face into my hands as the plane taxied up the asphalt runway. It was more out of exasperation and mental fatigue.

Hilaire touched me on the back. "Relax, man, you will be okay," he said. "Is this your first time on a plane?" he asked me, as I sat back, following the advice of the stewardess.

"Yea, but is all what happened this morning. I am tired," I told him, not really prepared to go through the events of the morning again.

The plane slowed down when it got to the top of the runway and then I felt it turn around. I realized we were getting ready to take off. The plane shuddered as the pilot revved the engines. I looked outside through the small window next to me. The propellers were spinning very fast. All I could see was a circular blur of white and black as the propeller blades spun and the noise of the engines got louder. The aircraft inched on forward and then started accelerating along the asphalt runway. The coconut trees alongside the airstrip zipped by as the engine roared louder still and the plane picked up speed. The grass on the side of the runway was just a blur of green. I held on tightly to the armrest of my seat as the plane lifted off the ground. I closed my eyes as a strange empty feeling came over me. I felt the plane bank to the right. My stomach boiled.

I opened my eyes and I saw the Marigot coastline and the airport runway disappearing in the distance as the plane flew over the Atlantic Ocean. I saw the giant waves crashing against the island's rugged coastline and ending in a mass of white froth among the rocks. *Wow!* I heard myself say as I saw Dominica's rugged coastline for the very first time from the air. I crossed myself one more time with the sign of the cross.

Hilaire looked at me, smiled and nodded his head. "You'll be okay, man!" he reassured me. "You'll be okay," he said again. "Trust me!" he said.

I nodded my head. "Okay! If you say so, man," I answered. I eased back and thoughts raced through my mind. I remembered my mother and wondered what she would be thinking. I hoped she was okay.

Barbados, here I come! I whispered softly, as the plane climbed above the clouds.

Somehow, I found the courage to smile.

Hurricane

As a boy growing up in Dominica, I could not remember the names of more than three or four hurricanes that had struck the island. Edith, Gloria and Dorothy and possibly Cleo were the ones that stuck in my mind. I could not recall any serious damage that these hurricanes had caused except to the banana industry, although it did not have to take a hurricane to do damage to the banana industry; any significant windstorm could do that. Sometimes there was damage to a bridge or two and then there was the occasional landslide. Usually, these hurricanes tended to inflict more damage on the other islands of the Caribbean than they would on Dominica.

For a long time we strongly believed that the towering fortresses—Diablotin, Micotrin, Trois Pitons and even in St. Joseph, Morne Pican—would continue to be our best defenses against hurricanes. In our bravado manner it was *"Just bring them on."*

Hurricane David proved otherwise when it slammed this country on August 29, 1979. Whether it was coincidental or the wrath of God striking the land, the 29th had not been too good to the country that year. First, there was the May 29th political uprising that saw the death of Philip Timothy and the toppling of the Patrick John Government and then the July 29th incident in Guadeloupe involving Dominican youths. Now this?

I lay on my bed the night of the 28th and listened to the weather reports from the Caribbean radio stations, more notably, the Montserrat-based Radio Antilles, and all reports painted a gloomy forecast for the country known as Little England—Barbados. All reports were indicating that this massive hurricane was taking dead aim at Barbados. Barbadians or *Bajans*, as West Indians love to call them, were being warned to take all necessary precautions against David. There was no way out.

I had no relatives or friends in Barbados, as far as I knew, but I had traveled to the country to get my visitor's Visa from the US Embassy so that I could visit the US on vacation and I had also stopped there intransit from St.Vincent during a CXC training workshop. I was therefore aware of how flat the island was. I shuddered at the thought of a hurricane of David's magnitude passing over the island. I stuck the transistor to my ears listening intently into the late hours of the night, but nothing changed. I went to sleep.

I awoke at approximately 6:00 a.m. the next morning and quickly switched on the radio to find out what had transpired overnight in Barbados. My mouth dropped when I heard the news reports. It seemed like a dream, but this was no dream. This was real. David had altered its course. Barbados had been spared and the hurricane was now taking dead aim at Dominica, Guadeloupe and Martinique, with Dominica likely to take a direct hit. I got up from the bed and awoke everyone in the house.

We were unprepared for the hurricane, just as many other Dominicans, I was sure. We had nothing set aside. No canned foods, no water, no bread, nothing! Daddy was planning to go to his plantation in the Layou Valley and he had to hurriedly change his mind. He had no time to let his helpers know, but he hoped they would use their judgement. There was no way he would risk his life in this weather. It was raining now, though not very heavily, but at a rather steady rate. But yet, with all this, there was the belief, based on previous experiences, that Dominica would be able to handle this one.

"Don't worry, those mountains will stop that," my younger brother, Simon said as we stood in the living room discussing what we had heard. My sister switched on the stereo and there was a minister of government addressing the country on the impending storm. But for all intents and purposes, we were all caught unprepared. Nothing, not even a nail, had been raised in preparation for this monster, packing winds of almost 150 miles per hour and moving like a giant elephant.

"Don't you have anything to put over those windows?" my mother asked my father. All the windows in our home were of glass and even the door was made up of glass louvers and panes.

"No, I don't have anything. Nothing at all," he said, realizing the hopeless position that we were in.

"God is good," said my mother as she went into the kitchen and began filling a few pots and pans with clean water.

I felt the tension in the house. Words were few and short as everyone realized the enormity of the situation. My sisters had planned to go to Roseau, but that plan was shelved as soon as they heard the news of the approaching storm. There was no way that anyone was going to leave to go anywhere.

Within an hour after I had awakened, thick dark clouds were skimming across the sky. There was this eerie feeling floating in the atmosphere and it felt like anytime something terrible would happen. I went to the verandah and sat on a table watching as people scurried about. My father, still in his nightclothes, joined me and stood in the doorway.

"It looking like this thing dangerous," he said to me. "How comes they did not know it was coming to Dominica?" he continued.

"It's one of those things. Just a little change and it could make a big difference," I told him, "And if it's big like they say, a little change is something big," I added.

We stood there, just the two of us, looking out, not saying a word. Inside was also very quiet, except for the radio from which the hurricane warnings and information were being given; alas too late to be of any real help. My mother moved around, taking down the photographs and the mirror that hung on the walls. She also cleared the top of her living room cabinet. She did not want any of her prized souvenirs and relics to be damaged during the storm.

"Look at this guy!" cried my daddy, pointing in the direction of a young man who was trying to take down a TV antenna from the roof of his house. "You mean somebody going to risk their life for a antenna?" he asked.

The wind was beginning to blow a bit stronger now and the young man was having a tough time trying to steady the antenna. To make matters even more frightening, he was just a few feet from the secondary electrical wires that hung a few feet above the roofs of the houses. After about ten minutes, the antenna snapped and crashed to the ground. Finally, the young man made his way down, clutching on to a tall wooden ladder that rested against the house, apparently held by someone on the ground.

The trees on Morne Pican, a hill above St. Joseph, were beginning to be blown about furiously. People on the streets began screaming as the wind was becoming stronger and some of them changed their minds and headed back home. My mother had lit the stove and made some coffee, but I did not have the nerve to drink. I sat on the table transfixed by what I was seeing. I watched as the leaves of a papaya tree were ripped from the top of the tree. The leaves floated crazily in the wind, spinning wildly. A few pieces landed right in the porch where I sat. The debris had traveled almost five hundred feet or more to where I was.

"My word," cried my father, as the pieces of leaves smacked against my face. "This is something. This is no joke. In all my time I never see that. Oh no! That's not good." Then he remembered his vehicle. He had parked his Mitsubishi truck on the side of the street along the riverbank across from our home. "Oh, boy, you know what? I better go an' park de van by de police station. If de river come down ..." Without completing his sentence, he hurried into the house to change his clothes. He was soon on his way.

The clouds grew more ominous by the minute and they literally whisked in all directions across the sky. I had never seen any clouds heading north before now. It was amazing. The rain intensified. It was scary to think of what could happen if this thing really hit land and was as dangerous and powerful as the radio personnel were saying it was. Would those mountains save us again, or would they succumb to the fury and power of the behemoth? "Only time would tell," I told myself as I stood up and walked to the edge of the porch to see what was going on. All about, the tree branches were being blown in all directions like loose kites in the sky.

Our house was located on the banks of the St. Joseph River, and I had a very clear view of houses on the Morne and others that were located in the flat in Autrobando. Not one house showed any sign that it had been readied for the storm. Here and there I heard the sound of boards and some old galvanize sheets being hammered as some villagers tried the eleventh hour thing. But it was getting to be too late. The mango tree, which was about twenty-five feet from the northeastern corner of our house, lost its crop as the wind increased in intensity.

Some workers who usually left their homes in the early hours of the morning and who had ventured out, unaware of the approaching storm, were now returning home, some telling other villagers of the threatening look that could be seen everywhere, especially over the sea. One woman tried to shelter herself from the rain using her umbrella and found this a very challenging exercise. Finally, in disgust, she threw the now damaged umbrella into the river and limped on in the rain.

The church bell sounded. Traditionally, it was sounded only for church activities, but it seemed that the sexton or the priest was now using it as a warning device, alerting people. Usually, the church was used as a shelter for people who feared that their homes were not safe enough to see a storm through and maybe the priest and sexton were reminding people of just that. Whatever the reason, the bell rang for almost five minutes before it stopped.

My father returned, soaked to the skin. We all listened to him as he told us of what he had learnt from the police when he parked his truck. "This thing really doesn't look good. It look like it change course last night and is still picking up speed. Everywhere you look all you see is darkness. The wind blowing everything and the sea is beginning to get very rough," he said. "I try to get something in Edna shop but all shop close already," he continued.

The wind gusts grew stronger. The trees were not just being blown about; their leaves were being torn off the branches. Some branches snapped. I saw the entire foliage of a sour sop tree completely sheared off. Pieces shot right for the porch. It seemed like this was the line of fire and I withdrew to a corner of the porch that was protected from the wind and rain.

"You better go inside, you know," my father said to me when he saw this happen, but I wanted to see what was going on. I had never really witnessed what a hurricane had done and even if I was aware of Edith and Gloria, I was asleep when these struck or maybe too small to remember in detail what had happened. I watched as the utility lines leading to people's homes strained to the point of snapping. Television antennas that had not been taken down from roofs snapped like matchsticks and tumbled to the ground or hung from the sides of the houses.

The radio suddenly went quiet. Then our house was in semi-darkness. Lights were gone. Now all contact with the outside world was gone. I could pick up other Caribbean stations on my transistor radio, which was battery operated, but DBS, the local radio station, was off the air. The stations that I was able to pick up painted a grim picture of Dominica's chances—and Guadeloupe and Martinique, too. This thing was so big that it engulfed these tiny islands within its giant claws. There was no getting away this time. The streets were now completely deserted. Everyone had sought shelter somewhere.

The first real wave of hurricane force winds drove me inside. I did not want to be a victim if I could avoid it. Flowerpots and other loose items were now flying missiles. The wind gusts hummed noisily as they whipped about. I heard the sound of objects slamming against houses as the wind picked them up and transported them wherever. Some pigs that were tied under the mango tree along the bank of the river, close to our home, squealed noisily as they felt nature's fury. Their fate was sealed—no one was goin' to get them out.

My mother and sisters moved to their bedrooms and so, too, had my youngest brother, Tony. My father stood like a guard at the door while I moved from room to room, window to window, looking out, making sure that none of the windows would get blown in. My mother was reading her prayer book and she held a rosary in her hand; my sisters just lay in bed saying nothing.

The wind seemed to gain in intensity by the minute. It howled like I had never heard before and it seemed to have a structure to it. I cringed as it tore through the branches of every tree in the neighborhood. They were left bare of any leaves and stood like skeletons waiting to be smashed to cinder bits. The rain, too, intensified. It was coming down in white sheets and water was being blown into the house through any crevice in the windows and the doors.

Ravines, drains and yards were flooded as more water was collecting than could be taken away. The St. Joseph River was rising rapidly and tree trunks, old vehicle chassises and even a cow—still alive then—washed away to the sea. The rising water began to overflow the banks and the road that led to Autrobando and the bypass was under at least four to five feet of water. The water also came close to our home which was just a mere twenty feet from the edge of the riverbank. My daddy spoke, concern in his voice.

"The water is coming up close to the house and it even covering the street. Is a good thing I take the van to the station," he said.

I assured him that the water would not affect us because that would mean having to rise another five feet higher before our house would be in danger. I could not see this happening, although I had to confess that I had no idea how high the river would get, based on the amount of rain that was coming down.

"Come and see this, come and see this," my father shouted.

I rushed to where he stood. Across the street from where we lived, part of a house had collapsed. The occupant of that house was an old woman.

"I wonder where the lady is?" my father said. "The house just bend one way and then the other and it just breakup" he continued, describing what he had seen.

Apparently, daddy was not the only one who had seen the house collapse. Four young men, who lived opposite the woman, braved the elements, ran out and pulled her out from under the rubble, taking her to the safety of the house where they were. It was a daring act in such dangerous conditions.

The door of our house throbbed violently and I was concerned that at any time the force of the wind would finally get the better of it. However, it stood strong even as it buckled every now and then. The water continued to sip in below the window frames and my younger brother used a cloth to wipe the water off the walls before it slipped to the floor. At times, it felt like the whole house was vibrating from the force of the wind. But it did not budge.

The village was so dark that it seemed like this was happening at sunset. However it was only 10:00 a.m. The dark clouds continued zipping across the sky. They seemed to be lower than before. Galvanize sheets tore off roofs and floated in the air like kites. I saw a sheet lift off a roof and travel westward through the air. I marveled. "How was this possible?" I asked myself. But this was only the beginning. I watched in horror as house after house lost its roof or all the sheets of galvanize, leaving behind only the rafters. In some cases, the whole roof went catapulting through the air.

This was nature at its fiercest and most ferocious. I felt scared and wondered if our roof would meet the same fate. And where would we go? I saw us as sitting ducks in this kind of weather if our roof went. I prayed silently just like I guess everyone else in the house was doing, especially our mother.

I watched in total disbelief as a sheet of galvanize hit against a telephone pole and was wrapped like paper around the pole within minutes.

"Boy, that is something. I have never seen something like this in all my life!" my father cried as he watched this amazing feat unfold before our eyes. "You would swear is paper," he said.

Telephone and electric poles, as far as my eyes could see, were snapped in half. Some stood askew while others lay strewn against houses. It was total destruction. I envisaged what was going on in the rest of the island. What was happening to places on the eastern and northeastern coasts where this storm had made landfall? I knew there was no way I would find out for a while. But for now, I could see devastation before my eyes. St. Joseph was taking a beating.

Suddenly, there was a loud bang. It sounded like an explosion coming from atop our roof. My sisters and youngest brother came running to the living room, their eyes wide open. My mother followed, but she said nothing, her rosary still in her hands. We all looked up to the ceiling, but the roof was still intact. My daddy and I went from bedroom to bedroom and checked every window in the house, but there was no sign that anything of consequence had happened. At least there was no water coming through the ceiling and that was a great relief.

"Maybe something fall on the roof," said Simon, as we returned to the drawing room.

"That could be," my daddy answered, as he retook his post at the front door. Everyone seemed to agree with the assessment and the girls and my mother returned to their retreat. Tony remained with us, although he said nothing. He just watched through the windows and shook his head, over and over again.

For almost four hours that seemed like an eternity, the storm battered the village. I surveyed the village from my window. Not a tree stood in places where they once stood. I could see houses that I had never seen before as others around them had been smashed to bits or sections broken off, scattering people's belongings far and wide. In Autrobando, the river continued to rise and there was about four feet of water everywhere; water splashing against the foundations and pillars of people's houses. Then it became quiet, like nothing had happened. A strange, eerie calm had descended upon the village.

"It's not finished. This is the eye passing over. It's going to start back right away," my father cried as we all gathered in the drawing room. I also heard people's voices and as I looked out, people by the dozens were running out from houses and under houses and seeking safety.

"Let me go and see what was that noise on the roof," I volunteered. My mother opposed my going out there, but Daddy informed her that it would be okay as long as I could do it real quick. I opened the back door, and with no shoe on my feet I stepped outside and climbed the little hill above the house and surveyed the roof. I saw nothing of concern. All the sheets of galvanize were in place. Our roof appeared to be in perfect condition. I went down and circled around the house but there was nothing except water rushing everywhere.

I looked towards the north and northeast at the hills overlooking the village, and in places where there was once green, all I saw were bare spots. The trees were gone and in some places there were mudslides. St. Joseph looked like a war zone. I looked, too, at the house

149

where my girlfriend lived to see if that was intact. The house looked okay. Marcella had traveled to Montserrat on vacation and I was sure she would not believe the devastation that was going on. I got back in quickly and gave a report of my findings. Everyone was delighted that our house was okay, but at the same time concerned as I explained what I had seen in the village.

"You see, maybe is that that happen," said Simon. "Maybe is a sheet of galvanize or something that fall on it and then it just keep going."

"Well, we will find out when this thing finish," said my father, a little relaxed now, no doubt happy that the roof was still intact. "In all my years I never see one like that. There used to be bad landslides and a lot of rain, but nothing like that," he added. He walked to the kitchen and poured himself a drink of brandy. We waited for the eye to pass.

I was extremely amazed that our windows had been able to withstand the force of the winds thus far. Our neighbor's house to our east served as a buffer, but still, those were strong winds. It was a taller house than ours and I believed that this was one of the reasons why such brittle one-eighth of an inch glass had not shattered from the force that I had seen displayed before my eyes that morning. I was still amazed, based on what I had seen outside when I went to survey the roof, that our house was intact. There was devastation all around. The roof of the Bylers' house had been damaged and they were all huddled together in the lower level of the house, shielded by the stone and concrete foundation.

It was not long before the winds picked up again. We braced ourselves for round number two. It was like a prized fighter working his way through his opponent. In this case, the opponent was unable to respond. The storm continued to batter the village. The water rushing down the river was now a dark, rusty-brown and it stank. It seemed like the land was being purged. I could hear the sound of stones, and giant ones at that, bouncing against each other as the force of the water drove them along. Some young people, unaware that the storm was not over, scurried for shelter, as they realized that the thing was back.

At one point there were peals of thunder and a few flashes of lightning mingling with the deafening scream of the wind and the whipping of the rain against the windowpanes. The heavens had really opened up and everything was now happening together. I heard screams, but I had no idea where they came from. Somewhere out there, people were crying out for help. "Isn't this a good thing this did not happen at night?" I said to my father.

"You right. That's true. Boy! Imagine if this thing had happened at night! How would people do in this darkness? We must say thanks God it happen in the morning," he replied. He moved from the door and went to one of the windows on the western side of the house in order to see what was happening out there. "I don't believe what I seeing there!" he cried.

"What?" I asked him, as I rushed to the window, followed by Simon and Tony.

"I see something like a whole roof, the whole thing flying up there. I telling you the whole thing just lift up like a plane and it was floating in the air with pieces of wood hanging from it. Boy, that is something else, eh," my father said, looking shocked by what he had just seen. He looked towards the ceiling to reassure himself that his roof was still there.

The roof had landed somewhere or was still in flight. But as some houses collapsed and others lost their roofs and roofing sheets, I could not but watch in wonder as a few small houses were still standing like nothing was happening. Ma Bernard's kitchen was still standing strong and so, too, was Vella's little house. I expected these to be lifted off the ground anytime and blown into the raging river, but they seemed to stand there and defy all that David threw at them. How was that possible?

For the rest of the afternoon, we stood watch, keeping our eyes on the front door. We knew if it ever gave way, this could be it for us. There was nothing that was going to stop the wind from coming right in. My mother had finished saying her prayers and she took her chances to boil some hot water on the gas stove so that we could make some coffee and tea. We had not eaten anything all day. No one had really cared about lunch. Surviving this monster was key. My sisters remained in their beds. There was nothing to do, nowhere to go and we seemed to be riding the storm rather okay to this point.

We had no idea what was happening in other parts of the village, but based on what I was seeing from where I was, I believed that the same or similar fate had befallen many others. One concern was whether any villagers had lost their lives in this barrage. It was hard to think of it, but that was a reality.

"I wonder how my mother is doing?" Daddy said loudly, as he passed his hand over his face, seemingly a bit weary. "I hope that little house stand up," he said, his voice dropping to a murmur. Daddy's mother, Ma Falanie, lived in Salisbury and her house was perched on tall stilts. It was a one-bedroom house and it was in a very vulnerable position. We knew that if the house fell off the stilts it could be disastrous. There was a valley below and if her house fell, it would be a miracle to prevent it from ending up at the bottom of the valley.

"I hope she went by somebody and didn't stay in the house. Anyhow, God is good. He'll take care of her," he said softly.

My mother, too, was worried about her mother who lived on Back Street. "If I had known that it was that bad I would have told her to come here," she said as a tear trickled down her face. For the first time for the whole day, the mood in the house was very emotional. It seemed now that there was urgency on everyone's part to find out what had happened to our grandparents. But before we could do so, we had to await the end of this storm, if there was ever going to be one. This was a marathon.

Everything that happened for the next hour seemed a repeat of something that had already happened. We seemed to be in a state of expectation. Whose house would it be or which roof? At this point it looked like this was inevitable and the longer the strong winds and rain kept up, the greater the chances of more houses being destroyed. The memories of Edith and Dorothy were now minuscule compared to what I had seen today. I realized that those mountains had failed and were no match for this killer.

"They didn't say our mountains would stop the hurricane?" contended Tony, at last saying something. "No mountains look like they could stop that non, pal," he added.

After almost seven hours (or was it eight?), the winds began to lose their intensity once again. The rain eased up and the clouds, though still dark and menacing, were no longer zipping by overhead. They just floated on. Galvanize sheets and other loose building materials only banged against the sides of buildings. It looked like the storm was heading out to sea in search of another victim. Guadeloupe was the most likely target now.

"It's dying down. It's dying down," my daddy said, a tone of relief in his voice. For the first time all day, he took a sit on the couch, his hands under his chin. My mother sat next to him.

"You tired now?" she asked him rather jokingly. My father looked at her and said nothing. "Ma Falanie is okay," my mother said, hoping to reassure him that our grandmother would be okay.

Everything was quiet now. An eerie calm hung over the village as if something else was going to happen. I opened the front door. There

152

was debris strewn all over the porch and there was a pool of about an inch or two of water. The river was rushing a mere two feet from the fence at the front of our house and by the look of the debris left behind, it had crested much closer at the height of the storm. We all were on the porch now, regardless of the pool of water. That would be taken care of later and this was the least of our problems at the moment.

People, especially the younger ones, were out on the water-covered streets. I could see the look of exasperation and bewilderment on the people's faces. There were some who simply just didn't know what to do or where to go. Everywhere was devastation. The hills above the village, above the bypass and towards Caswen were naked in spots where trees had once stood. In some spots, landslides had taken place and I could see the exposed rocks and cliffs.

"Let me go an see what happen in Senjo. I need to go and check the library too," I said, as I walked back in to change into suitable gear to deal with the conditions out there. (I ran a voluntary library service in the village and I had hoped the building had survived this monstrosity. If not, well I knew what I would have to do).

"Where you going already? Be careful!" said my father, hoping that he could persuade me to stay home. But nothing was keeping me back.

"I'll come too," said Simon. "Wait for me."

We walked along a narrow track along the bank of the river and the first sign I had to believe what Daddy had said about a roof being blown away stared me right in the face. The roof of Mr. Heldon's house was completely gone. The whole thing, rafters and all, had seemingly been transformed into a UFO. Now the search was on to find out where it had landed. The community library had taken a direct hit and most of the roof was gone. Books were strewn all over the floor and chairs and tables knocked over. I could not bear the pain to watch hours of work gone! I moved on. And then there was the church. The building where many had passed the time during previous hurricanes, and maybe this one too, was in shambles. I guess those who were there had sought shelter somewhere else. Almost every single sheet of galvanize had been torn off the roof of the church. But the steeple, with the cross at the top, was still there. The walls of the building still stood firm. After satisfying ourselves that it was a safe thing to do, Simon and I gingerly crossed over Jubilee Bridge above the surging river. The arched bridge was built by one of the early Catholic priests so that the parishioners could have easy access to the church. Today it stood strong against the biggest hurricane to hit us in a long time.

We joined the hordes of people who had gathered on Main Street. I had my first look at the Caribbean Sea. It was pounding at the shore with fifteen to twenty foot waves. I had never seen this before. There were boats and nets in the streets away from the shore as the owners and fishermen had dragged them away from the hungry clutches of the sea to safety. Yet, by some miracle, it seemed that not one single house perched on the shoreline was dragged out to sea nor was damaged by the raging waves.

I stood and watched in awe at what had happened. All around me were damaged houses, telephone and electric poles, broken tree limbs, parts of houses; anything that you could think of, all lined up on Main Street.

The village was no longer as dark as it had been earlier in the day. It was getting brighter, although the day was coming to an end. I beckoned to Simon. We turned around and headed back home. I had seen enough. I hoped I would never be a witness to a repeat of this. I knew one thing though: Mother Nature is a powerhouse!

A Thief in the Night

Mr. Philip heard the commotion in the yard and knew that the person was back again. Whoever it was who had been stealing his chickens those past few weeks was at his old tricks again. This was it! He had had enough and he felt that he had to deal with whoever it was. He touched his wife who was lying next to him. "*Moun la viwè encore, Cecilia. Yo pwen nous encore,*" he said to her in hushed tones.

"*Sa'w sa fè ? Bondyé ké bon pou yo,*" she replied, as Mr. Phillip got up from his bed and made his way to the living room. He went to the window and softly turned the bar that kept it shut. He opened the window just a bit and peered into the darkness, looking for an intruder. But he saw nothing and he heard nothing. Whoever it was had already gotten what he wanted and fled. There was not a sound coming from the yard. Dejectedly, he made his way back to bed.

Mr. Philip and his wife, Nurse Philip, lived together in their two-bedroom wooden house in Autrobando. They had no children between them although Mr. Philip had four children with two other women in the village. They had been married for almost forty years and for a number of years they had raised chickens, mainly for the eggs that they sold in the community on a daily basis. Every now and then, when they felt like it, they would sell a hen or rooster to someone who was having a christening, first communion or who just wanted to cook a *mess*. It was just enough to keep the two of them, especially Mr. Philip, occupied in his older years.

Mr. Philip had been a headmaster before he retired ten years ago. He spent most of his teaching days in St. Joseph except for a few years in Massacre and Colihaut. His wife, Cecilia, was a nurse before she, too, retired about five years ago. They were both very popular in the village, especially Miss Cecilia, or Nurse Cecilia, as almost everyone in the village referred to her. She always boasted that she was the person who had delivered almost everyone in the village. She spent almost thirty-five years tending to the sick people of the village and being the mid-wife to almost all of the women in the village. She always said that although she never had any children of her own, she was mother to every child during her day because she had helped to deliver them.

Mr. Philip liked the idea of raising chickens from the time he was a boy because his father also raised chickens. In the afternoons, after school, he would split some dry coconuts and grate the meat he tore off the shells. Sometimes he gathered vines, especially *zeb coowess*, which he hung with twine from the roof of the chicken house, thus adding a bit of variety to what he fed the chickens. That was his job every afternoon. He was the only child of his parents, and when they passed on he took over and kept his father's tradition alive. When he married Cecilia, he got her involved since she was the one who was home the most.

Mr. Philip was known as the "chicken man" or the "egg man" of the village and he took it seriously. It was not only a hobby but also a source of income. Villagers would go to his home to purchase the eggs, and even though they complained at the price he charged for an egg, they still bought from Mr. Philip. They believed that one of Mr. Philip's eggs was better than two of the imported ones that were sold in the shops. They preferred the brown shell of Mr. Philip's chickens more than the imported white ones. At the very least, the villagers believed that the brown ones made a better *chodo*. It was their opinion that Mr. Philip's eggs were more nutritious while, at the same time, they believed that the imported ones were somewhat artificial. Mr. Philip always believed that if one person did not want to pay the price he asked, there was always someone else who was walking to his home to buy that same egg. Thus, he hardly ever bothered to argue with any of these villagers when they complained of his so-called steep prices.

But lately Mr. Philip was getting worried. On two occasions in the past, someone had broken into the chicken house and on each occasion had stolen one of his roosters. The first time it happened was on a night when there was a thunderstorm and apparently the thief had used the bad weather and the noise of the thunder as a cover to commit his crime. Mr. Philip was of the belief that this was just a random act and he decided to let it go without reporting it to the police. He was a kind man and there was hardly a bone of ill will in him. His wife, however, did not feel the same way as he did.

"You should make a report to the police. We work so hard and people come to steal your rooster in the middle of the night in all that bad weather and you letting it go!" she warned.

"But we don't even know who did it and when. I don't have any witnesses who can say they see who did it, so I cannot point my finger at anyone," Mr. Philip replied.

"Philip! That is not right. You should go to the police and make a report. What if it happens again? You want them to carry the whole chicken house away before you do something?" she pleaded. But Mr. Philip was not going to take any action.

"One cock will not kill me. Let whoever steal it eat it. What will it do for them? Nothing! Don't worry with that, Cecilia. God is good," he said to her.

It looked like it was open season on Mr. Philip because, one month later, just as his wife had forewarned, someone struck again. Mr. Philip was very surprised that Sunday morning when he went out to feed the chickens to find that most of them were outside in the backyard. He checked the latch on the gate, but the padlock was on and the latch was in place. "Oh, what did they do to me this time?" Mr. Philip asked as he began to search for the escape point. He found it. Someone had cut through the wire at the back of the chicken house.

"I told you that you should have gone to the police," Nurse Cecilia said to him when he told her what had happened. "You see, we trust them too much. Give them a foot and what do they do? They take a mile. Nobody has respect for people's property anymore. I want to see if you're not going to the police this time," she said to him.

"Yes, I will," replied Mr. Philip. "I will go after I am finished feeding them. Let me block the hole before I go," he answered.

Mr. Philip searched the yard and found a piece of tin sheeting. He quickly made a crude patchwork, hoping that it would be sufficient to deter the thief. He would try to get someone to do something more permanent when he had the time. He opened the door and then threw food into the chicken house luring the birds back in. He shut the door and stood silently for a while pondering what he should do next.

"Cecil, I gone," he shouted to his wife as he worked his way through the yard toward the street and headed to the police station. Just then, the church bells were being rung, signaling that it would soon be time for Sunday service. Usually, at this time of the morning, he would be preparing to make his way to church with his wife. However, the events during the night had derailed his plans. His wife would leave him behind this morning. He knew that his absence would be noticed, he being such a prominent member of the church community, but he had to get this thing out of the way. He didn't want to keep dealing with it any longer.

At the station house, Mr. Philip gave an account of what had happened to the officer who was manning the desk. When he was finished noting Mr. Philip's complaint, the officer accompanied him back to his home to make a visual inspection of the damage to the chicken house. He left with a promise to follow-up and asked Mr. Philip to let the police know of anything that would help them in nabbing the culprit or culprits.

"So what happen?" Nurse had asked him when she returned from church.

"They just took a report, that's all," he answered.

"Well! Wait and see what happens next. I don't know what to say myself," Nurse said in resignation.

"You know what I'm wondering, Cecilia? I'm wondering if they're not even stealing our eggs, too. I never really check, you know."

"It's not impossible. Those people so bold. They can do anything. Now, the last thing I hear is that somebody is breaking and entering shops in the village. Two nights ago it was Ma Hughes and Ma Georges, and last week Mr. Lamber. Who knows, maybe it is the same person. It's not impossible!" she said. "If they're stealing our chicken, maybe next time they will enter our house. Maybe we should get a dog!" she cried out in exasperation.

———————

That was where it stood until this morning. As Mr. Philip lay back in bed, a million thoughts went through his mind. He thought of trying to entrap the person. He thought of trying to do away with the chickens. He even thought seriously of entertaining his wife's suggestions from a few days back—getting a dog. But would a dog be of any use now? What he needed was a full-grown dog, not a puppy. He would have to train an old dog to guard his yard the way he wanted and he didn't see this happening. That was not something he could consider. He prayed for morning to come so that he could see what had happened. He was not going to go out there at this time of night.

Mr. Philip was up at the crack of dawn. So, too, was his wife. She made some coffee that they shared between them. Then Mr. Philip went out, not sure what to expect. Three of the birds were in the yard. He stiffened. What had happened now? He looked into the chicken house and saw the gaping hole where another bird was trying to jump through. His patchwork had not held. There and then Mr. Philip made a vow. He was going to catch that thief. He had had enough. He was not going to get the police involved again. It was he and the thief or thieves from now on.

"Philip, you alone cannot catch the thief. Leave that for the police," his wife urged him, as he stormed back into the house, vowing to carry out his threat.

"But so long I made a report they have not done anything! All they do is sit in there and play domino all day and night and have a nice time. I am sure there are people out there who know who's doing that but they don't give a damn. Now is my turn."

Nurse Cecilia was about to say something to Philip but she changed her mind. She, too, was a bit infuriated with what was happening. After a while she broke out. "So what they see with us? It seems like all of a sudden somebody has a taste for eating our chicken! So why don't they go somewhere else. Well ... I shouldn't say that, but you know what I mean," she said, feeling guilty for wishing ill unto others.

"This must be the second coming of Mally," Mr. Philip said. "I hope I don't have to end up doing to that person what they did to Mally," he offered.

"You think that was really true? I heard that somewhere but I cannot believe that really happened. It sounds too much like a Brer Anancy story," his wife said.

"I don't know. Some people say is a joke, some say it really happened and some people say it wasn't the chicken that killed him, but there was something else wrong with him."

There is the story in the village that there was a notorious thief who went about stealing people's roosters and while everyone was asleep he would be awake, cooking up a *mess*. It is said that he was so brazen that he usually told the people to their faces that he was coming to steal their chicken and those who didn't believe he could, believed when they got up the next morning to find the roosters missing. People were scared of him because he was supposedly a violent character. It had gotten so bad that some people had begun setting traps in order to snare him, but that did not work. But what worked, as the story goes, was that after he threatened a man that he was going to steal his prize bird, the man went in search of a bed bug. He slit the chicken, and like a surgeon, implanted the bug into the meat of the chicken. Just as he had said, the thief stole the man's rooster and cooked it, unaware that it was set up for him. Three days later, he died. But no one has been able to verify this story to this day.

As he pondered on what had to happen, Mr. Philip planned his next move. He was going to booby trap his chicken house and attempt to stay up during the night to see who it is who had been robbing him. But Nurse Cecilia was getting worried. Her husband was consumed with trying to save his chickens, while, at the same time, he was destroying his own life. She had to do something.

"Philip, you are losing your head. Don't do that to yourself. You could get yourself hurt, maybe even killed and for what? Why all that for a few lousy chickens? Please leave those animals alone. Only animals can act that way. This person is sick. Society is sick. Nobody respects what is not his or hers anymore. Look at us. We shouldn't have to be going through this at our age," she moaned.

Mr. Philip listened as his wife spoke and anger boiled within him. He was a man who was very slow to anger and even when he was very hurt, he hardly raised a finger. That was one of his strong points as a school principal. But today, he was angry. He sat on the step that led into the house, his hands under his chin, contemplating his next move.

Not too long after, one of Mr. Phillip's friends, a fellow by the name of Pasco, dropped by to say hello. Pasco was very unsteady on his feet that early in the morning, suggesting that he had either awakened drunk, or that he had already had his fill for the day. Pasco was a heavy drinker and on many occasions he took in more than his body could control. Pasco's real name was William Pascal and he and Mr. Phillip were old classmates and buddies. But while Mr. Phillip had gone on to do well, things did not go the same way for Pasco. His love for the bottle caused his downfall and the subsequent separation from his wife. He was unemployed and did not seem too concerned about getting a decent job. He did the odd jobs for villagers whenever they needed someone to help them. He had become a "slave" to the bottle and his whole life seemed to revolve around it.

"So what you doin' sittin' dere on de step all by yourself that early, man?" he asked Mr. Phillip.

"And what are you doing drunk so early this morning?" Mr. Phillip countered.

Pasco smiled. "You don't answer a question with another question, Teach. You look like someting botherin' you. I jus' come from de bayside so I say let me stop by you a little. I take de smell of de coffee so obviously I stop," he said as he sat down on the step next to Mr. Phillip. "Nurse, morning, oui," he shouted, hoping that Nurse Cecilia would hear him from inside.

"Morning, Pasco. I hear you oui, papa! Look like we in business early this morning eh," she answered, as she came to the door.

"Not really, nurse. I jus' come and see de mister and get some of your hot coffee. You know you make de best coffee I ever drink in all of Senjo," he answered rather flatteringly.

Nurse Cecilia prepared him a cup of hot black coffee. Pasco sat down and sipped it bit after bit, slowly savoring each sip. "Nurse, dat is real coffee, you know! Not de fing dey hav' sellin' in de store dey call instant coffee. Humm! Dat always remind me of my father; God bless his soul. Dat man use to make some good coffee! Oh, yes! You could smell it from here to Coubarie. Thanks, Nurse, and you too, Mr. Phillip, before you get jealous," he said. He laughed a bit, spilling some of the hot coffee unto his pants. When he was through drinking the coffee, he turned to Mr. Phillip again and asked, "So what is really wrong, Teach? You don't look yourself all de time I dere with you."

"Do you really want to know? Maybe you would not believe what I am going to say, but is true," Mr. Phillip said.

"What? De madam threaten to leave you like mine do me? But your madam love you too much and again you too old for dat," said Pasco, a mischievous smile on his face.

"That's not it, man. Somebody's been stealing my roosters and it's not the first time," answered Mr. Phillip, a tone of disdain in his voice.

"You talkin' joke, man; dat cannot be!" answered Pasco, rather shocked at what Mr. Phillip had told him. "You of all people, Teach. Oh no!' cried Pasco.

"Is no joke, Pasco," replied Mr. Philip. "I even go to the police already, but the person is not satisfied. Come with me let me show you what they did last night." They climbed down the steps and walked towards the back of the chicken house and Mr. Philip showed Pasco where the thief had entered.

Whether he was sober enough to comprehend what was going on did not seem to show on Pasco's face. He looked at what had happened and shook his head. Then he spoke. "You know something, Teach! I have an idea. I think I know about de stealin' chicken business, but I don't know if yours is part of it."

"What? You heard something or you see something about them?" asked Mr. Philip.

"I don't know who it is, but I hear somethin' de other day about some guy who was up all night cooking a *mess* while everybody was sleepin'. It sound kine of funny, but who know? Doh say is me, but is dat I hear, Teach. I even hear de police checkin' on him."

The two men walked back to the steps and talked about the situation and a few other topics of gossip until Pasco decided that it was time for him to leave. "Got to go, Teach. Got some business to take care of. Know what I mean, eh. But jus' leave it to me. I will see if I get some information for you. Tell Nurse I go, eh," he said and made his exit from the yard.

Mr. Phillip watched as his friend made his way out unto the street, making every conceivable effort not to appear drunk. Mr. Phillip shook his head in amazement. "What a life!" he said aloud, as Pasco disappeared around the corner and headed down the road heading quite possibly to Coubarie and to one or two of the "speak-easies" over there; undoubtedly, to get a *shoot* of his favorite beverage—Macoucherie Rum.

It was almost a week before Easter, in fact the Saturday before Palm Sunday, and nothing had happened since the early morning visit of Pasco. No more chickens had disappeared or had been stolen, and the police had told Mr. Philip that they had no clue as to who had stolen his chickens because no one would talk. Life had continued its normal course till now and he was relieved. He was out in the late hours of the afternoon tending to the chickens while his wife sat on the step, now and then dozing off, when Pasco stopped by.

"Hi, Teach. How we doin' today? Hello nurse," he said as he took a seat on an old bench in the yard, his breath reeking of alcohol. "So what's new, Teach?" he asked Mr. Phillip.

"You have all, Pasco. You have all. I am trying to help myself and they are destroying me. What else can I say?" Mr. Philip replied, a smile on his face. "Not a damn thing happening, man."

"Sssh," whispered Pasco. "I hav' some news for you. I hav' a suspicious individual in mind and dat is de same individual I was thinkin' of when I tell you about what I hear."

"Since when you use such big words? You had a little extra *nannie* this morning?" asked Mr. Phillip. Nurse Philip laughed aloud.

"If you want to say dat, Teach. If you want to call it so ..." he paused. "I extricated some information for you," he continued. Mr. Phillip laughed.

"So what do you have?" he asked Pasco, rather humorously.

"So you doh hear dat?" Pasco asked him.

"Hear what?" Nurse Philip asked.

"I thinkin' allyou was pullin' my foot. But in all seriousness, Teach. Dey say some people was chasin' a fella las' night. Dey say he clime de *zaboca* tree in Ma Leanne yard where her fowls and dem does sleep and a branch break with him. It seem he was goin' an' steal Ma Leanne rooster too," Pasco told them. He continued, "Den people begin to chase him until he *sharpè* in de darkness. Some people say dey know who he is even though he was dress all in black. Now dey have de police checkin' it out. De police say dey hav' to ... what you call it? Inves ... invest ..."

"Investigate," Mr. Phillip helped him.

"Ya, dat's it, Teach. Dey say dey hav' to invesgate de situation before dey can arres' him."

"But who is him?" asked Mr. Phillip. "You just keep saying him, him, him. Does *him* have a name?" he asked Pasco.

"Ummm ... I think they call him *Mal*," answered Pasco, a frown appearing on his face.

"Are you sure what you're saying is true?" asked Mr. Phillip.

"Is dat I hear but I not sure," replied Pasco. "I jus' de messenger, Teach. But I will jus' keep my ear open. But one fing! If I was you, I would keep my eyes wide open as Easter comin' because you know dose guys ..." he paused a while, making sure he said the correct words, "You know dem already, Teach. You know what I mean," he continued, as he winked at Teach. Once again, like he always did, he made his way out the yard on unsteady legs; legs that were getting weaker as he progressed in age.

"What you think?" Nurse asked her husband.

"About what?" he answered.

"About the story he just told you. You know, I don't trust him too much with those stories. It sounds like he is making them up. Something tells me it's not true," Nurse replied. "How comes we didn't hear anything. Maybe he is beginning to hallucinate. The rum must be getting into his brains," she laughed.

"Well, I don't know. I don't even know what to think of him those days," Mr. Philip confessed.

Mr. Phillip became a bit more concerned after Pasco's warning. He considered laying in wait for the thief under the cover of darkness.

"How can you think of doing something like that?" his wife exclaimed. "You're letting this thing get to your head, Phillip. How can you do something like that?" she asked again. "You think you can catch anyone."

"How are you sure I cannot do it? All I want to do is see the person's face so I can go to the police," he answered.

"You know, we're too old for all that problem. If is trouble, let us sell all those fowls and let the person give somebody else the trouble. I don't want to get no heart attack or have my pressure go up for no old fowls. Let us sell them or give them to somebody, Phillip," she pleaded.

But Mr. Phillip was not prepared to lay back and roll over to any thief. "You mean after all those years, I am going to let them do what they want with me? No! No! Tonight, in rain or no rain, I am going to wait outside. I am going to buy some batteries for my flashlight so when the person comes I will shine the bright light in the person's face," he said adamantly.

However, commonsense prevailed over his machoness and instead of laying in wait outside, Mr. Phillip decided, upon the urgings of Nurse Cecilia, to sit at the window and keep an eye on his chicken house. For five consecutive nights, starting at ten o'clock or thereabout, he sat at the slightly opened window, his eyes peeled on the chicken house; his ears tuned for any sound. In the meantime, his wife slept, unmoved by what was going on. After the fifth night, and after beginning to feel the effects of not going to bed on time, Mr. Phillip decided to give up his all night vigils. The odds were not in his favor. Every now and then he dozed off and he would awake with a start to see if he had given a window of opportunity to that thief, but nothing had happened.

"But I tell you, you wasting your time, Phillip; just let us give it up," his wife pleaded with him again. "We have no right to make ourselves slaves to this thief," she exclaimed. Mr. Philip said nothing in defense of his actions.

It was the Saturday of Holy Week and the Easter Vigil Service was to be held at eight o'clock that night. The village was predominantly Catholic and a large number of villagers usually participated in the Easter celebrations. Mr. Phillip and Nurse Cecilia were no exception. However Mr. Phillip was worried. He had to make the decision to stay put and protect his birds from the thief, and deciding to go to church. However, he had an obligation to the community because he served as an usher at church. Nurse, on the other hand, was a lector. They were quite involved and they hardly ever missed going to any sort of church service. Tonight shouldn't be any different.

But Mr. Phillip could not bring himself to telling his wife what his fears were. All throughout the day, he counted and double counted the number of roosters and hens that he had. He made sure that the latch was secure; he checked the wires to make sure that there were no areas of escape for the birds. He even wrote the number of chickens that he had on a piece of paper and placed it on the table in the dining room. Finally, there was nothing else to check, but he still was not sure if all was well.

As he walked to the church service with Nurse, his mind was on that chicken house. Somehow, Pasco's warning had come home to roost. He even, for a while, wondered if his dear friend Pasco was not involved in the whole scheme, but he brushed that aside. He doubted Pasco had the heart to do something like this to him.

The church service seemed like an eternity to him and he was pleased when the priest gave the final blessings. He could not wait to get back home. He tried as much throughout the night to disguise his emotions and feelings, but deep down he was on edge and kept wondering whether his chickens were not part of someone's Easter meal. The usually relaxed, unperturbed and calm Mr. Phillip was not himself tonight and the good old nurse had noticed that.

"But Phillip, why you acting so funny? Something tells me your mind on that chicken house. Lord, you going to stress yourself out!" she cried, as they made their way home.

"I okay, I okay," Phillip answered.

"No, sir! Not true. Believe me. I know. And it's all about some lousy fowls. This is it, Philip. I think so. I think I am losing you," she said, as she hastened her pace.

As soon as he got home, Phillip went to a cupboard drawer in the kitchen and got his flashlight. He went back out, and headed straight to the chicken house. It was strangely quiet and Phillip was startled as something moved infront of him in the dark. He stopped cold. He swept the light and two bright eyes glared back at him. He stood upright and realized that it was a cat. He was sure it wasn't the one stealing his roosters. He gathered himself, moved on and shone the light of the torch into the chicken house. Some of the hens cackled and jumped down from their perches, looking rather disoriented. Mr. Phillip checked the latch on the door. He stiffened. The latch had been snapped right off.

"That son of a bitch! God forgive me," he cried, almost immediately. He checked the chickens. The rooster with the black and white tail was missing. He slammed the door of the chicken house, causing pandemonium. Mr. Phillip was raging mad. He tried to restrain himself; tried to behave in a manner to dignify the religious season, but it was difficult. He blurted out a few curse words.

Nurse Cecilia came out when she heard the commotion. She looked on as Mr. Philip paced about. When he finally stopped she spoke calmly to him. "Phillip, this is Easter! You just come from church. You forget yourself? Today you make confession. Hear you now. What is wrong with you? You're allowing Satan to get into your head."

Mr. Phillip slammed the flashlight to the ground, destroying it in the process. "You're right! Yes, you're right Cecil. I think I had enough. I am going to give this up. I too old for the trouble it's bringing me," he cried in resignation.

"And me too!" Nurse added.

As they stood together in the yard pondering the future of the chickens and the chicken house, they heard a commotion coming from the street. Nurse made her way to the front gate of the house to find out what the commotion was all about at this time of the night. Just as she did, a breathless Pasco walked up to her.

"Nurse, where Teach, where Teacher Phillip?" he asked, gasping for breath.

"What you want Teach for?" Nurse Cecilia snapped.

"You hear all dat noise? Teacher lose any chicken tonight?" Pasco asked, his eyes bulging from his head.

"Yes, he lost the rooster with the black and white tail," she replied. "But I don't think you want to talk to him now Pasco," she warned. "He is not in the best of moods now. The thief came back again," she added.

"Well, maybe is it de police have in de bag," offered Pasco.

"You not serious, Pasco. Is joke you making," said Nurse Cecilia, quite surprised by the news.

"Cross my heart, Nurse; cross my heart. Dey say de police get a *sipsyon* dat Mal was de one dat stealin' people fing. So tonight dey was walkin' on Back Street and when de officer see Mal he aks him what he had in de bag and he just start runnin'. He drop de bag an' it begin jumpin' an' de officer an' his pardner chase Mal all in people yard until dey ketch him hidin' under Ma Sylvian house an' dey put him in handcuff."

Mr. Phillip heard Pasco talking to his wife so he joined them. He stood spellbound as Pasco related his story. He did not say a word, as he watched the spectacle that was developing on the street. The crowd laughed and mocked the young man who was being held by the waist of his pants by a young officer.

166

"Teach, you have to go an' identi...amm...identify your belonging at de station because de police have to keep it as evidence. Officer, Officer!" Pasco broke off, as a second officer followed behind, holding the bag that the young man allegedly used in the robberies. "Dat rooster is Mr. Phillip rooster, you know. He jus' lose his rooster and I sure is it dat in de bag."

"We know, we know. Teach has already made a report, so we know," the officer answered.

"Oh, you guys good, you guys on de money, officer," Pasco chuckled.

"But what do you have to do with this anyhow? How comes you are the one talking?" the officer asked Pasco. "I know Teach. He can talk for himself. Did you have one too many tonight, Pasco?" the officer mockingly asked Pasco.

"Well we is friends ... school buddies, and he kind of ... you know what I mean officer," Pasco retorted. Some of the onlookers laughed.

"By the way, Teach, we will need you to come and identify the rooster that's in the bag so we can make a case against this guy," the officer continued.

"You no need no case officer. Jus' tell de magistrate to sen' him to Stock Farm for a few years, dat's all," Pasco said, offering some legal advice. The officer looked at him and smiled.

"Okay, officer. I will come over in a while," said Mr. Phillip after Pasco had said his bit. He looked at Nurse Cecilia and she just shook her head without muttering a single word. After a while she spoke up.

"I am not coming, non. I am going to sleep. You alone can go if you want, or take Pasco with you," she told him. "I had enough already," she added.

"I guess I don't have to worry about losing any more chickens for a while," Mr. Phillip said, somewhat apprehensively though, a smile of relief on his face. "Just like Pasco say, they should just send him to Stock Farm tonight," he muttered.

Nurse looked on and said nothing. A number of thoughts flashed through her mind. She sighed deeply. She shook her head slowly from side to side. She looked at Mr. Philip and neither said anything. Nurse turned away and made her way towards the front door and up the steps into the house while Mr. Phillip walked out the gate and followed behind the crowd towards the Police station. Along with him, stride for stride, was his buddy Pasco, a broad, mischievous smile on his face.

The Pilgrim

"Wake up boy, wake up!"

Jason thought it was a dream. He rolled over and heard the voice again as the imposing figure of his mother stood over him.

"Wake up boy, wake up!" he heard again. At that same moment he heard the sound of the old alarm clock resound through the room until his father banged his hand on the knob at the top of the old contraption, stifling its sound.

It seemed quite earlier than usual. His brothers and sisters were all snuggled together among the bedding on the floor in the two-bedroom frame house. He wondered why he was the only one who was up or being awakened from bed. "What happen?" he asked his mother, somewhat incoherently.

"What happen what?" his mother snapped back. "Just wake up. We goin' on a pilgrimage," she replied.

Jason sat up and yawned lazily. He had never been on a pilgrimage before. His mother had gone to many of them before, usually with members of her church group, but she had never taken him or any of his siblings along with her. "We goin' to La Plaine. Get up and put your clothes on you. I put them on the hanger above the door in the drawing room."

Jason, his parents and his four siblings lived in the village of St. Joseph. His mother was a member of the St. Joseph Social League of Catholic Women. She was a very devout member of her church and attended Sunday mass regularly. She was also present the remainder of the week at the five o'clock morning service. She was also helpful in decorating the church on Saturday evenings in preparation for service on Sunday mornings. His father, on the other hand, was quite a different individual. Nothing about church related to him. He was one of those who believed that church and religion was a woman's thing. But ironically, he made sure that all his children attended church on Sunday. There was no excuse for anyone to stay home. His Sundays were spent playing dominoes with his friends under the mango tree in Mr. John's backyard or sitting under the flamboyant tree next to the Catholic Church, watching a game of cricket or soccer on the village playing field.

He said nothing as Jason and his mother got ready for the trip to La Plaine. He got up and walked to the kitchen. There, he poured some hot water from the thermos flask into a large enamel cup and added about four teaspoons of ground coffee. He then added some Nestlé condensed milk and two teaspoons of brown cane sugar. He then stirred them all together with a large tablespoon. He then poured the coffee into three smaller cups: one for him, one for Jason, and one for his wife. He placed theirs on the table and went to the dining room where he sat at an opened window and slowly sipped the coffee.

"You ready, boy?" Jason's mother asked as she sipped the last bit of coffee and placed the empty cup on the table. "You drink your coffee?" she asked.

"Yes ma, I ready. I drink de coffee already," Jason answered.

"Come on, let's go before they go without us! Come on! Outside!" she said.

She went to the door and turned the wooden bar that kept the door shut. It was still very dark outside. The streetlights were few and far apart and in the area where they lived, the inhabitants were not lucky enough to have such an amenity. She bid goodbye to her husband who grunted in reply. She and Jason stepped outside. The neighbor's dogs barked as they made their way between the houses that led to River Street. They moved quietly, trying to avoid making any noise to attract any more attention than they would need to at this time of the morning.

Jason's mother was dressed all in white and on her head, the large white hat, the one that she had bought at J.E. Nassief's store the last time he had accompanied her to Roseau. This was the first time she was wearing it to go on a pilgrimage. He had on a pair of black pants and a white shirt. They smelt of mothballs. The last time he had worn them was at the funeral of his grandmother (his father's mother), who had died about six months ago. For a while, he remembered the face of his grandmother as she lay in the coffin. He was scared to go close to her body but he finally summoned the courage and knelt beside her coffin. He shivered a bit as he remembered that day.

Jason and his mother made their way along the semi-dark street to Main Street where they were to meet with the other people going on the pilgrimage. Jason was scared but he said nothing. He somehow believed that his mother's presence would protect him from anything evil. He had heard so many stories about *jombies, soucouyans* and *la diabless* being out in the early morning, sometimes blocking the way and preventing people from going about their business. But he said nothing to his mother.

As they walked down the street, the sounds of the early morning were everywhere. Dogs barked as they saw them or heard their footsteps. Mr. Shalto's donkey brayed noisily and all about the village roosters were answering each other with their noisy crows. They passed Mr. Samuel's bakery. There was activity in there as Ma Bonnie was preparing the oven to make her first batch of bread of the morning. For a while, Jason imagined the smell of the hot loaves. He wouldn't be there this morning to buy bread.

Every morning, at seven o'clock, he would be sent to the bakery to buy two dollars worth of bread for breakfast. Almost every time, Ma Bonnie would add an extra loaf, just for him, and he would munch on that loaf on his way home. He would take his good old time and enjoy the bread as he walked home. He was going to miss that loaf today.

As they passed the bakery, he saw a figure standing against a telephone pole about fifty feet ahead of them. His heart skipped a beat. His hair stood on edge. He felt a shiver go through his spine. Was it what he believed? Why would anyone be standing out there at this time of the morning? He heard his mother mutter something under her breath, but he did not hear clearly what she said. He didn't have to worry too much because just as they got closer, the shadowy figure moved furtively away and disappeared between the houses. His mother muttered something again. Jason wondered whether it was a *lougarou* or a *la diabless* that was trying to do something to them. He moved closer to his mother.

A few minutes later they arrived at Main Street and met the group of people standing together next to Ma George's shop. Some of them greeted his mother and one of the ladies, Ma Mabel, who seemed to be the one in charge, informed her that they were waiting for the truck driver to show up.

"You think he forget?" his mother asked Ma Mabel.

"No, I doh think so. I speak to him las' night an' he say he comin'. Maybe he sleep a little too much. You know dose man already. Saturday night dey up all night." His mother nodded her head in agreement.

Jason realized that most of the ladies, including his mother, were members of the Social League. There was also a handful of men, among them Rushing. Jason wondered why Rushing would be here. He was not a churchgoer, although his mother was a member of the League.

Rushing's real name was Rushford Paul. He was a very popular young man in the village, but he was always accused of hanging out with the wrong crowds or displaying that "bad boy" mentality. A few months ago, there was a shooting over a woman at a dance in the community hall. One of his friends was alleged to have wounded another with a gunshot to the leg. The gun used in the crime was never found. Rushing was accused of disposing of the evidence. He was arrested and then released on bail. His case was due to be heard at the High Court in Roseau in a few months.

Jason thought that Rushing was on this trip simply because of that incident. He wondered for a while whether the pilgrimage he was going on was for Rushing. He was convinced that this was the reason. Why else would he be here? He felt cheated. He should be in his bed, not here for this guy. He believed his mother had deceived him. His thoughts were interrupted as the box truck that would take them to La Plaine came around the corner and pulled over to the side of the road next to where they were all gathered. One by one they climbed in and took a seat. Jason tried to take an end seat but his mother would have none of it.

"No! Mr. Jason! You not sittin' at no end. Come over here," she commanded as she pointed to a space next to where she sat. Jason grudgingly complied.

Ma Mabel inquired whether everyone was aboard. Someone made a quick head count and realized that Ma Scot was missing.

"Dat lady always late," one of the ladies said.

"Doh say dat," replied an older woman who was rolling a rosary in her hand. "If it was you, you would be happy we waitin' for you."

"Is true, is true," another lady said, in defense of Ma Scot.

Ma Mabel spoke to the truck driver, Chance, and asked him to hang on for a while until Ma Scot came. If she did not show up in five minutes, they would leave. They did not have to wait too long. Two minutes later, Ma Scot came rushing around the corner. In her hands, she held a bouquet of white lilies and a large leather bag. Along with her were her two daughters, Theresa and Marissa.

"Sorry everybody, I had a little problem with de mistah as always," Ma Scot said as she made her way into her seat. Everybody understood, even Jason.

"Where you get dat nice bouquet?" asked Ma Mabel. "It nice oui!"

"Oh, Marissa buy it in market yesterday. Is for me to put in front of de Blessed Virgin when we get in de church," Ma Scot answered.

Ma Scot's husband was a Catholic who had converted to the Adventist faith. He and his wife had squabbled quite a bit because he wanted all members of his family to become Adventists, but Ma Scot and the children had held fast and that did not go well with Mr. Scot. At times he berated his wife in public about her "devilish" works and practices and blamed her for the fact that they were not a united family going to church together on Saturdays like some other Adventist families did. But Ma Scot remained steadfast to her faith and beliefs.

"Somebody hav' de time?" Ma Mabel asked. "Is time we go; who miss us is their fault."

"Four o'clock," answered Rushing. Some of the women looked back, a bit surprised when they heard his voice. Jason smirked a bit. His mother nudged him and gave him the eye.

They were on their way as the truck slowly made its way through the village. Some of the women, including his mother, crossed themselves with the sign of the cross as they passed the village church whose giant form loomed in the darkness. Jason always wondered why people crossed themselves when they passed the church building. He wondered if they really felt blessed when they did that or whether they were convinced that the sign protected them from harm. Rather belatedly, he hurriedly crossed himself too.

Within a few minutes they were snaking their way up the Layou Valley along the Transinsular road that hugged the Layou River. It got much cooler as they proceeded farther into the heart of the island and the strong breeze that whipped through the open truck did not help either. Some of the ladies seemed to have expected the cold conditions: they were wearing sweaters. A woman who was seated at the front started to pray and the rest of the group joined in spontaneously. She repeated phrases and the group answered. Then they would stop and Ma Scott would start with another prayer.

Jason listened, a bit sleepy though, and although his mother nudged him every now and then, he just listened without saying a word. The women continued praying. They would start loudly but by the end of the prayer, their voices would fade a bit:

Hail Mary, Full of Grace
The Lord is with thee
Blessed art thou amongst women
And blessed is the fruit of thy womb Jesus.

172

Holy Mary mother of God,
Pray for us sinners
Now, and at the hour of our death
Amen.

They repeated the prayer, it seemed, forever. Then Ma Mabel started singing the *Ave Maria*.

Jason had to catch himself from giggling when Ma Mabel seemed to have started at too high a note. She choked on the song and his mother picked up from where Ma Mabel stopped. He could hardly remember when he last heard his mother sing. He looked at her somewhat amused, but she was not. She pinched him on his legs and he knew what that meant.

After they had traveled for almost half an hour, it started to rain. The ladies undid the rolled side curtains of the truck. The curtains flapped noisily against the side of the truck as the wind whipped them about. It was a heavy downpour and it only helped to make the outside darker. The truck driver slowly maneuvered his vehicle along the flooded roads, his wipers hardly able to keep up with the volume of water. The praying and chanting became louder as if the women were imploring the Lord to help them through the downpour.

Through all this Rushing was almost quiet. He simply mumbled the prayers and hummed the songs that the ladies sang. It almost looked like he felt out of place among the pilgrims, but if their prayers were going to help him, he did not mind. He sat with his face buried in his hands and every now and then he rubbed his hands over his face. Maybe he, too, was sleepy.

The truck became a chapel on wheels. The women were not allowing anything to deter them. The constant repeating of the Lord's Prayer and Hail Mary's and some other prayers that Jason had not heard before, began to sound monotonous. He asked himself again why his mother had taken him along. This was no fun. He could not appreciate the outside because it was still dark. Besides, the curtains made them prisoners of themselves.

The drone of the truck as it climbed hill after hill along the island's rugged terrain drowned the prayers and songs of the pilgrims, but it did not matter. Jason began to understand the reason for Rushing's presence when Rushing's mother began to mention his name in her prayers. She and another woman even turned back and laid their hands over him as they prayed. The whole spectacle was beginning to get amusing to Jason. He giggled to himself.

"So that's it, eh," he said to himself. "He do what he do an' now dey praying for him an' makin' pilgrimage for him." Jason felt betrayed by his mother. "Why she bring me along to help pray for dat guy?" He cut short thinking of anything unpleasant about Rushing as the truck hit a bump that sent a shock through his spine.

"Ouch," he said softly.

He was not a fan of Rushing. He remembered the day that Rushing spat in his face. He never told his mother about it, fearing he would have been punished for having been where he was when he had the confrontation with Rushing. He wondered if he should tell her about it now and embarrass Rushing in the presence of everybody. He had felt humiliated then when Rushing had done the act and dared him to do anything about it. Maybe now he should humiliate him too. Quietly, he felt happy that Rushing was in the predicament that he was in; maybe the hand of God had turned on him.

They had traveled now for almost an hour and dawn was slowly approaching. The light of day slowly began to emerge as they drew closer to the East. This was his first trip to this part of the island and he was unaware of the villages they passed until every now and then someone uttered a word or two that hinted where they were.

As the light outside grew brighter, some of the ladies, aided by Rushing, wrapped the flapping curtains. The rain had stopped for a while now, but because they shivered from the cool mountain breezes the women had asked that the curtains be left down until now. Jason could see the rays of the early morning sun shining atop the very tall trees helping to brighten up the morning.

The ladies had grown quiet now and many of them, including his mother, were rolling beads of their rosaries between their fingers and whispering softly to themselves. The truck rounded a bend and in the distance before him Jason saw the white caps of the Atlantic Ocean. He smelt the salt and freshness and saw the windswept almond and coconut trees standing along the rocky ledges of the cliffs below. He had heard of it so many times, but this was his first view of the Atlantic. He heard the roar as the waves continually crashed toward the shore and splashed against the giant rocks.

The sun was up now and its rays bathed the side of the truck. This was the same way it looked when the sun set on the western side, but there was a different feel. The sun was coming up instead of going down. Just as they neared the village, the truck slowed down and the driver pulled to the side of the road. As if on cue, Ma Mabel began to pray again. "Brothers and sisters, let us thank God for a safe trip today.

Let us thank him for every thing. We ask God to help our brother as he face his troubles an' hope everything will be okay for him. Yes, Lord."

"Amen," they all responded. But Jason said nothing. He realized that his suspicions were true about Rushing.

Ma Mabel continued. "An' we pray for our family, Lord. I pray for my husband an' for all our husbands, open their eyes; open de eyes of all men, Lord," she pleaded.

"Yes, Lord. Yes!" the other ladies answered.

Ma Mabel paused and then calmly said, "Let us bow our heads an' pray." Together they recited the Lord's Prayer. Jason, surprisingly, joined in, his head bent low and every now and then stumbling to say the correct words.

When the women and men had finished praying, the driver got back unto the main road. After having traveled for almost twenty-five feet, he turned right unto a secondary road and drove up the hill that led towards what Jason believed was the village of La Plaine. The truck wound its way slowly along the bumpy, unpaved road and drove up towards the village. A few minutes later, it stopped next to what looked from the outside to be the village church. Again the women crossed themselves with the sign of the cross, confirming Jason's suspicions.

Jason was in awe. He couldn't believe the location of the church. It was close to homes. Banana, coconut and breadfruit trees surrounded it. It was different in his village, where the church was apart from the main village. All around the church were flower plants. As he gazed about he heard the peal of the church bells beckoning the faithful to come to worship. He disembarked from the truck, stretched, yawned and almost tumbled over. His mother slapped him over his left arm and admonished him. "Why everywhere you go you showin' your bad manners, boy? You cannot close your mouth as you yawnin'. A fly should go in it, aksing God pardon," she said, as she fixed her large-brimmed white hat over her head.

"But I tired, ma. My leg cramp, oui," he answered.

"Aks God to uncramp it when you go in church," his mother playfully said to him.

Rushing was close by and Jason's mother's comments amused him. He smiled. Jason glared at him and felt like answering him but he somehow could not muster the courage to do so. Again Rushing had won.

The pilgrims, some with bags in their hands, others with bouquets of various kinds, began to file into an almost empty church. An old man was going about lighting the candles around the altar and an organist was practicing a few tunes. Rays of sunlight sipped in through some of the open windows. Jason's mother tugged at his shoulder and motioned for him to follow her. She stopped before a statue of the Blessed Virgin and started praying in whispering tones. Jason stood silently, saying nothing but wondering to himself what was going on.

His mother placed a few coins into a coin box and lit a candle that she had taken from her bag. She gave him a few pennies and a candle and asked him to do the same. She then knelt before the statue and opened her hands in supplication. Jason felt embarrassed. *Why she doin' dat?* he thought quietly.

His mother then made the sign of the cross. She stood up, kissing her thumb as she did so. Jason smiled. Ma Scot and her daughters then joined them. Ma Scot placed the bouquet of lilies that she had brought along at the foot of the statue of the Blessed Virgin. She and her daughters knelt down, and with her arms wide opened, Ma Scott began to pray. Jason watched intently. He looked at his mother, but she did not look at him. He turned his face and smiled.

Jason wondered what were the other people thinking of his mother and Ma Scot, but a quick glance around the church did nothing to help his concerns. Almost every one of his fellow pilgrims was kneeling or praying at a Station of The Cross or kneeling before the altar, their hands opened wide in supplication. Rushing was standing before the altar with his mother and Ma Mable. The ladies had their hands over his shoulder and seemed to be praying over him. "They would never do that at home," Jason said to himself. *Did they have to come all the way up here to ask God to forgive him?* he pondered.

His thoughts were interrupted again as his mother pulled him along and led him to a seat in the fifth row of pews, next to Ma Sambo. By that time the church was almost filled with worshippers. More people were filing in slowly and taking their seats in the pews. It felt so different in this church than in the church in St. Joseph. There was an air of piety, calmness, and in the background, the distant rumbling of the Atlantic Ocean. He could not help but gaze about the church building, looking at the way people of a different village behaved. He felt the calm and the peace, too, and for a while he stopped worrying about his fellow pilgrims all clad in white sitting in the front pews and also about Rushing who was sitting somewhere else.

The officiating priest was a man of very slim stature, short and gray-haired. He looked very frail. He was assisted by two adults who acted as servers. Jason was accustomed to seeing young kids serve as altar servers, not older people. He was even approached by his pastor to serve as an acolyte but he felt he was not ready to take up this responsibility, even if his mother had tried to encourage him to do so. He did not feel he would be able to get out of bed to go to church in the early mornings. There was nothing better than being in bed, especially if it were raining!

At the commencement of the service, the priest, speaking with a French accent, welcomed the pilgrims to La Plaine and asked them to return again and told them how nice it was to have them celebrate Mass with his congregation. Jason smiled. "If only the priest knew why they were here," he thought. Some of his fellow pilgrims smiled while others seemed embarrassed as the priest made mention of their presence, but what difference did it make, anyway? They were all noticeable with their white dresses and hats all flocked together up in the front rows. "*Why white anyway?*" thought Jason. "Was there something special about wearing white clothes at a pilgrimage?" he wondered. "So why was he dressed in black and white just like Rushing was? "Were the men supposed to dress differently?" he asked himself.

Maybe his thoughts were very loud or his mother was reading his mind, but just as these thoughts flashed through his mind, she gave him that look. Jason knew she was ready for him.

"You better not say nothing!" she whispered. He looked at her, wide-eyed, but she did not budge an eyelid.

Seventy-five minutes after it had started, the church service was over. The small choir seemed louder than it had been all throughout the mass as they sang the recessional hymn, *To God Be the Glory*. Jason's mother and her fellow pilgrims joined in, some of them shaking their heads from side to side. Jason just watched in bewilderment. "What happen to dose people?" he thought. "Where dey think dey be?" he asked himself.

As the congregation filed out, following the priest and his altar servers, he kept gazing around the church. It seemed so quaint. He felt a nudge as his mother tried to urge him out of the pew so that she and other pilgrims could get out. He stepped out and he felt another pull on his shoulder as his mother reminded him to genuflect before leaving the house of God. He obliged but he was not too happy about having to be scolded in the presence of the other people. Soon he was outside with the other congregants.

The sun was up and its brilliance shone all over the village. The white dresses of his fellow pilgrims and of the other churchgoers dazzled in the sunlight. His fellow pilgrims were about making acquaintances with the villagers. The priest was still out there shaking hands, too, and talking to all who wanted to express their greetings and best wishes.

Jason pulled away from the crowd and stood under a tall breadfruit tree across from the church. He did not want to be among all the hoopla and what he thought was "put on" and not real. From where he stood, he saw Rushing's mother approach the priest and shake his hand. She spoke to him and then they moved aside from the crowd. She pointed to Rushing and she called out his name. Rushing walked over to meet them.

What she tellin' de priest? Jason thought, and he smiled again. *Maybe she aksin' him to make a mass for Rushing. I wish de priest would say no,"* he prayed. Jason watched as the three of them moved away and headed to a small building next to the church surrounded by a variety of flowers: red and white roses, hibiscuses, lilies, and croutons. They were neatly laid out and looked beautiful in the sunlight. The area around the building was neat and well kept. A narrow concrete path led from the main road to the building. Jason realized that this was the presbytery. He had an idea what must be going on. He smiled. *You think I have to come all the way up here to pray for mistah?* he asked himself again. *An' why my mother bring me up all de way up here to see their macakwi?* he pondered. He did not believe that they could have done the same thing in his village because the village priest knew what Rushing had allegedly done.

Although concerned about these things, Jason was still happy to have taken the ride with his mother. Not too many children from his village had traveled that far. At least, this was something he could talk about at school tomorrow. This, even at the risk of having his classmates poke fun at him for having been with a group of old ladies on a pilgrimage. Maybe they would even think of his mother as one of those 'strange' ladies. But he did not think his mother was a strange lady. She was just a woman deeply rooted in her spiritual beliefs and he knew she was proud to profess her faith.

Most of the churchgoers had departed to their homes and the only people left on the church grounds were his fellow pilgrims, now congregated around the truck they had traveled on. Rushing and his mother returned from the presbytery. They were both smiling broadly, seemingly enjoying a joke. They joined the rest of the pilgrims.

"Everybody dere?" Ma Mabel asked after a while. No one answered. "Anybody missin'?" she added.

"Ma Sambo go with a lady. She say she comin' jus' now," Ma John answered.

"Okay," answered Ma Mabel. Surprisingly no one seemed worried. People had nothing bad to say about the petite lady. She was always cheerful and very nice to everyone. They knew she would be back soon.

"An' where Ma Philip?" someone else asked.

"Oh yes, where her?" they all asked in unison.

"She maybe beggin' somebody for their flower. Dat lady cannot go nowhere an' doh go an' get a piece of bush to plant in her yard. She maybe have flower from every part of Dominica," Ma Louisa said. "Everywhere she pas' she mus' to pick up something," Ma Louisa added.

Ma Louisa was Ma Philip's neighbor. She knew all about her love for plants. Ma Philip grew all types and even sometimes sold plants at the market. There were plants in every corner of her little yard both in the ground and in pots. She seemed to have a green thumb. Whatever she planted grew. And her love for plants transcended to what she did at church. Every Saturday afternoon she led a group of women in decorating the church for Sunday mass. Or if it were a feast time, like the feast of St. Gerard, she was there too. Ma Philip was the flower lady of the village.

"I hope she know we cannot stay too long. We hav' to stop somewhere for us to eat a little something," Ma Scot added.

Less than five minutes later and just like everyone had expected, here came Ma Philip carrying a bunch of plants in her hands. She had a broad smile on her face as she approached.

"Way papa," Jason's mother exclaimed as Ma Philip took her load to the back of the truck. "You bring for everybody, non?" she asked jokingly. Ma Philip looked at her and said nothing. The truck driver helped her secure her plants.

A few minutes later, Ma Sambo came walking down the road accompanied by an older lady. The ladies recognized her. She was the wife of Mr. George who was once the headteacher of the St. Joseph Government School. They had once lived in St. Joseph for almost five years. Ma George was also a teacher at the school.

"I wish I knew all you were coming to La Plaine," she said as she greeted everyone. "And I know this gentleman. I remember you," she said as she pointed to Rushing, who had an innocent child-like look on his face.

"Yes ma'am, I was in your class." Rushing answered.

"This is what I thought. What is your name again?" she asked.

"Rushford Paul" he answered, after a momentary pause.

"Yes, that is your mother. I remember you," she said as she smiled at Ma Paul. "And you, mister ..." she paused as she tried to remember the driver's name. "I used to travel with you to Roseau. You used to live up the river, isn't that so?" she asked.

"You got that right, Teach," Chance answered, a broad smile on his little round face. "Is me self."

"Well I'm really sorry I didn't know. Next time you are coming to La Plaine send to tell us. Anyway, I will not keep you too long," she said. "I know you have a long drive back. Say hello to all my people and have a safe trip back. Take care, eh," she said.

"Yes, Miss George, we will," Ma Mabel answered. "Tell de husband we say hello," she added.

"I will," Miss George answered. "Take care of everybody, eh Mr. Driver," she said to Chance, as she patted him on his back.

"I will, Teach," Chance answered. "They in safe hands," he boasted.

Jason stood quietly listening to the conversations between the adults, without saying a word. When Ma George turned her back and headed back home, he turned to his mother. "Who was dat lady, ma?"

"Why didn't you ask her yourself?" his mother answered.

"Because you tell me I not suppose to talk to strangers or ask older people questions," he answered.

"She not no stranger. She was in Senjo for five years. She an' her husband was teaching at de school. Her husband was the head teacher. You wasn' born yet," his mother replied. Jason shrugged his shoulders. It did not really matter to him.

One by one, the pilgrims re-boarded the truck and took their seats. Jason climbed in from the back and took an end seat. He wanted to have an unobstructed view as he headed back home. His mother tried to get him away from that seat but he pleaded his case until he got some of the ladies to get his mother to relent.

"Merci Bondyé!" someone said as the truck backed down the slight slope.

The driver swung around in the empty schoolyard and changed directions for the journey home. Everyone, including Rushing, seemed to be in a happy mood. Slowly, the truck eased down the hill towards the main road.

Jason turned to his mother. "Ma, I hungry," he said. His mother looked at him and said nothing, but he persisted. "Ma, my stomach hurting me," he whispered this time.

"Stop troubling me, boy. When we stop you will get something to eat. Why you so greedy, non? An' doh trouble me again," she said sternly.

He felt a bit embarrassed and looked around to make sure that no one had noticed the exchange between him and his mother. And as fate would have it, his eyes fell in line with Rushing's. They looked at each other and for a while neither of them said anything. Jason spoke first. "You remember you spit in my face," he blurted out at Rushing. "You remember de day up school?" He was startled by what he had said. He did not mean to say it but it seemed to have just slipped out.

For a moment Rushing said nothing. Then he answered. "What you talkin' about? What's wrong with you?" he snapped at Jason.

"You know what I talkin' about, doh do like you don't know!" Jason shouted back. "You playin' like you is a saint but you not no saint." Rushing glared at him but said nothing more. There was anger in his eyes.

By now everyone on the truck was shocked by what was going on. Jason's mother looked rather perplexed by what she had just heard. Rushing's mother looked horrified as she stared back, unable to say a word, her hand over her mouth.

"Yes, he spit in my face the other day because I see him take a mango from Ma Sylvia tray and I tell her he take de mango," Jason cried out, now assured that he was getting back at Rushing.

"I don't know what de boy talkin' about," Rushing answered, now visibly embarrassed by what had just transpired.

"You don't know! Aks Timothy for Ma Dorian. Is me an' him dat was together," Jason countered.

"Okay! Okay!" Ma Mabel interjected, taking charge of the situation. "Allyou, here is not de place for dat. Whether you spit in de child face or not, or whether you take Ma Sylvia mango, dat is not de time an' place for us to talk about it. We just come out from takin' communion and askin' God to help us. Allyou should talk about dat when allyou get back home."

"Is true. Is true," some of the ladies answered, nodding their heads in agreement.

"But how he can say things about me?" asked Rushing.

"Well, I don't know. I wasn' dere," replied Ma Mabel. "But somethin' happen between allyou. So Ma Paul an' Ma Mary allyou an' dose two boys should get dat thing straighten out. Allyou agree?" Both mothers shook their heads in agreement; both visibly upset and embarrassed. "When allyou get to Senjo allyou should speak with de boy for Ma Dorian an' clear up dis whole fing," Ma Mabel added.

"I agree with dat … is a good idea," answered Ma John.

"Is true, is true," some of the other ladies answered in unison, once again.

"Okay!" Rushing's mother replied, seemingly resigned to deal with the situation as it was. "Dat okay with me!"

"I too," added Jason's mother, looking extremely perturbed by what had transpired.

"Okay, let us bring dis fing to a end, "Ma Mabel said as she turned to look at Rushing and then Jason. "I not takin' no side here. All I want is for us to respec' each other. Allyou understand?" she said.

One after the other, Rushing and Jason and their mothers, nodded in agreement with Ma Mabel, who had taken full control of the situation and was commanding the attention of all aboard.

"Okay, den. Is up to allyou now," she ended.

Just as Ma Mabel was finished speaking, Ma Philip, who was sitting next to Rushing's mother, started singing:

"Peace is flowing like a river,
Flowing out to you and me,
Flowing out into the desert,
Setting all the captives free."

One by one, the pilgrims all joined in, singing and clapping as they wound their way up the winding East Coast Road. Rushing did not join in. He just kept shaking his head. This wasn't what he had expected today.

Jason looked out as the truck zipped past the windswept sea grape, almond and coconut trees one more time. The sound of the Atlantic, roaring against the cliffs below, was almost drowned out by the ladies' voices. Then all became silent. For a moment Jason wondered whether he had started more trouble than he could handle and he wondered what his mother would say about this situation when they got home. More importantly, he wondered whether he had ruined his chances of going out on another pilgrimage with his mother. He had surprisingly enjoyed this one until that incident. Tears dripped down his face and he wiped them away with the sleeve of his shirt. He shrugged his shoulder like he always did. Only time would tell for the young pilgrim.

A Father's Hope

It was the end of the school year. The University of Cambridge General Certificate Exams (the GCE's), were now completed. It was not yet time to worry about the results since they would not be back from England until some time in August. For a number of graduates, job-hunting was now the name of the game. Applications, interviews, wait and see what happens, became the order of the day. Most of these graduates needed time to relish the moment if that were possible or to begin to work their way into the job market. Others, on the other hand, hoped that the results would make it possible for them to enter the Sixth Form College to prepare themselves for entry into one of the three regional campuses of the University of the West Indies and eventually attain a degree.

Michael was one of those in the middle. He was not sure what he wanted to do. He could not wait too late to decide whether he should get a job or see what his results were and then enroll at Sixth Form College. In fact, he was not sure whether he wanted to go to Sixth Form. Though he hoped he could attend university, he knew the odds were stacked against him. He was not sure that he would do well enough to get a scholarship and he also knew that his parents were not in a financial position to pay his way to university. There was no one who could assist him to pursue a college education. If he got grades that were good enough to enroll and further his academic education, then he would make that choice; but for now, getting a job was his better choice. He could not depend on his parents to make that decision for him. He believed that he was mature and confident enough to make the correct decision when that time came.

Michael's father had other ideas. His world and Michael's were two different ones. He had his own dreams and aspirations; Michael had his, too. A farmer and an agriculturist, his father loved the soil, the plants, or anything that grew from the ground. He was retired from his job as an Agricultural Officer with the Ministry of Agriculture and now spent a lot of his time tending to his plot of land, growing bananas and other cash crops.

Michael saw it differently. He saw his father and many others like him in the village and throughout the island laboring for a few dollars in poor and primitive conditions. He saw no future in this life. He saw nothing but pain and heartache. But his father wanted his children to follow in his footsteps: take to the plow and join the hustle.

Michael sat across from his father in the living room of the three-bedroom wooden house he shared with his parents and his two sisters. He was alone with his father today. His mother was at work in Roseau and his sisters were attending a Youth Division sponsored camp in Vielle Case. He had participated in a number of such camps during the past five years but had decided against participating this year. He wanted to devote as much time as possible to job hunting. His father had gone to his garden plot in Carholm earlier that day and had returned after only a few hours.

His father was sipping some rum and coke from a glass. The strong smell of the booze filled the little room. His father had no shirt on his back and only a pair of khaki shorts on. This was a common habit. Later, he would make his way to the center of the village where he would meet with his friends. They would then play dominoes in the back of Mr. Ossie's shop until the late hours of the night.

For a while they sat avoiding eye contact as they listened to the cricket game between the West Indies and England being played at Kensington Oval in Barbados. Michael sat on the couch while his father sat in his old rickety sofa that needed being replaced. His dad had resisted his mother's efforts to replace the old thing with a new model. The game was being broadcast on the local radio station. Michael and his father had done this a number of times before, even at nights, when the West Indies team was down under in Australia. Today did not seem any different.

Every now and then his father hissed in disgust if a play did not go the way he wished. He was a cricket fanatic and Michael, too, had picked up some of his father's love for the game. He was a member of the local village team, the Beach Rovers, and he had aspirations of some day representing Dominica in the Windward Islands Tournament. He was a very good batsman and showed a lot of promise. His father played every now and then for the village's Married Men's team. Like so many West Indian men, cricket was in their blood.

After a while, his father spoke. "Are you coming with me tomorrow?" he asked.

"Where?" Michael answered, knowing quite well that his father was asking him to join him to harvest bananas.

"What do you mean by where?" his father answered, as he wiped his mouth with the back of his right hand. "Are you coming with me to cut some bananas tomorrow?" he repeated without looking at Michael.

"No, Daddy, I can't," Michael responded, after a momentary hesitation. "I have some things to do," he added.

"So what is so important that you cannot do it another day?" his father asked, somewhat disgusted at his son's answer.

"I have to go to do something in the afternoon," Michael replied, pausing a little to listen, his attention focused on what the cricket announcer was saying. "I have some business to do in town," he continued.

"So you mean to tell me that after all those years you spend at school, the one day that you not at school, you cannot come and help me cut some bananas?" his father queried, the tone of his voice raised a bit.

"I don't know," Michael answered, staring his father straight in the eyes. His father stared back without batting an eyelid.

"How comes you don't know? Who you think I working all this time for? For you and your sisters! Not for me!" his father shouted back.

"But, Daddy, you don't understand. I am not interested in doing that kind of work. This is not my cup of tea. I cannot see myself in this day and age doing something that has no future for me," Michael said to him, knowing quite well that he was only causing his father to get angrier.

"How you mean it has no future?" his father snapped back.

"Because the government is not interested in helping the small farmers. They need to spend more money to get agriculture moving in the right way," Michael told him.

Michael's father took another sip from the glass and laughed mockingly. "So you are one of those communist or leftist, whatever they call all you, who talking about the government not doing this and government not doing that?" he asked. "So why don't you and all the others move to Cuba if all you like the leftist system so much?" he asked sarcastically.

Michael had touched a nerve. His father was a strong supporter of the ruling political party and in his eyes the government could do no wrong. This was a topic that, as kids growing up, he and his sisters dared not talk about while they were in the house or when his father was present. If they did, his father would shut them up.

But Michael believed that since he had graduated from high school, he had gained the right to express his political view whether his father liked it or not. He was approaching his eighteenth birthday and soon he would be able to vote. So, why couldn't he voice his political opinions?

"No, I am not a communist nor a leftist. I just don't think that in this day and age I have to struggle to make a decent living. I don't want to do like all the people like you doing and then later have nothing to show for it," Michael countered.

"Is that why I send you to school for all those years, boy? Is that what you have been listening to when you and you friends meet and to come and tell me about the future? Is this my thank you after all those years? After all, did I waste my time? This is what is wrong with all you young people. All you think all you have answers for everything. This is what is wrong with the world now."

Michael said nothing for a while as his father fumed and muttered to himself. After a while, he spoke.

"If you want to think that way Daddy, is up to you. I have other ideas and farming is not part of it. Furthermore, you yourself know that I cannot carry too much load on my head. It hurts me and that's why the basket fell last week."

"The basket fall because you didn' give a damn, not because your head hurt. Is because you didn' give a damn about all the work I put getting food down here," his father shouted. "So you going to go to Roseau while I have to pay an extra person to help me when I have a damn big man like you doing nothing to help me! When I cannot go to the garden again, who will take care of it? You really think I work all that time just to let it sit there and let grass grow and take over the place? You really think so?" his father asked as he got up from the sofa and stood looking at Michael.

Michael sat still, his ears tuned to the radio, shutting off his father for a while. Then he spoke again. "I don't know what you're thinking about, Daddy, but I don't think that this is what I really want to do. I went to school in an effort to get something better in life, not to struggle like you have to. Why they cannot give you guys better roads so that you can drive up to your estates? Why does Geest have to tell you how much he's paying you for your bananas when you own it and then you cannot even get a penny for yourself? I hate to say it again. You don't like me to say it but this is the truth and I am not getting into it," Michael said, trying his best to control his anger and emotions. This was *his* father. He respected him, but he had to let him know that he was not going to allow him to dictate his future.

His father looked back at him. Michael could see disgust and unhappiness on his father's face. His father kept shaking his head from side to side and sucked his teeth a number of times. He stared at Michael and for about a minute or two said nothing. Then he started again. "You know I never ever dreamed of the day when I would hear you speak to me like that. I never imagined that a day would come when you would turn your back on the soil that has made you what you are."

"The soil has not made me anything, Daddy. It has made you something. It was the thing when you were growing up, but it is a different world today. How many young people you see going up and cultivating land? How much money can you make selling bananas to Geest? Just think of it, Daddy. Think of the rip-off that is Geest! Think of all the people who have filled their pockets on the back of the poor farmers, including you!" Michael answered.

"I know that was where you were heading, mister! I knew that all the time," his father said, a tremor in his voice. "From the day your mother told me you said you did not want to go to garden anymore I knew something was up. This is what those leftists have brainwashing you guys at school and saying they teaching for the future and blaming the goverment. Just make sure that nobody talk about politics here. When you have your house you can do it, but not in mine," he scowled at Michael. "I, William Bernard George work hard for what I have and nobody going to come here and think they saying what they want. No sirry! Not here, Mr. Michael; and that going for all of you," his father warned.

"Why do you want to blame anyone for me not going up to cut bananas? I just don't want to do it. It has nothing to do with government, or leftist. It has everything to do with me, Daddy; that's all. You just don't understand!" Michael answered, this time a little angry with his father.

"How you mean I don't understand? What is there for me to understand? What makes it so difficult for you to help me, just one day, just to show your appreciation for all I have done, for all I sacrifice all those years so you can sit in this damn chair and tell me about communist and goverment and the future! Umm? What makes it so hard to help your own father?" he ranted on.

"Because I have a job interview tomorrow morning and one in the afternoon," Michael said without looking at his father. He did not think that his father heard what he said because just at that moment the cricket commentator announced that one of the players on the West Indies team was out; caught in the slips.

"Oh shucks! Oh no! You mean those guys going to lose the game?" his father cried as he stared at the radio, as if speaking to the commentator. "Why they didn' pick Boche instead? They picking who they want and see what happening! They cannot even win a game!" he continued, as he placed both hands on his head. "Those damn selectors; they so biased. Big island against small island and they calling it West Indies team! Who they think they foolin'?" he asked, as if speaking to the announcer on the radio. "Why they not picking Boche? Eh, why?" he asked emphatically. Michael wanted to laugh, but he had to control his emotions lest he made the situation more volatile than it already was.

Satisfied that he had made his point, his father sat down and took another drink from his glass. Michael said nothing, but he was burning inside with laughter. He found it amusing the way his father was behaving. He fought himself to be calm lest he caused his father to get angrier at him.

Boche was the nickname of one of the island's best cricketers, Irving Shillingford, who many, including Michael's father, believed had been passed over and over again by the West Indian selectors in favor of cricketers of seemingly lesser ability from Barbados, Trinidad, Jamaica and Guyana. It was a small island, big island syndrome. It pained his father the more as he listened to the way the team was being beaten by the English bowlers.

Eventually, he seemed to have resigned himself to the fact that Michael had made up his mind and he was not going to be able to change it. He got up and walked slowly to the kitchen, shaking his head, the now empty glass in his hand. He dropped the glass into the kitchen sink and muttered to himself as he walked back to the room. He sighed deeply as he took his position on the rickety sofa.

Michael was not sure whether his father was muttering at him or at the poor showing of the team. It did not matter anyway. Michael was an example of what was happening in a country which was experiencing changes in various aspects of its development. He had seen a number of his friends immigrate to other countries in search of education and better opportunities for themselves. He was not prepared to remain stuck. This was a beginning. Who knows what would follow?

His father was a tradionalist, a man who had paid his dues and enjoyed life in the country when life was different. Today things were not the same and Michael wondered whether his father was prepared to accept the changes.

He looked at his father slumped in the sofa. *What had made it so tough to get through to his father?* he thought.

"Daddy, why do you speak like this?" he asked his father. "I am only telling you what is good for me. Why are you against it?" he continued.

For a while there was silence, as if his father was thinking of what to say.

"Ask yourself," snapped his father. "Ask yourself. Ask those friends of yours. All you think all you know everything, but all you don't know nothing. You don't know about life boy!" he reiterated.

Michael looked at his father again. He wanted to say something more to him, but he thought otherwise. He had had enough. He stood up and walked to his bedroom. He took his denim jacket off the top of the door and made his way back through the living room and out of the house, as his father followed his every move. He walked down the steps out into the afternoon sunlight without uttering another word. He had said what he thought was right. He had spoken his mind and if his father was not happy with it, well, so be it.

Michael knew that the situation he had just experienced was going to stay with him for a while and he felt that he was prepared to live with it. He shrugged his shoulders and pulled the denim jacket over his back. To him, tomorrow was what mattered most and he was not going to allow his father to cause him to change his mind. His father had had his time but now his future was his to carve and his only. No one, not even his father, was going to change that today.

Abòlò	A large ground lizard.
Ackra	A fish cake delicacy made using a mixture of flour batter and titiri and fried in oil.
Bèlè	A local folk dance believed to have originated from Africa.
Copra	The dried meat—using a kiln to do so—of a coconut.
Chodo	A breakfast drink made with the white of eggs, milk, grated nutmeg and cinnamon. A favorite of many families after church on Sunday or on special family occasions.
Common Entrance Exams.	The annual exam held to by Government to determine the eligibility of children to attend high school.
Konpè	Name referred to a man who was a sponsor for a child at baptism or confirmation by that child's parents or vice versa.
Conte	A short story told in Creole. It usually starts out with these words: "Mesyé! Kwik!"
Country bookie	A reference to a person from a rural area who is not familiar with the "city life."
CXC	Caribbean Examination Council.
Gardé	To look into the future.
Jombie	An evil spirit.
Kabawé	Rum shop.
Kay Kaka Chyen	"The House of Dog Excreta." The name given to a building on Main Street in St. Joseph originally owned by the late Alvin 'Paton' Armantrading.
Ki moun ki la.?	Who is there?
La diabless	A she-devil who is believed to use a disguise (beauty) to snare her victims.
Lapeau kabwit drum	A drum made from the stretched dried skin of a goat.
Macadam	Crushed stones used in the early construction of roads in Dominica.
Macakwi	Foolishness; nonsense.

Makoumè	Name referred to a woman who was a sponsor for a child at baptism or confirmation by the child's parents or vice versa.
Malè	Bad luck or misfortune.
Mango anmè	A mango with a bitter skin.
Merci Bondyé!	Thank God!
Mepuis	Slanderous language, sometimes accompanied by profanities.
Nannie	Spiced rum—Rosemary.
Néyé	Drown.
Obeah	Devilish works and practices specifically meant to create harm to someone else.
Pawèn	Godfather.
Poto Catolic	A staunch Roman Catholic christian.
Quadrille	A local folk dance.
Sharpé	Escape.
Socouyan	An evil witch who supposedly sheds her skin and flies on a broomstick at night. She is also believed to suck blood from unsuspecting victims while they are asleep.
Seine	Big net used by local fishermen.
Senjo	The creole name for St. Joseph.
Shalviwé	Overturned or capsized.
Soula	A drunkard.
Titiri	Hundreds of tiny fish (Goby family) that enter rivers from the sea to spawn.
Vep	A free ride on a motor vehicle.
Zaboca	Avocado pear.

www.ingramcontent.com/pod-product-compliance
Lightning Source LLC
Chambersburg PA
CBHW020423180626
46812CB00003B/1129